Praise for the #1 Kindle Bestselling Historical Fantasy,

EMBERS IN A DARK FROST

"*A magical tale! If you love fantasy settings, a budding romance, and a reluctant heroine, I would urge you to try Ms. Keaton's ethereal Embers of a Dark Frost.*" Night Owl Reviews. 4 1/2 Stars, **TOP PICK!**

"*There is no denying Kelly Keaton's writing, she has a dark and languid style that is both captivating and addictive.*" Parajunkee Reviews

"*This is why I take a chance on indie books... because you find ones like this. Embers In A Dark Frost is thrilling, magical, and sexy!*" Shortie Says.com

"*With characters that immediately captivate, there wasn't a moment that I wasn't caught up and lost in the story . . . I highly recommend this title for fans of fantasy and "New Adult" and everyone who's looking for a bright shining star of a book. Enjoy!*" A Life Bound By Books

Read the Young Adult Series School Library Journal calls, "*part "Lightning Thief," part "Twilight," and part "Maximum Ride."*

DARKNESS BECOMES HER

"*Unforgettable, complex, and unique. I could not put this book down.*"#1 New York Times Bestselling author Christopher Pike

"*A page-turning story with a multidimensional heroine and an atmospheric near-future setting.*"Publisher's Weekly

**"*Keaton creates a New Orleans setting rife with Gothic rot and decay…*"
Booklist, starred review

A BEAUTIFUL EVIL

"*If I could become a character in a fictional world, I would pick this one. Action and romance combine with good storytelling and an alluring world. More, please!*" Melissa Marr, bestselling author of the Wicked Lovely series

"*Packed with action and hints of romance, [Kelly Keaton's A Beautiful Evil] pairs well with fans of Rick Riordan and Stephenie Meyer.*"
Recommended. Library Media Connection

"*Percy Jackson meets Anne Rice.*" School Library Journal

Enter the thrilling, urban fantasy world of Kelly's critically acclaimed Charlie Madigan Series, written as Kelly Gay

SHADOWS BEFORE THE SUN

"*Fate, sacrifice and the refusal to say die all collide in the newest terrific Charlie Madigan adventure. This is an epic rescue tale fraught with magical hazards that will push Charlie to her limits. Gay's evolution as a marvelous storyteller is on full display in this frightening and exhilarating ride. It's time for Charlie to kick some major butt!* RT Book Reviews, 4 ½ Stars, TOP PICK!

THE HOUR OF DUST AND ASHES

"*With a compelling heroine, sarcastic humor, and gritty action, The Hour of Dust and Ashes is perfection!*" Night Owl Reviews

"Sizzling. . . . A whirlwind of suspense, tension, and action. . . . Dark and gritty urban fantasy. . . . The chemistry between [Charlie and her partner, Hank] is sexy and hot and the dialogue is humorous with a sensual undertone. . . . The conclusion is heart stopping." Smexy Books

THE DARKEST EDGE OF DAWN

"What do you do when your first book is one of the most highly praised urban fantasy debuts of the year? If you're Kelly Gay, you follow up The Better Part of Darkness with The Darkest Edge of Dawn, and force reviewers everywhere to try and find a better way to describe amazing." All Things Urban Fantasy

THE BETTER PART OF DARKNESS

"This gritty urban fantasy . . . is extraordinary." Booklist

"Captivating urban fantasy. . . . Intricate world- building and richly complex characters mix with a fast- paced plot to create a standout start to a new series." Publishers Weekly

BOOKS BY KELLY KEATON

Embers in a Dark Frost

The Gods & Monsters Series:
Darkness Becomes Her
A Beautiful Evil
The Wicked Within
Heart of Stone

Writing as Kelly Gay:

The Better Part of Darkness
The Darkest Edge of Dawn
The Hour of Dust & Ashes
Shadows Before The Sun
Carniepunk: "Hell's Menagerie"

EMBERS
IN A
DARK FROST

Kelly Keaton

Chapter 1

O*ne day you'll be accepted, Deira, by every being of this darkening land. You'll see. Even the creatures, big and small, will love you."*

My eyes closed and my mind opened to the memory of Mother's softly spoken words, of her sweet-smelling breath as she pressed her cold lips against my cheek and cradled me in weak arms. *"You'll see."*

I sighed deeply and opened my eyes, seeing the never-ending snow carried by the wind. A strong gust lifted my loose hair and sent it billowing around me.

If only her words had been true.

Above me, the white and gold banners of my House snapped in the steady current. From my vantage atop the highest tower, Murias—once a shining city of warmth and light—lay buried beneath a thick blanket of snow. Once, vibrant green hills and forests, terraced temples and fountains prospered under a brilliant blue sky. But that was long ago. The cold had crept so slowly across the land, stealing the warmth and turning the days into a dull, solemn gray.

Death loomed over Innis Fail. Our world was dying. *We* were dying.

And I was to blame.

"Daydreaming again, Deira?"

I straightened, turning to lean against the stone ledge of the tower as Lidi inched her slender frame onto the battlements. "I'm finished with my duties," I said over my shoulder, prepared for the coming lecture.

Mother's only confidant, Lidi had witnessed my birth and then, when I was left alone, she'd taken me from the Woodlands, through the great Plains of the Thunderer, and across the lake to the island of Murias where she continued to watch over me.

She tucked her straight silvery hair behind one ear—something she always did right before a lecture. "How many times must you be told?" She grabbed my shoulders, turned me away from her, and began pulling my hair into a tight bun. "Your hair must be kept up. And where's your veil? Left to float on the breeze, no doubt. I don't know what draws you here…"

Despite the cold, I loved the tower, loved letting my hair down in defiance.

"Ow! Don't pull so hard!"

"You're lucky I brought another veil. Lucky no one knows you come up here. You know how much trouble you'd cause if anyone saw you?"

Aye, I did. But then, I didn't care. "The veil doesn't hide everything. They all know what I am." A monster.

"And I've heard this argument how many times? Everyone here may know what you are, but they don't want to be reminded. Besides, our visitors do not know and best to keep it that way."

I rolled my eyes even though she was right. If they saw my head uncovered and my red hair flowing in the breeze—evidence of my mixed blood, for red hair was purely a human trait—I'd spend the next two moons up to my elbows in some undesirable task.

As Lidi tugged on my hair, I admired the view of the other snow-covered islands in the lake and beyond our own shores, the Plains. And perhaps beyond that the path my father, Conlainn Mac Roich, had taken to be free of my mother's kind, the Children of D'Anu.

What I wouldn't give to be free of them too, I thought bitterly.

I let out a heavy breath, wincing as Lidi pulled my hair again. "Do you think he made it?" It was a question I'd asked ever since coming to Murias in my sixth year. It was now my twenty-first.

Lidi's hands stilled for a spell before continuing in earnest, using pins to attach a spare black veil to my head. "You must stop thinking of him." She yanked my hair to emphasize her words.

"But there were others before the war who made it back to Eire."

"Legends all." Lidi stepped beside me, taller than me by a head. "Whether he made it back to the human realm or not, he abandoned you, *leann*. Do not give him the honor of remembrance.

He had to know what your life would be like without him..."

An embarrassment to the ruling House of Anu. A life of being shunned and looked upon with disgust, fear, and prejudice.

A slow burn spread through my chest. What else was I to do but defend him? Believing he loved me and had left me for a purpose was far better than the believing he'd abandoned me.

"Look there." She pointed to the far shore where tiny pinpricks of light appeared. First just a few, then more until the lights swarmed like thousands of angry fireflies above the snow. The faint rhythmic beat of war drums carried across the lake. A tingle swept beneath my skin and lifted the hairs on the back of my neck.

Lidi gripped my arm. "The Legions of Sydhr," she whispered in awe. "The Fire Breathers have come."

I swallowed, my eyes riveted on the illuminated shore. "Sydhrs don't breathe fire any more than you or I."

"Perhaps." She paused, staring out over the frozen landscape before turning to me with her usual prim expression. "At least now we have a chance. With the House of Sydhr finally allied with the Houses of Anu and Taranis, we have a chance to defeat Nox of Annwn and fix the damage those horrible humans—" Her cheeks and the tips of her ears flushed red. "Oh, Deira, I'm sorry I didn't mean..."

I shrugged and the smile I tried to give her faltered. "You speak the truth." The cold had begun to sink in, deep inside to my very bones. "I can't help what happened in the past any more than I can help what I am, though I wish I could."

Her arm slipped around my shoulder. "I know. And I'm sorry for what I said. One day this war with Nox will be over. And they'll forget."

But we both knew no one would ever forget.

I, with my red hair, short stature, and tainted blood, was a reminder to every Danaan in the land. I alone reminded them of loved ones lost, of greed and betrayal. I alone carried the blood of a people reviled and hated by those of this world, for it was my human ancestors who stole the Light, the Lia Fail, from our world, causing the darkness and frost to creep across the land and steal the glow of eternal youth from our cheeks. And now the House of Annwn, the Underworld, had broken peace and taken advantage of the darkness to wage war.

No, they would never forget or forgive me for the half-blood that ran through my veins or the blight on my soul because of it.

With the added protection an alliance with the Fire Breathers brought, travel restrictions would ease, making it easier for me to find a boat. From there, I'd return to the Woodlands and claim Mother's abandoned estate for my own. All my earlier petitions to leave Murias had gone unanswered or had been denied. But no more. I was grown. The time had come for me to leave, permission or not. And the distraction of visitors coming and going would make it easier to get off the island.

"We should be getting back. If the Legions of Sydhr have arrived, the Council will convene and we must feed them all."

She groaned. "It's going to take forever to restock the

storehouse after this."

"Aye," I replied, feeling hopeful at last. Things were about
to change.

* * *

The tension and heat from the kitchen struck me as soon
as we entered. Most days I aided Lidi there, salting meats and fish,
or pounding raw roots and plants into pastes, or drying them for
use as herbs. Other days I apprenticed to the scribes in the Hall of
Records.

Knowing my duties, I washed my hands in the basin,
snagged an apron off the hook nearby, and set to work washing
and chopping greens.

Before long, the heat grew and so did the ache in my feet.
I'd chopped, washed, kneaded, cleaned, and swept. Servers dressed
in white tunics trimmed with gold cloth finally arrived to take the
first of several courses to the Great Hall.

Even though this ritual had taken place every night since
the House of Taranis arrived to discuss an alliance, each time the
servers lifted their trays and filed through the wide double doors a
sense of longing and wistfulness filled me. When the doors opened,
the energy of the Great Hall seeped through; the low hum of many
voices blended with the sweet sounds of music and laughter.

"Deira!"

I jumped.

"Stop lingering at the door." Bressia wiped her long, flour-covered fingers on her apron with sharp movements, eyeing me speculatively. Then she laughed. "Want to attend the Council, now do you?"

Heat shot to my cheeks. "No. Why would I?" But she'd seen my look.

"*You* in the Great Hall. Ha! That'll be the day. Finish cleaning the pans and then see to the fires."

My teeth clenched. I was so weary of being told what to do. Sometimes I wanted to rip my veil off and scream. In front of everyone. I missed Mother. Missed feeling loved and valued. Once it became clear how my mixed blood was viewed by my family, I learned quickly the value of indifference. But today was not one of those days.

Perhaps it was the anxiety in the air. For the first time in ages, three of the five ruling houses of Innis Fail had aligned, Anu, Taranis, and, hopefully, Sydhr, to fight against one of our own. More Danaans would die in the assault against Nox of Annwn. Nerves were raw. Everyone was on edge. As was I.

Keryn, one of the servers, hurried into the kitchen flustered and out of breath. Quickly, I poured her a cool glass of water. At least if I did it first, I wouldn't be ordered to do it.

"There aren't enough of us," she said after a deep drink. "We need more servers."

"Well, you won't be taking my staff. Servers do little good without food to serve," Bressia shot over her shoulder as she left to direct the making of breads and pastries.

I leaned against the counter. "I could help." My heart

skipped at the suggestion.

Keryn's perfect silvery eyebrows rose. "You?" She said it with such disgust that I wanted to hit her. My fists clenched at my sides, but I forced down the anger with proficiency; I'd had years of practice, after all.

Suddenly, I wanted nothing more than to serve—just because they didn't think me good enough to do so. "There are so many in the hall, no one will even recognize me. I have my veil. I'll keep my head down and serve, and only the other houses."

Keryn's eyes narrowed. She scanned the kitchen. Everyone was busy with a task. As long as I'd been in Murias there had never been a gathering like this, never been this many visitors, this much importance, this much work… It was an unusual time for everyone. Hope rose as she considered my words, but fear quickly set in, for I'd never been in the same room with more than a handful of my own family much less the rulers, prefects, and warriors of other houses.

I pushed my trepidation aside. I had to do this. In the hall, I could eavesdrop and find out the state of travel, the best roads to take, and how things fared in the Woodlands.

"I suppose you could serve the other houses," Keryn said. "Keep your head covered, don't look anyone in the eye, and just do your job. No one spares a glance at the servers anyway. Don't give them a reason to. Understand?"

I kept my head down. I could barely hear through the blood rushing through my ears. "Of course."

In the long corridor that separated the kitchen and the

Great Hall, Keryn slipped a soft white tunic over my head and then belted it with a leather tie sewn with gold threading. She handed me a heavy jug of ale from one of the tables that lined both sides of the hallway. Servers bustled around me, jostling, but never looking.

"Go." She pushed me toward the hall. "Don't forget what I said."

Immediately, I was swept up in the wave of the servers pressing forward into the Great Hall. I couldn't see over those in front of me, so I followed until, suddenly, I was there and the servers thinned out, hurrying to the long tables.

For a moment, I couldn't move. I was in the Great Hall, surrounded by Danaans, by the swell of music and the heady aroma of food and drink.

Colorful banners hung from thick beams high overhead. Tapestries depicting great battles lined the walls. Bright gowns and jewels adorned the females. Warriors practically glowed in shining, silver chain mail and the vibrant tunics of their houses. My jaw went slack. I'd only seen occasional visitors and those who worked in the palace; my teachers, the scribes, and my grandfather. I'd seen the Legions of Anu from afar, but never like this. So close, so imposing.

My hands trembled as I took a deep breath and followed a line of servers to one of the long tables at the far end of the hall, away from my family's table. It was so crowded, so many milling about and talking in groups, that I knew I'd be safe.

A hand seized my arm and jerked me back into the shadows.

"Deira, what are you doing?" Lidi hissed in my ear as she pulled me against the wall.

I leaned close to her, wincing because her fingers dug into my upper arm. "Leave me be, Lidi."

She glanced around nervously, trying to shield me from view with her body. "Come back into the kitchen." She pulled, but I didn't budge.

The energy in the Great Hall surrounded me, making me feel hopeful and intoxicated. No one would make me leave. "No. You go back. I'm staying."

"Have you gone mad? If your grandmother sees you..."

I yanked my arm from her grasp. "I'm not mad." My voice rose, but it didn't matter; no one could hear me amid the music and the noise of the crowd. "Don't you see? I'm tired. I walk these halls like a shadow. I want to live, to feel, to take my life in my hands and do what I will with it. I have that right." My cheeks burned. My tone and eyes, I knew, were fierce. I calmed myself. "Please, go back to the kitchen."

Her gaze softened into worry and resignation. Perhaps even pity. She inclined her head before slipping away. I watched her slim form disappear into the crowd, knowing I'd hurt her with my harsh words.

But they were words of truth. I'd always been a thing, a mistake kept hidden.

Someone bumped into me. The ale in the jug sloshed over the edge, waking me from my thoughts. I blinked back the sting of tears as I headed down the length of the wall. I had to leave

Murias. Otherwise, what was the point of my life? I had to make a stand now for myself. Because I knew no one else would.

As I stopped behind a table and began filling ale mugs, two servers went by, giggling.

"They're so big! Did you see the color of his eyes?"

"Breathing fire might not be a bad thing," the other said before erupting into more giggles.

I moved back against the wall. They spoke of the Fire Breathers. I admonished myself for using the term. Lidi had me thinking of make-believe again. On the tips of my toes, I looked in the direction the two servers had come. Far down at the end of the table, sat the officials and war leaders of the House of Sydhr, descendants of the god of fire.

I kept refilling mugs, staying in the background as much as I could, but making my way farther down the line. A few servers recognized me. I saw the flicker of shock, but they said nothing. It was too busy to lodge any sort of complaint at my presence.

Suddenly a lone drumbeat brought the hall to silence.

Everyone froze, as though the sound had suspended time.

Dancers swept into the center of the room, tall, lithe and as pale as moonlight, with hair the color of night. They were not the silvered-haired beauties from Murias. No, these must be from one of the other houses. The drums began again, heavy and steady. The servers resumed their work more quietly than before.

Riveted by the scene, I watched the dancers, their sheer blue gowns flowing and rippling like gentle water over smooth stones with each timed movement. It was a dance celebrating the form. There were six of them. All female. All perfect. All true-blooded Danaans.

The sound and vibration of the drums pounded through me, making my cheeks hot and my limbs weak. I'd never seen a dance like this. Never heard music like this. Demanding. Overwhelming. Mesmerizing.

I forced myself to continue down the line, stopping to fill mugs and trying to focus on my task, to overhear conversations, not realizing at first that I'd come to the Fire Breather's table.

Leaning between two warriors, I trained my ears to their words, but the drums were so fast now, beating loudly in time with my heart that it was all I could hear. The entire hall was spellbound, all eyes on the dancers undulating in harmony to the frenzied tempo.

And then it ended with one enormous drumbeat that echoed in the stillness of the hall.

The crowd stood to honor the dancers while I watched, horrified, as my jug, knocked by the two warriors as they rose, slipped from my hand, flipped over the table, and hit the stone floor where it shattered into pieces.

All eyes turned to me.

I froze; my body and hand stretched out where I'd tried to recover the jar, feeling as though the blood drained from my face and down to my feet where it ebbed from my body.

The crowd remained silent and staring. I hurried in between the two tables and knelt to gather the pieces. No one helped me. Tears pricked my eyes, but I blinked them back, concentrating hard on my task, willing my hands to stop trembling.

The scrape of a chair. Footsteps. Black boots on the floor in front of me. My breath caught. Why wasn't the music starting? Why weren't people talking, eating? Jars broke all the time...

Dear Dagda, what have you done?

A black-clad knee bent down in front of me. Close. Too close.

I raised my head and looked straight into fire.

Chapter 2

The blood I thought lost came rushing back with a roar.

From a strong face, eyes the color of lit amber bore into mine. An aura of war and power, of an iron will and a predatory nature held me still.

His black hair was cut short. He wore polished black chain mail under a black tunic with a silver raven on the breast. A thick silver torc hugged his neck and a black tattoo climbed, like entwined flames, from beneath his tunic, up the left side of his neck where it clipped his jaw, earlobe, and the tip of his ear before continuing up his temple to disappear into his hairline.

I heard no noise from the Great Hall, only the sound of my breathing and his. His sharp black brows, like the wings of a crow in flight, dipped just a fraction. His penetrating gaze searched my face.

Then, his hand snaked out and snatched the veil from my head.

I bit back a cry as the pins yanked hair from my scalp as

they came away with the veil.

A collective gasp rose to the rafters. Chairs scraped against the stone floor as Danaans stood in shock, anger, disgust—I knew not which, for I couldn't pull my eyes away from the stranger in front of me.

"Hair the color of flame." His voice was quiet and thickly accented. A tic began in the muscle of his shadowed jaw. "You're human."

My life was over. I had disgraced not only the House of Anu, but also the entire ruling council of Innis Fail.

Still, the dark warrior stared at me, his face a mask of fierce thought even as his hand pulled the remaining pins at the back of my head, releasing the tight bun Lidi had arranged. My hair fell around my face; the ends pooling on the stone floor.

A murmur rushed through the crowd. Cloth rustled near me. A shard from the jar cut into my palm, but I didn't move.

"Forgive her." My grandfather jerked me up by the arm so quickly my vision swam. "She has a faulty mind and forgets her place."

I gasped and gave him a sharp look. His hand squeezed my arm, warning me to be silent. For once, I listened.

"What is this, Lairgnen?" Another male stepped forward. Long, blond hair flowed freely down his back, save for the two war braids at each temple. Torch light reflected a myriad of tiny sparks off the silver chain mail he wore over a vibrant blue tunic. I knew him to be Mael, descendant of Taranis the Thunderer, leader of his house, King of the Plains and Master of Air.

Never had I seen such a gathering of beauty. Everywhere I looked was perfection, on the faces and forms of trueborn Danaans. I wanted to crawl under the nearest table.

The warrior who'd unveiled me straightened, standing taller than my grandfather, taller than Mael.

I realized with yet another degree of humiliation and fear, this had to be Balen, leader of the House of Sydhr.

No one had to tell me. He had the age of heroes written in his eyes and the weariness of it, too. Lidi had been right, and I wondered if the legends and myths were true. How long had he lived?

My grandfather spoke. "This is the daughter of Ariannon, Priestess of Anu, who passed to the Place of Souls fifteen moons past." He paused, took a deep breath and then said reluctantly, "My granddaughter."

The murmurs grew louder. Mael stepped forward, eyes scanning me from head to toe. "She's blighted. There's only one thing worse than a human and that's a halfling." He grabbed my grandfather's arm and whispered fiercely, "Dear Dagda, Lairgnen. Why was she not killed at birth?"

My grandfather's tone was tight. I'd pay for embarrassing him. "My daughter hid her until the child's soul was firmly bonded. You know the law, Mael. Once an innocent soul has firmly bonded to the body we cannot take a life."

Mael stepped closer to my grandfather, lowering his voice. "Aye and she is damaged, her soul is blighted because of *human* blood. You know it as well as I. It's why we made it unlawful for this kind of union; they are dangerous and too unpredictable... This one will be no different than the other halflings who came before her."

Fear knotted my stomach. I knew I was unwanted. I'd heard it nearly my whole life, but I never understood why.

Mother had held on to so many secrets. She never told me what I was, only that I was special and loved. Not even Lidi knew what the blight on my soul meant and what, besides the theft of our Light, had happened in our history to make one such as myself so reviled. We'd both searched endlessly in the Hall of Records at Murias, but found nothing of others like me. It was as if the halflings of so long ago had never existed. Only the council seemed privy to the lost history, to a time when Danaans and humans mingled freely.

Because Mother was a priestess of Anu and beloved daughter to Lairgnen, I'd been given a home, an education, meals and clothing to wear. I should've been grateful for their charity, but I wasn't. I was angry. And my anger had grown every day, little by little, just like the darkness and frost creeping across our land.

I met Balen's eyes, for they'd never left mine, and I saw a flash of something. Pity? Anger?

"And the father?" Mael asked in a tight voice. "The gates have been closed since the Old War, since they stole the Light from us. How did he get in to sire this child?"

My grandfather shook his head. "I don't know. He disappeared soon after Ariannon passed."

There I stood before three rulers of the land. And, aye, I

was a halfling, but I was also D'Anu. I was the only daughter of my mother and that alone should mean I had the courage to face whatever came next. I was already caught, already revealed. So let them look and have their fill of my oddity. Perhaps then, they'd move past it and I could proceed with my life.

My grandmother approached, a reigning beauty of Murias, but hers was a cold, hard, silver beauty that made my insides curl. Lairgnen released me as she snatched my wrist. "I will take her. Please," she said graciously, "continue with the feast."

At the first tug on my arm, I glanced desperately at my grandfather. His stern profile remained unchanged. He wouldn't look at me; he rarely did. Instead, his attention had focused on Balen.

The Fire Breather spoke, his gaze never faltered, never looked away from me. "An alliance will be forged. Let us speak of terms."

Balen's words, words everyone had wanted to hear for so long, hung in the air.

It wasn't Balen's words that made my stomach clench and a cold sweat prick the small of my back, it was the way he studied me, confident and calm. Too calm.

"Take her to her room. Lock the door," My grandfather said to his wife before turning toward Balen. "Let us speak of this in private."

Dazed, I didn't fight as she dragged me from the Great Hall, down the servant's hallway toward the kitchen while I tried to keep up with her swift stride. Her fingers dug so deeply into my

wrist that the small tendons and bones grated together. The servers
stopped, their backs pressed against the wall to watch our
progression. I ignored them, knowing I wouldn't find any friends
there.

Despite the pain in my wrist, I pulled against her. "Please
stop, Grandmother. Please."

She didn't. I stumbled, trying not to trip on the long hem
of her shimmering indigo gown. We barged into the kitchen to the
startled gasps of the cooks and Lidi's blink of astonishment.

The room Lidi and I shared was only a few doors down
from the kitchen. My grandmother shoved me inside with such
force that I nearly fell. Quickly, I recovered. "Wait!"

She paused in the doorframe, her chin high and her wide
blue eyes full of loathing. "Balen of Sydhr might be of fire, but he
has a heart of ice. He will not forgive this . . . mockery you've
created. We should've left you on the rubble pile a few more days,
but your grandfather has a soft heart like his daughter."

"What?"

She slammed the door. The lock clicked.

"No, wait!"

Her words rang in my head and made the hairs on my
arms rise. I sat on my bed, trying to make sense of her tirade. The
lock clicked again. Lidi rushed in and threw her arms around me.

"Oh, Deira! What have you done?" Tears and panic
muddled her voice. "Why don't you listen? Why?" She moved
back, smoothed the hair away from my face. Her glassy eyes grew
larger and rounder. Even in her sadness she was painfully beautiful.

"What were you thinking?"

I hung my head. "I don't know. I just wanted to see. I wanted to find a way to leave..." Lidi held one of my hands and patted the top. I winced. My wrist throbbed. "Grandmother said they left me on the rubble pile. What did she mean? I have memories. But I kept telling myself they were just dreams, nightmares... Is it true, Lidi?"

"I've always wondered when you'd ask," she said quietly. "I never should've brought you here."

"They left me to die."

She nodded, unable to look at me. "I couldn't stop them, to tell them you were innocent, just a child, but they wouldn't listen. They abandoned you, left you on the hill, left you to fate."

With the garbage of Murias. I felt sick.

"Why?" Pain squeezed my chest. I hugged myself, remembering those awful nights that weren't dreams, terrified to move, exposed to the elements and not an ounce of power in my being to save me.

"After a fortnight, your grandfather was overtaken by guilt. He sent his guards to bring your body back, to give you a proper burial, but when they arrived, you were still alive." She looked at me then, her face stricken with so much guilt and confusion. "You were so small. Do you remember?"

I put my head in my hands. My temples throbbed. I saw flashes of myself as a child, curled up amid the garbage of our great city, crying, while the wind lashed the rocky hill. The bugs. Calling out to Mother. The nightmares. The dead birds and animals that mounted up as each day passed.

"They say you stole the life from every living thing around you, that's how you survived."

"No," I choked out, stunned and sickened by what she said. "That's… No, I couldn't."

"So they brought you back. No one knew what to do with you. They were more afraid of you than ever, afraid you'd do the same to them if they harmed you."

No, I hadn't done what she said. I couldn't have. I didn't remember doing something so foul. "Lidi." I lifted my head to look at her. "How could I do that? What *am* I that I could do that?"

"I don't know. No one knows except those within the council. I think, long ago, when humans traveled freely between our lands and others like you were born, they did terrible things, had terrible powers like yours. That's why, when they saw you, they feared you. But they don't know your heart, like I do, Deira. They were blinded by whatever happened in the past. It was a moment of madness, unlawful, what they did."

We stayed together on the bed for a long time as I tried to process what I'd learned and accept the things she'd said. But I couldn't. I couldn't have done what she said.

"Perhaps it's not as bad as we think," she said after my tears had dried. She placed a finger under my chin, forcing me to look at her. "Your mother once told me you were meant to be in our world, and I believe her still. You have a purpose, Deira. We don't yet know your fate."

I jerked my chin away. "I know it. To be roasted to a crisp

by a Fire Breather."

She smiled. "I thought you didn't believe in those myths."

"What's going to happen, Lidi?"

Her arm came around my shoulder. I leaned into her. Our sides pressed fully together from shoulder to knee. Scenarios crammed my mind until I couldn't think anymore. Where was my goddess in my time of need? From the first moment I drew breath, Anu had turned her back on me. I'd never felt her power or her blessing, yet I found myself bereft at her absence all the same.

Earth. Air. Fire. Water. Every Danaan could claim descent from one of the creators, the four Ageless Ones. Two gods: Sydhr of fire and Taranis of air. And two goddesses: Anu of water and Dagda of earth. Our four Houses.

But there was another house. The House of Annwn. The Underworld.

The legends claimed its ruler, Nox of Annwn, everything from a direct offspring of the gods, to an Ageless One himself, a holder of a fifth element, that which was unknown and unseen but existed in everything. Some claimed it was the power of the spirit, some claimed it was the life force running through us all. Whatever it was, it gave him dominion over the Deadlands and the Place of Souls.

And me? I possessed nothing. I, who was the daughter of one of the greatest priestesses of Anu, couldn't even summon a raindrop.

Hours passed it seemed, until the door opened once more to reveal my grandfather's regal form. "Lidi, please help Deira gather her things. She will leave immediately. The House of Sydhr has agreed to the alliance. And they are taking Deira with them."

As I sat there stunned, Lidi rushed at him. "You'd trade her to win your war? She's your granddaughter!" He grabbed her arms, but she jerked free. "After all you've done to her. How could you do this?" She fell to her knees crying.

My grandfather straightened his tunic with shaking hands. "Aye, Lidi. I have traded her. The Legions of Sydhr may be the only thing to stop Nox of Annwn from taking over. At least then we will grow old in peace, or perhaps find a way to stop the darkness."

"I want to go with her."

"She goes alone."

Desperate and afraid, Lidi hurried to my side. On her knees, she cradled my face and touched her forehead to mine. "There must be another way," she barely whispered. "Escape."

Escape was for the brave, and I wasn't feeling brave; I was feeling resigned. Detached. Lidi wouldn't let go until I gave her the hope she needed, so I met her look and gave her a quick nod, though I had no idea what I'd do or where I'd find the courage to move forward.

"Gather what you can carry," my grandfather commanded gruffly.

My limbs were weak and shaky as I grabbed my notebooks, writing supplies, and my father's books, shoving them into a satchel with Mother's pendant. Once I was done, I donned the heavy gray cloak lined with fur—a gift from Lidi.

Lidi went with me through the palace, my grandfather ahead of us, the guards behind us. With every step, fear quickened. As we stepped outside, frigid wind tangled my cloak about my legs and stung the wet tears on my face. My steps faltered. I tried to stop, to go back. "I've done nothing." I struggled against the two guards, digging my heels into the snow, anything to prevent my short journey across the courtyard. "Please..."

People were gathered there. I scanned the courtyard, searching for help, for mercy, for someone to come to my aid, but no one did. They were all strangers staring back at me, whispering of me, staring with curiosity or disgust. How odd I must look to them with my bright red hair whipping around against a backdrop of fresh white snow.

Lidi ran in front of us, stopping the procession. She hugged me hard for a long moment. Against my ear she spoke, her voice thick. "Deira." Just my name. Nothing more.

I struggled to swallow the grief, and steeled myself. "You'll catch a chill without your coat," I told her. "Go back inside."

With a deep breath, I moved around her and didn't look back.

As I stepped through the outer gate, a blast of cold wind pushed me back a step. I pulled up my hood and gathered the cloak at my throat. My grandfather managed to face me. He reminded me very much of my mother with his clear blue eyes and his thick, straight hair the color of daylight and sea foam. Eternal youth still clung to him, but not as vibrant as it should have.

With a long sigh, he surveyed the city below and far off

into the distance. "Your fate is the will of Anu now." Regret came into his eyes. "What I've done, Deira, I have done for all of Innis Fail. You understand?"

I didn't. "I understand."

Then he hugged me—a stiff, awkward embrace and a whispered, "I loved your mother."

Coward. He'd part ways with me here at the palace rather than leave with the memory of forsaking me to the Fire Breathers. Cowards all. And I hated them all. Perhaps he was right. Perhaps one day I *would* betray them, not out of blood, but out of retribution. I might be leaving Murias for an uncertain fate, but I'd find a way to survive and even prosper despite them. And, one day, they'd regret what they'd done to me.

My anger bolstered me as a guard led me away from the palace to a group of waiting horses and more guards. I rode through the city, villages, and meadows to the docks of the great lake where another escort waited to take me by boat to the far shore.

I'd gotten my boat after all, I thought, nearly laughing aloud at the irony as I dismounted and climbed aboard.

Chapter 3

The quiet of the water, the creak of the boat, and the gentle dip of the oars had a lulling affect that seemed fitting as I watched the island grow distant. Mother had often talked of her home, her family, and of the island, but I never saw much of it since I was kept within the palace complex. Would that I'd had the time to truly see it, the whole of Murias, at my leisure and by the dim light of day. But even by moonlight the island looked beautiful, cultured, and grand, reminding me so much of Mother.

I turned away, finally, and faced the shoreline.

By my estimation, more than an hour had passed since I'd boarded the boat. My bottom ached, and I was sure it had frozen to the hard bench. As we drew closer to the dock, the lights from the sprawling camp grew brighter, outlining the small mounted party waiting by the water—riders with torches.

Sydhrs.

Warm breath swirled like smoke from the horses' nostrils. The torch flames flashed off polished black armor. A light blanket of fog covered the ground, making the air damp and thick. I clutched my cloak tighter around me. The thin sheet of ice that had gathered by the shore cracked and split as the boat glided to the dock.

No one helped me from the boat, but then, I didn't expect they would. As I climbed the three steps to the dock, my heart pounded and the very beginnings of panic began snaking beneath my skin. There was little escape from the docks unless I wanted to plunge into the frigid water, so I had no choice but to turn my attention to the Fire Breathers on their dark horses.

The boat shoved off behind me. I held the satchel against my breast, as though it would protect me.

A rider separated himself from the group, directing his mount right onto the dock. Its hooves echoed like thunder on the boards, and I could feel the vibrations beneath my feet. The bridle jingled as the horse gnawed on its bit and came closer and closer.

The beast halted before me, so close its muzzle inches from my forehead. Warm breath stirred my hair. The rider leaned forward and offered me a black-gloved hand. *Dagda give me strength.*

I lifted my chin and met a pair of brilliant amber eyes. Balen of Sydhr.

You're strong, Deira. You've been through much worse than this and survived. You can do this.

"Come, Deira. No harm will befall you." He leaned over the saddle. "Take my hand."

In my years at the palace, I'd become adept at reading disgust in the eyes of those around me. I saw none in his. But that didn't mean much. Balen was a warrior, a king, and as such, he'd be an expert at concealing his true emotions. And even though it felt like he was giving me a choice, it was clear I didn't have one. An opportunity to leave might present itself in the camp. I'd have to focus on that, have to bide my time. And the farther I could forge into the Grasslands the better…

My grip on my satchel eased, and I reached out. He did not take my hand, but instead, leaned down, caught my waist in both hands, and in a flash, I was swept onto the horse, my cry of surprise stuck in my throat.

Securing me in front of him, one arm tightly around me, Balen spun the beast around and it cantered off the dock, passing the other warriors, who fell in behind us. I held onto my satchel and Balen's arm as though my life depended on them.

Harsh wind stung my face as we galloped down a main road, passing legion after legion. The Legions of Taranis and Anu. Pennants and banners flew. Fires from torches and campsites blazed everywhere. The smell of horses, snow, mud, and wood smoke hung low in the air.

Before long, we arrived at the outer edges of the encampment where the Legions of Sydhr had made camp. The horses slowed to a canter as we veered down a narrow track lined with tents, and finally came to a stop at the end where three large tents formed a half circle. Balen lifted me off the horse and then dismounted.

The atmosphere was quiet and tense.

The wind snapped and pushed at the tent roofs and

riggings. A large fire burned in a pit in the center of the half circle. The snow had melted away, making the ground a soup of mud, snow, and ice. Wood planks made walking from tent to tent easier than slopping through the mud. No one spoke except in the lowest of tones.

With a light hand on my back, Balen directed me to the large center tent. I glanced over my shoulder, feeling the somber gaze of the warriors on my back. Inside, warmth rushed over me and I forgot about the unnerving stares. Balen's large form followed me in and seemed to steal most of the air in the tent. I moved out of the way, watching and waiting as he went to a table, and began removing his leather gloves. The gloves landed with a soft plop.

He leaned one hip against a long side table, black eyebrows drawing together, as though he faced a problem he could not yet solve. "The washroom is through there." He tipped his head to the right. "There's drink on the side table. The bed is there. Get some rest. We ride at dawn." He spun on his heel and strode past me.

"Wait!" He paused just short of the tent's entrance. "Why am I here? What are—" I forced down the lump in my throat— "your intentions?" I was already thinking the worst, and he could see it plain on my face.

"You are not here to warm my bed, Deira. Or the bed of any other. You have my word. You have nothing to fear from me or my men."

Balen might be a king, but he was a stranger, one whose word—royal or otherwise—I had no reason to trust. "Am I to be your servant, then?" Perhaps he wanted an oddity to serve him. Perhaps he collected strange things and wanted to show off his prize. "Don't you care that I'm a halfling?"

"No, I don't care. Sydhrs aren't so quick to fear as others. We'll speak of this later." With that, he ducked under the tent flap.

I stayed there unmoving for a time, unsure of what to do or think, unsure of the things Balen said. Everything had happened so quickly. Too quickly. And now that I was warm and safe, for the time being, weariness settled over me. I removed my cloak, found a peg to hang it on, and then drank two mugs of cool water before ducking through a narrow flap to find a small room set up for dressing and bathing.

There were no luxuries here, yet Balen was king. Where were the servants, the fine rugs and tableware?

I'd experienced very little of my own world. I'd been sheltered by my mother and then hidden by my family. And while I'd read and studied scrolls and books on every subject imaginable, finding myself thrust in the outside world was frightening. And exactly what I'd wanted. I'd dreamt of seeing the world, travelling, experiencing all those places and cultures I'd read about.

But not at the cost of my freedom. Or my life.

There was a flap at the rear of the bathing area. I pushed it back and ducked my head outside, expecting to find a guard. But there was no one. Male voices, low and unintelligible, carried through the camp. Shadows played upon the tents on either side of mine, but there was nothing or no one to bar my way, just the wide expanse of Grasslands.

My swift footsteps were muted by the light dusting of snow upon the grass. Any moment, I expected someone to shout as I slipped away from the tent.

Then I ran, struggling over never-ending clumps of grass until my lungs burned and the clumps gave way to tall grass and even ground. I slowed my pace, coming to a stop to catch my breath.

Behind me, the glowing camp appeared bright and warm, nothing like being alone in the cold night, surrounded by a sea of waving stems. But I never minded being alone.

Being alone meant I was free.

I started moving again, my heart pumping with the promise that lay before me, with exhilaration that quelled my fears and fueled my courage. I ran until my lungs stretched and strained, until I fell to my knees, gasping and then rolling flat onto my back to stare at the stars.

My life was my own.

And as soon as I caught my breath, I'd run again.

The soft hiss of stems rubbed together in the wind along with the scratchy, high-pitched call of nighttime animals. The tips of the grass swayed gently into and out of my line of sight.

I'd always imagined what it would be like to run wild, to let my hair down and be free. It was better than I thought.

Joy bubbled inside me, and I laughed.

A large shadow blocked the moonlight from my view. "Are you drunk?" a deep, gravelly voice asked. It was close. A few feet above me.

My laughter died.

The shadow moved, cocking its head. The sound of its breath reminded me of the horses at the docks. Stems rustled and broke as it shifted, but I heard no other sounds. The nighttime animals had gone silent. As it moved, I saw its eyes, large, elongated ovals that blinked slowly.

"Drunk?" I managed.

"Aye. An odd creature I find, on its back in the middle of the Grasslands, smiling stupidly at the moon. Or perhaps your heart pines after a male? I hear love makes people stupid. Is that true?" Its breath came out in cloudy tendrils of warm air. It moved closer, peering at me until my back pressed deeply into the grass.

"I frighten you," it said, curiously.

"Aye." I gulped, my heart racing. "Aye, you do."

The dark shadow of its head, larger than my entire body, rose up away from me. I let out an uneasy breath. A cold sweat broke out on my forehead and at the small of my back.

I knew what it was as surely as I knew the thread of my life blew thinly in the wind. Extinct, I remembered, feeling a little sick as I stared at the rarest of creatures. A creature made for war, forged from fire, wind, and magic. War Raven.

Chapter 4

In dragon form, the War Raven's chest, underbelly, neck, and head were fashioned of thick muscle covered by black skin said to be tougher than enchanted chain mail. As it cocked its massive head, I noticed a thin white stripe, which ran between its eyes and went back over its head.

It stood over me, trapping me where I lay on the ground. "Perhaps this is better."

The shadow receded and moonlight returned. Standing at my feet was a slender Danaan-like figure. Its skin color hadn't changed, but now it was smooth-looking and with a luminous blue hue wherever moonlight struck. Despite the long white hair that flowed over its slim shoulders, its features weren't elderly; they were of a young adult. Though, the thick hum of power, like the buzz of honeybees, spoke of old, ancient magic.

Fear rooted me to the ground. This was no War Raven I'd ever read about. Never once had I read or heard about its ability to turn into anything but dragon and raven. I swallowed, trying to find my voice. "What are you?"

It shrugged; the gesture odd and Otherworldly, the movement too slow, too calculated.

"What are *you*?" It countered. The voice had changed as well. Softer, breathier.

The creature stepped back, allowing me room to scramble to my feet. I adjusted my cloak, realizing I must indeed look drunk or lovesick. My hands were so cold I couldn't feel my fingers. "I'm— Well, I'm just on my way home." I glanced around. "That way. My father, he waits for my return." I backed up and it didn't follow, so I began walking slowly toward the direction I'd indicated.

Somehow I was sure that running would appeal to the predator. Running would get me killed.

My footsteps, my breathing, even my heartbeat seemed obscenely loud. I wondered if it could smell my fear.

There was movement beside me.

The creature kept pace next to me, its hands tucked into pockets of a long, deep blue cloak. It didn't look at me. "I can make it on my own," I said, attempting a friendly voice.

"As can I." The corner of its mouth stretched into an unnerving grin.

How long could I walk with this thing beside me? How long would it toy with me? There was no father, no home to hurry to. I didn't even know if there was a village or dwelling ahead. But then the creature knew that already. It was simply playing with me.

Finally I stopped, facing the mysterious figure that

mirrored my movements.

Taller than me, but not by much, it blinked, regarding me without any emotion or guile in its slanted yellow/green eyes.

"I won't eat you, you know." Teeth flashed with its wide smile. "Not now, anyway."

My stomach dropped. I couldn't out run it, couldn't fight it, couldn't do a damn thing if it decided to attack.

Its smile turned into a frown. "You have no sense of humor."

"There's no humor in being a meal for a War Raven."

The lights from the encampment were mere specks now, but they called to me—a safe haven I never should've left. But then, how could I have predicted this?

The War Raven was staring at the lights, too. "You should return. You have much to do."

I drew back, surprised by the words. "Will you force me to go back?"

It shrugged. "You need to go back."

"Why? I'd rather take my chances out here." Provided the War Raven let me go.

"Would you now, Light Bearer?"

It chuckled, the unnatural sound causing goose bumps to spread along my arms. I saw the flash of white teeth again and a glimmer in its eyes. *Light Bearer?* I opened my mouth, but it spoke before me.

"Travel another hour and you'll be sorry, Deira D'Anu. Don't expect me to save you from the thieves and cutthroats that use the high grasses to hide. Go back and you'll not die this night, or the next, or the next... A champion has given his word, and you must return to face your path. It'll take you to the Woodlands. Be patient. There is nothing out here, but rape and slavery and death. The *choice* is yours," it said, humor lacing its last words.

A great whoosh of wings and a blast of wind hit my face, lifting my hair in all directions.

It was gone.

Slowly, the call of night birds and insects returned to their songs. The relief that washed over me sent me to my knees, my stomach so tightly knotted I nearly retched. The horror of staring death in the face, and the utter astonishment that I'd survived it, made tears spring to my eyes.

Its warning rang in my head.

Should I heed it? Did it have a reason to lie?

Weighing my chances with Balen and his word with potential thieves and worse had me rethinking my path. The War Raven claimed I'd reach the Woodlands. How had it known? How had it known my *name*?

Never would I have guessed, standing atop the tower earlier, that I'd be here now alone in the Grasslands, having met such a creature, and still alive to tell the tale.

I'd been a daily visitor at the Hall of Records ever since arriving at the palace. I'd read of war, of history, of the five houses, and of our myths and legends. Not once had I read about a War Raven able to shift into anything more than a dragon and a raven. So what was it? Something else?

Or perhaps the records didn't know everything there was to know about the creature.

Travel another hour and you'll be sorry, Deira D'Anu.

I shook off those haunting words and with shivering hands opened my satchel to root for a pen and my notebook. I wrote every impression and fact of my strange encounter until my frozen fingers were barely able to scratch in the two odd words it had called me, Light Bearer. Perhaps there was mention of it in the Fire Breather's history. Perhaps they, too, had a vast library.

What I wouldn't give to peruse another Hall of Records, to learn about a people and history so new to me. For the first time in my life, possibilities, a future stretched out before me.

If Balen was to be believed, my differences were not feared among Sydhrs. Should I find Mother's estate in ruins, I might be able to secure a place for myself within the community of the Fire Breathers. I'd need a profession, a skill to ensure my place and the means to provide food and shelter. The Hall of Records would work nicely. There I could scribe. I could research and learn more about the strange creature, the changeling War Raven.

Perhaps write a story, a great work of fact or fiction. Become a celebrated weaver of tales.

Every Danaan adored a good play, a good tale...

I placed my instruments back into the satchel, so that the pages of my notebook lay smooth and unbent, and then pushed to my feet. I chewed my lip, weighing my options. I'd always been focused on running away, but perhaps there was another path, a new life, a new profession with a people who accepted me. And that didn't seem as lonely as living in the old estate, still shunned and disliked by the world.

There was no more adrenaline or fear left to heat my body. I was depleted and knew I had to make a choice. Balen's image flashed in my mind, the closeness of his face as we'd knelt on the Great Hall floor, the unrelenting expression as he stared at me for what had seemed like an age, but, in truth, had only been a mere moment. His very being had overwhelmed me. Though, that wasn't surprising. He was a leader, a king, a champion who had lived longer than most.

He'd simply left me in his tent. No guards. No bindings.

I hadn't been a prisoner.

Making my choice, I started back.

No alarms had been raised, no activity abounded as they searched for me. It was quiet in the encampment. The scent of meat roasting on an open fire made my mouth water. Low voices drifted on the wind. I followed the back row of tents until I came to the one I'd left, stopping just short of going in to brush off my cloak. Once that was done, I lifted the back flap to the washing tent and ducked inside.

Blessed warmth greeted me. I stayed there for a long time, rubbing my hands together and letting the heat seep into my frozen body, before pushing the heavy tent material aside to enter the main area.

Balen sat at the table.

His amber gaze rose from his plate to study me before placing a piece of meat into his mouth and chewing it slowly, never taking his eyes off me.

I was too startled to move.

He leaned back, entirely too big for the chair, in a relaxed manner. But I wasn't fooled; the power coiled beneath the surface was unmistakable. "Did you enjoy your walk?"

My shoes were muddy and the hem of my cloak was dirty, stained, and adorned with small pieces of grass. Heat crept up my neck and into my cheeks. I blinked hard, mentally preparing myself for what I'd come back to do. I lifted my chin and looked straight at him as he grabbed a goblet from the table and drank.

"Aye, I did, thank you."

I fixated on the way his fingers held the goblet, the thumb rubbing up and down the curve of the cup as he considered me. This was a patient leader, one who thought well his words before he spoke them. A calculating male.

"You wish to know my intentions, Deira D'Anu?"

I wanted to bite my tongue and follow along, but that was never my strongest trait. "Aye. I do. But—" My nervousness burst force, rushing my thoughts. "Let me tell you mine. I'm a scribe, a good one. A *very* good one. I'm dedicated. I work hard, and I'd be an asset to your house. I can scribe the languages of three houses: Anu, Taranis, and Dagda, as well some letters of the ancients. I'm familiar with the inner workings of a palace, but I'd be just at home in a village, city or, preferably, a Hall of Records."

By the time I was through, I was out of breath and probably more red in the face than I'd been before. His thumb had stopped rubbing the goblet. His whole body had stilled. His chest rose, then fell on a deep exhale, drawing my eyes to the silver raven embroidered on his black tunic.

One corner of Balen's mouth twitched, creating an indentation in his cheek. Odd that such a small movement would change his features. But it did. The reactions of the servers in the Great Hall came back to me. Now I understood better their giggles and excitement, their claims that breathing fire might not be a bad thing, but a very wicked thing indeed.

"Let me understand correctly," he said, and I wanted to roll my eyes at the fact that I now noticed how deep and rich-sounding his voice was. "You wish to *work* for me?"

"Aye, of course. That's what I do, work."

His eyes remained hooded, completely unreadable. "I already have a scribe. Several, in fact."

"Oh." The small, disappointed response escaped my lips before I could prevent it.

He drained the goblet, set it on the table, and waved a hand to the empty seat nearby. "Please, sit." He threw a quick look over his shoulder and called, "Orin!"

Sitting at the table brought us closer together.

For once I wished I had my veil. At the palace I'd gotten used to the stares on the rare occasion when my veil came off or I was caught without it. But under Balen's intense scrutiny . . . it felt different somehow—more embarrassing, more hurtful. I gave myself a mental shake, reminding myself that I'd been studied like this before. It was no different, nothing new, nothing worth getting red-faced about.

"Why do you smile?"

I jerked. It wasn't a smile on my face, but a smirk at my own stupid thoughts. I sat straighter, wiping the expression off my face, grateful the servant Balen had called came into the tent, bringing with him the murmur of voices gathered outside.

Orin was larger than Balen, a warrior dressed in the same tunic as Balen. A long scar ran from his forehead to his left temple. One would never know the different stations between the two, though Balen was without the full beard. My grandfather, even out of battle regalia, always wore the finest clothes, always stood out among his men. Balen did not and Orin was unlike any servant I'd ever seen.

"Aye, Balen?" Orin asked, though his eyes were on me.

The wariness and wonder of his look made me cast my eyes to the tabletop. If just one person would look beyond the red hair, just one! I drew in a deep breath and let it out gradually.

"Please bring a plate for Deira. I believe she's hungry after her walk."

After Orin left, I regarded Balen with the same outright intensity that he'd bestowed upon me. "Why didn't you stop me?"

Balen filled an empty goblet and offered it to me. "Where would you have gone? There are leagues of Grasslands between camp and the nearest town."

"You don't think I could've made it." I took a long drink.

He smiled wide, not answering. He was even more beautiful when he smiled. I hated him for it. I hated myself for thinking it.

"I would've managed," I muttered.

Typical male Danaan. He might look different than those of my house, but he was just like the rest, bloated on his ego. Balen's smile deepened. Light flashed into his eyes.

Orin returned with a plate piled with meat and greens, the savory scents making my stomach grumble. I glanced at Balen's man. "Thank you."

"An honor to serve you Deira D'Anu," he replied easily then dipped his head to Balen. A look passed between them, something significant, as he left the tent.

"What did he mean by that? Why is it an honor to serve me?"

"Eat." Balen gestured to my plate, dismissing the question.

I gripped the edge of the wooden table, leaning forward. "You say I'm safe. You give me shelter, feed me... Yet you haven't told me why."

Lidi always said I was never good at holding my tongue. Balen had no obligation to tell me anything. I was at his mercy. Yet it was easy to forget my place when he lived in a simple tent, with simple food, and simple clothes.

Darkness slid across his features, reminding me of a fast gathering storm, of thunderclouds rolling in on themselves. Turmoil flashed in his eyes. He rose. "You must trust me, Deira."

Frowning, I went to speak, but he held up his hand. "Eat and rest. Tomorrow we leave for home." He crossed to the entrance.

I shot to my feet, the chair toppling over behind me.

"Home? But you can't go home. You just made an alliance to stay and fight."

Again that sadness in his eyes, coupled with a heavy breath and a grim set to his jaw. "We will fight, Deira, and end this war without your grandfather and Mael ever leaving their lands." He ducked under the flap and disappeared into the cold.

Chapter 5

I righted the chair, sat down, and ate, irritated at Balen and vowing that the next time he entered the tent, I'd get my answers. Once my stomach was full, I finished off the wine in the jug then pushed away from the table to examine the room.

The area was sparse, only furnished with a large trunk, a wide desk, and the table and chairs, which appeared to be made from local wood—an army this size didn't travel with an abundance of furniture; they made their own.

Another makeshift table in the corner served as a desk. A large map was spread on the rough wood surface. The language of the Fire Breathers was similar to all Danaans, though certain words, meanings, and inflections varied. Reading the map wasn't a struggle for me, though there were some words I couldn't translate.

I slid onto the chair, soaking up the beauty in the carefully drawn lines, symbols, and writing. Mountain ranges, valleys, rivers, lakes... The artistry was stunning. I loved maps. We had several in Murias, but nothing this old. The thin leather was aged to a soft yellow brown. All four ends curled up slightly. The map had been well-used for a very long time. My fingers traced over the Woodlands and then over the Grasslands and Plains to the Lakes. I found the island of Murias easily as it was the largest island in the largest lake.

I traced the path that led to the Bren Cara Mountains, home to the descendants of Sydhr, the Ageless One who gave them the gift of fire. Balen's home. I'd get to see those mountains for myself.

Not only would I write about the War Raven, but I'd write about my journey. I'd scribe a great work of adventure, things no Islander had ever seen or read of before.

Orin entered the tent, holding the flap open for a female, carrying two towels and a pile of clothes followed by a young male with two buckets of steaming water. "This is Nuallan and her son, Ferryn. They'll prepare your bath."

If Orin was surprised to find me sitting at Balen's desk, studying his map, he didn't show it. I pushed to my feet.

Ferryn was shade shorter than Orin, but his black hair was longer, falling to his shoulders. A lock of hair fell over one eye. He blew it out of the way only to have it fall right back where it had been.

It was rare to see a young one, male or female. Danaans, as a whole, weren't nearly as fertile as the plants and animals around us. In my small corner of Innis Fail, *I* was the young one; there hadn't been a child born to the House of Anu since I'd come into the world.

"We're pleased to serve you, Deira D'Anu." Nuallan said. She was tall, slim and beautiful, with high cheekbones, pale skin, and amber eyes. A red tunic covered black leggings and soft black boots. She reminded me of the dancers in the Great Hall, and I wondered if she'd been among them.

She bowed her head, cast an anxious eye to Orin before proceeding toward the bathing area.

"No, wait." I stepped into her path. Balen might not have been forthcoming, but perhaps the servants would be. "Why do you serve me? I'm a halfling, a servant, too."

Nuallan's eyes widened. The look she shared with Orin was one of wariness and sadness.

"What?" I asked, my concern growing. "What is it?"

"You don't know?" Ferryn asked, surprised.

"Ferryn, hush," Nuallan whispered. "It's not for us to tell."

Orin's heavy black brows drew together so deeply that it made his scar wrinkle. "He hasn't told you?"

"Told me what?"

Tension filled the tent. I looked from Orin to Nuallan and back again, my frustration mounting. "Orin…"

"Nuallan's right. It's not for us to tell." His look said otherwise. His look said he didn't agree with all the secrecy.

"Am I to die? Is that why I'm here?"

Ferryn fumbled with one of the buckets, nearly dropping it. Water sloshed onto the rug. His face reddened as Orin's twisted in a flash of grief. "Only one person's death is sure," Orin muttered, "and it's not yours. Yours is not yet written."

With that, he gathered the dishes from the table and left. Nuallan had already disappeared into the bathing area, Ferryn following quickly behind her.

I hurried after them.

Ferryn was dumping the hot water into a small bronze tub as his mother laid out the towels and clothing. She straightened and smiled at me as I approached. "Would you like assistance with your bath?"

Determined to get an answer, I stopped in front of her, wishing I towered over her to glare her into submission. But I was the one looking up, as usual. "Do you have any idea what it's like to be taken from your home, without a choice, without knowing *why*? Please. Help me to understand."

She gestured for Ferryn to leave the tent. After he was gone, she regarded me for a long time. Clearly she wanted to tell, but I guessed loyalty to Balen won out over that desire. "I'm sorry. I cannot. Balen will tell you . . . when the time is right. I know this must be hard. But you can trust him. He protects those in his care." Her eyes went sad at that. "There's soap on the stand by the tub. The clothing is for you. This might be your last hot bath for a while."

My shoulders sagged in defeat. "How long will it take to reach Bren Cara?"

She moved behind me to help with my clothes. "Two months, give or take."

Once I was bare, Nuallan plucked a few pieces of grass from my hair. Then, I stepped into the tub and eased into the hip-deep water as Nuallan left the tent.

The bath was a luxury, one I was exceedingly grateful for. I soaked for a while and then washed before the water grew cold. After rinsing, I wrapped a towel around my body and inspected the clothing Nuallan had set out for me.

There were soft, form-fitting leggings, matching socks and leather shoes. I picked up a white blouse and tunic, both softer than anything I'd ever worn. The gold trim around the tunic flashed in the light. Carefully, folded the tunic and set it aside.

The white shift for sleeping, I set aside as well. The delicate material was nearly see-through and not something I planned on sleeping in; the leggings and blouse would do just fine. There was a gown as well. I held it up. When the light hit the shimmering fabric, it shone like silver. It was a regal gown, something my mother would've worn. I folded that too, choosing to don the leggings, blouse, and a simple copper-colored tunic.

I finger-combed my hair then braided it into two braids that I coiled into two low knots behind my ears. Instinctively, I reached for my veil.

I had no veil.

For once, I didn't need one.

I stared at my reflection in the oval mirror that hung on the high back of the washing table. In the steady glow of the lanterns, I tried to see the Danaan in me. But I only found the human. Even the shade of my skin was different; darker than the pale perfection I saw on everyone else. My cheek bones weren't high and royal; they were softer, and my eyes were the exact shade of mud.

Despite my differences, I did not see the capability to steal the life from other living things, as Lidi had said I'd done as a child. I saw nothing *that* horrible in the face staring back.

I shoved the thought from my mind.

While they seemed to think my presence was an honor, I wouldn't make the mistake of believing the Fire Breathers welcomed me. I had to protect myself, had to focus on making a life for myself. That was all that mattered. Resolved, I sent a silent prayer to Anu and Dagda before entering the main tent to call for Orin.

He stepped inside so quickly he must have been waiting just outside the entrance. "Aye, Deira D'Anu?"

"Deira. Deira is fine." I drew in a quick breath and then started working on my future. "Tell me, Orin, is there anyone in camp who needs a scribe? Someone to read or write letters?" He blinked as though I'd spoken a foreign language. "I'd like to get out of the tent," I told him. "I'm used to keeping busy, and this is something I'm trained to do." He still said nothing. "Am I forbidden to leave?"

"No, no. Of course not."

I gave him an encouraging smile. Quickly he stepped aside, lifted the flap, and I walked through. I was allowed to leave, but apparently with an escort. Orin fell in step beside me.

"Perhaps you'll have luck in the female's tent," he offered, clasping his hands behind his back.

Sparks from the fire pit flew into the night sky. Two men

lifted a thick pole holding a slaughtered stag, headless and skinned, and placed it into the grooves of a roasting spit.

I'd always imagine the legions to be rowdy and boisterous, but here the mood was quiet and tempered. Men came and went from tents, some carrying supplies, others with bath towels thrown across bare shoulders. Between the spaces in the tents, I saw simple things. Laundry hung out to dry, a man sitting on a log cleaning a saddle. As we went down the wide pathway of stamped grass and mud, I heard snippets of conversation and the muffled sounds of music and laughter.

"Your culture is much different than what I'm used to. My grandfather never sets foot in the stables or serves himself wine."

"Balen is our leader, but he is also Sydhr." Orin's pride was evident. "If he can do for himself, he does. That is our way. We serve him not because we must, but because we choose to. It is an easy thing to do when he protects us, fights for us, would die for us. He puts the needs of his people first."

Orin stopped in front of a tent that looked like all the others. He cleared his throat loudly. "Females! I'm coming in!" He lowered his tone and said to me, "I've learned my lesson. Last time—" he shuddered—, "left me bruised for weeks. One thing you should know about Sydhr females, they are—"

"Are what?" Nuallan stepped from the tent with a challenging gaze leveled at warrior, though there was humor there too.

Orin let out a martyred sigh. "Nothing I say will be right." He shook his head then promptly changed the subject. "Deira wants to read or write something. I thought this was a good place to start."

I wasn't sure whether to laugh or frown at Orin's summation of what I'd asked. Nuallan rolled her eyes at him, placed a hand on my arm, and directed me toward the tent. "Males," she shot over her shoulder.

"Females," he returned as the tent flap closed behind us.

Now *this* was the tent of a king.

Curtains, walls of shimmering color threaded with gold and silver, hid the drab gray of the tent cloth. There were tables and chairs and side tables full of trinkets and food. Luxurious couches and pillows of the deepest jewel tones filled the space and were occupied by the beautiful Sydhr dancers I'd seen in the hall.

It was the tent of a queen.

A *queen*.

I hadn't thought of that. How could I have not thought of it before? Of course, Balen had a queen.

Nuallan dropped her hand from my arm. Silence filled the tent. I smoothed the front of my tunic as they regarded me with speculative eyes.

One of the dancers rose gracefully from the couch and approached. She scrutinized every inch of me so thoroughly that each second passed tediously slow. Then her eyes filled with tears, her hand went to her mouth to stifle a sob, and she ran from the tent.

The others crowded around me, all with somber expressions. I looked to Nuallan for answers. "Did I do something wrong?

The shortest woman of the six tilted her head. "You don't know?"

"No." Of course not. No one would tell me!

They burst into murmurs, speaking too quickly for me to follow. The one who'd spoken stepped closer. Though the shortest of the dancers, she was still taller than me, but not by much. Her shiny straight hair was tucked behind both ears and she had an impish quality to her face. She smiled. "Your hair is truly the color of flame." She led me to one of the couches, plopped down behind me, and began uncoiling the buns.

The others joined us, sitting on the couch, the floor, or in the chairs nearby.

Nuallan settled next to me and rolled her eyes. "The one who is so rudely taking down your hair is Ciara. The others are Bryn, Daya, Mab, Edanna, and the one who fled is Ixia."

"Is she your queen?"

Ciara's hands stilled on my hair. "Ixia is closest to Balen," she said in an uncertain tone. "She's the eldest and has known him the longest."

"But she does not love him anymore or better than we do," the one called Edanna said from the chair next the couch, her long legs thrown over the arm, the blue gown riding high on her thighs without care.

"Does it wave like this on its own?" Daya asked from the floor, rising up to touch my hair, which was down now thanks to Ciara.

"Aye."

"She has eyes the color of polished copper." Was that Bryn or Mab who spoke? I couldn't tell them apart.

There was no disgust or superiority in their regard. In fact, I felt more like a fine material they might inspect for a gown.

"Tell us about the House of Anu," Edanna said. "Is it true you possess power over water? We've heard the priestesses can bring rain and flood, and control the tides."

"Aye, it's true. But only the most powerful can control the tides. My mother was High Priestess of Anu," I said with pride. "But I only remember the water games she played with me."

"Will you show us?"

Suddenly, I was not so proud. I had no power. Unlike the direct descendants of Anu, I held no control of her precious element. "I cannot."

"Please," Daya said, sitting forward.

"I'm a halfling. I have no power." The words hurt coming out. "There were others like me . . . before during the Old War. Do you know about them?"

They shook their heads in unison. Then, Daya said, "You have no power at all?"

My face grew hot. "None."

They were quiet. I closed my eyes, trying to enjoy the luxury of having my hair combed and ignore the embarrassment I felt.

"Well," Ciara said gently, "everyone has power. Perhaps you haven't discovered yours yet."

"No, I'm like my father. The power of the goddess doesn't run through my veins."

One of the women sighed. "What I wouldn't give to see a man, a human."

The others laughed. Nuallan rolled her eyes at them. "They find favor in tales of old, in the days when our two peoples mingled freely, and—" She gave them a stern look— "in things barbaric and forbidden, no?"

Several chuckled in a low, intimate way.

I considered telling them the things my father had written about in his books and papers; all the things he'd loved, the history he knew.

But I didn't tell them.

I remembered, sitting up straighter, I'd left my satchel and all my writing instruments in the tent. The comb pulled. Ciara scolded the sudden movement with a soft cluck, gently working out the tangle I'd just made.

I went to inquire about writing services anyway—surely they had parchment and pen with them, but Ixia entered the tent with Balen and my inquiry went unspoken.

Her eyes were red. Her arm was linked tightly with his, unmoving as he gently tried to free himself. He dipped his head and whispered something in a low, comforting tone.

They looked so . . . perfect together.

One by one, the dancers left me and approached Balen, giving him a small curtsy and then a warm kiss to his hand or cheek. My hands itched to twist up my hair into a veil. Out of sight.

And away from the fiery eyes that locked onto mine.

He stared at me for what felt like ages, before giving a curt nod to the dancers and leaving the tent.

Shaken, I rose, ready to go back to the tent, to be alone with myself and away from their teary eyes.

I'd had enough for one night.

Nuallan led me to the exit. Ixia didn't move aside as we approached. For a moment, I thought she'd strike me, but her words were far, far worse.

"He dies because you live." She swept her long hair behind one shoulder, pushing by me. "I wish we'd never come here."

Chapter 6

Ciara and Nuallan escorted me outside. "What did she mean?"

Ciara drew in a deep breath. "You were foretold by our queen, Balen's mother, at his birth. She was mad, but her foretelling, they were always right."

"With hair the color of flame, she will return the Light and deliver the land from darkness, and the champion will fall in her stead," Nuallan spoke, reciting words of old.

"Balen will die." Ciara's voice was grief-stricken. "His fate has been written. You've been found, and soon he will be no more."

The anguish in their eyes elicited the same feeling in me. The memory of Balen's expression and words came back to me. The sadness I'd seen in Orin's eyes. The mood of the legions. They all believed Balen would die.

No. There was no way in Annwn I'd ever believe it. "I make my own fate, my own choices. And so can Balen. He won't die because of me I can assure you. I'm not this person you speak of. I'm a halfling. I have no real power to deliver the land from darkness. I can't even summon a raindrop."

Their jaws dropped. Their eyes widened. And I left.

I paid no attention to the path I took or the activity around me as I relived the past few hours, letting the reason Balen had taken me set in, and determined to set whatever foretelling they spoke of on its head. No one, not even a mad soothsaying queen, would make my choices for me. I'd be a scribe, *not* a savior. And that was that.

Aye, I was determined. I had my freedom and my own path to follow. No one would die just because I'd been found.

Pain shot through my scalp as something snagged my hair and jerked me back. "Ow!"

Fire balls lit up the night sky.

The camp erupted in shouts and screams.

Arms wrapped around me. I screamed as Fire Breathers appeared in the lane.

But their attention was fixed beyond me. Fire grew from their bare palms and generated enough wind to shift the hair off their stark, confident faces. That same hot wind blew over me as they launched the fire overhead. It hit behind me and exploded with a loud roar.

Splinters flew like missiles as I struggled, kicking my feet and fighting against the arms that held me. But I was dragged into a dark spot between tents as the Legion of Annwn swarmed down the avenue and into camp.

My gut tightened as I realized what held me. A member of the fifth house of Innis Fail. A Fallen warrior. The dead.

Holding my breath, I looked down at the arms around me and found nothing but sinew and bone. My screaming and struggling began anew, fueled by the terror of what held me so close.

The ground shook from pounding hooves. Shouts and cries echoed. Smoke billowed around us, making its way into my lungs as I coughed and gasped for air. The Fallen kept pulling me deeper and deeper into the darkness. If it succeeded in getting me away from camp, I'd never make it back. I had to do something.

Thinking quickly, I ceased struggling and threw my weight with my captor instead of against it. It lost balance and its hold eased. As soon as it did, I buckled my knees, dropped out of its bony arms, then darted forward. I ran, my heart pounding, adrenaline flowing quick and hot as I dodged horses, fire, Nox's army of Annwn, and his creatures of the Underworld.

I narrowly missed colliding with an enormous white battle hound with ferocious red eyes as it lunged at a group of three Sydhr warriors. In the panic and chaos, I realized I was lost. All the avenues and tents looked the same. I had to get back to the tent, had to get my satchel—it held the only things of value I had in the world.

I skidded to a dead stop, trying to get my bearings.

There. The half circle of tents.

I ran into Balen's tent, found my satchel and slung the strap across my chest. I made for the back of the tent, but fire hit, exploding one side of the tent and sending me flying. I landed hard, the breath knocked out of me.

Flames ate up the material in a loud, crackling frenzy.

Heat stung my face as I struggled to get up.

Coughing and attempting to shield myself from debris and flames, I staggered outside.

The lane was blocked by fire.

Another tent erupted into a ball of flame. Then another, until I was trapped in a ring of fire. I spun, pulse thumping wildly, searching for a way through. The heat was scorching. I covered my mouth. If only I could summon water!

And I tried. I stood there and tried with my whole body, mind, and heart, but nothing came except the sting of frustrated tears.

I scanned the flames, looking for a weak spot. I was going to get burned, I knew. But burned was better than dead. My fists clenched at my sides. I found a spot and readied myself. I took two steps toward the flames when, suddenly, they wavered and Balen, clad in black armor, stepped through, larger than life.

He never faltered, never hesitated, just marched right up to me, picked me up before I could move, threw me over his shoulder, and strode back toward the flames.

We didn't make it.

A white hound leapt the flames and landed squarely before us.

Balen set me down, pushing me behind him. "Stay back," he said as the hound crouched down, the hairs on its back stiff and straight. Its lips pulled back in a bloody snarl as Balen drew his sword. Flames danced in the reflection of the blade.

The hound leapt. Balen waited . . . waited . . . then he rolled forward, came up on one knee, and stabbed the hound in the belly as it sailed over him. The blade slid in effortlessly. Blue flame spread from the hilt of the sword, down the blade, and into the hound's body, engulfing it. Almost instantly, it became ash, which fell softly to the ground.

Balen shook the ash from his hair and then held out his hand. But I couldn't seem to move.

"Deira!"

I jumped at the deep command, sliding my hand into his. He tugged me close, wrapping me in his arms, his big armored body protecting me as we walked through the flames.

Beyond the flames, a group of battle-ready Sydhrs, Orin included, waited atop eager horses, two of which were without riders.

"Orin!" Balen shouted above the chaos. "Secure the encampment!"

Balen lifted me onto one of the horses then mounted the other. Orin moved his mount close to Balen and they clasped hands. "May the blessings of Sydhr go with you." His features were set in grief, his eyes bright with it. "It has been my honor to serve with you."

"And you, Orin." Balen reined the horse around to face

me. "Keep your head down. Stop for nothing."

I needed no other encouragement. I hadn't really ridden since my father left, but I knew enough to grab a handful of mane, dig my heels into the horse's sides, and hold on as the large beast charged down the avenue with Balen beside us.

"Where are we going?" I shouted, surprised when we veered into the Grasslands and away from the battle.

"Home!"

Stunned, I sat straighter and pulled my mount to a stop. It danced, tossing its head, eager to continue. Balen spun around and cantered back to us, a thunderous look on his face. "Now?" I asked, incredulously. "In the middle of the fight?"

"I told you before we were going home."

"With the rest of your people! Are you mad? We can't leave. They're back there fighting, dying."

Fury hardened his features. "You think I don't know that? You think this is what I *want*?" he shouted, angling his horse closer to mine as the beast pranced and pawed the ground. "Stop thinking and questioning everything, Deira," he said coldly. "You and I have a battle far greater than this. My legions were never going to accompany us tomorrow. I don't leave them lightly. I leave them to save them—their families, their children, their world."

He slapped my mount on the rear and galloped on.

We rode hard, the Grasslands seeming to go on forever. Eventually, the panic of our flight gave way to weariness. Sweat darkened the hair behind my mount's ears and along its long, muscled neck. The coarse mane tangled in my grip. I was grateful with every stride that Father had insisted I learn how to ride.

I glanced back and could no longer see the light of the camp behind us. We were entirely alone.

Until a shadow glided overhead and then soared upward with a screeching cry.

The War Raven.

* * *

My horse munching loudly on grass woke me. Whiskers tickled my ear. A soft nose nudged my shoulder as the beast's teeth tried for a clump of grass beneath me.

I rolled to the side, giving him what he wanted, and pulled my knees to my chest, using my arm for a pillow. My face and eyes were puffy, my body stiff, and the insides of my thighs ached.

I hadn't ridden a horse in so long; just drawing my legs to my chest had hurt. Warm breath blew on my cheek. My hair was tugged as my horse mouthed the strands.

I sat up and removed my hair from his mouth. "That's not grass, you fool." I scratched the white star between his eyes, not yet wanting to rise and knowing how much it'd hurt when I did. The gelding stuck out his nose to breathe in my scent then returned to scavenging for grass.

I raised my arms over my head and stretched, then bent forward to touch my toes until my muscles lengthened. "Oh sweet Dagda, that hurts." I rubbed my eyes, noticing Balen's horse grazing nearby.

We'd camped in a dense grove of trees where small blue flowers carpeted the ground. Birds chirped and flitted from tree to tree. While the cold had come upon our land slowly, it seemed as though the wildlife in this spot was too stubborn to admit defeat. Give it another year or two and no matter how hard life wanted to bloom, it would not.

We were getting close to the Woodlands—deep, ancient forests, home to the descendants of Dagda, goddess of nature and the one house that remained neutral in the fight against Nox.

Tipping my face to the dim light above, I soaked in what little warmth there was, knowing with a heavy heart that soon it would fade forever. Our world would cease to exist, frozen and forgotten and dark.

Nox had chosen our time of greatest weakness to wage war on us all.

Standing, I stretched once more and then approached Balen's horse. I trailed my hand over the blue flowers, glad they had forced their way into the world even if for a brief time. Flashes beyond the trees drew me to a small stream.

Balen crouched by the edge of the stream. His armor was gone, revealing a simple padded tunic in black, his leggings, and boots. He splashed water onto his face three times then dragged his wet fingers through his hair.

I stopped behind him, nervous in the light of day. "You really believe in this foretelling?" I said at length.

He rose, not answering, as I went to the water for a drink. After I had my fill, I turned to find him sitting on the bank, resting his back against a rock, one knee drawn up.

"All of my mother's foretellings have come to pass," he said as I found a flat rock to sit upon. "This one will, too."

"Even if it means your death?"

A weary exhale blew past his lips. His gaze shifted to the water. He leaned forward, resting both elbows over his knees. "Aye, even that."

"You would accept it so easily?"

"You assume I have. Did you not ride to the docks thinking the same—that you might die? Yet you rode toward it as surely I will ride toward mine. It is never *easy*."

"I'm sorry. I know it's not... What does the foretelling say exactly?"

He eyed me for a long moment before pushing to his feet. As he stopped in front of me, my nerves leapt to life once again. Then, surprisingly, he lifted a curl from my shoulder. "It is truly like flame." His voice was low and filled with the reverence all Sydhrs had for fire.

I struggled with my reaction, hoping he couldn't see the whirlwind taking place inside me or the confusion it brought. He was beautiful, strong, and powerful—I'd seen plenty like him in my life, but none had looked at me without bias, without hate or disgust or fear.

Sadness crept into his eyes, but fled as quickly as it came. "The foretelling says only a being of both worlds can find the Lia Fail. Such a person can bear the Light and bring it home." He tugged on my hair and gave a wry smile. "That person is you."

I slid off the rock. "It's not me. I don't know what to do, where it is, or how to get it back. I have no power. None." None that mattered, anyway.

Frustrated, I glanced around us, wishing the grove was as it should be—vibrant and greener and flourishing in perpetual summer. But bringing back our Light, defeating Nox? That was a quest for a champion, for an army, not me.

Balen's brow rose as he crossed his arms over his chest, my words apparently having no weight at all. "That's why it must be you. Name another with hair such as yours. Do you know how many years I've waited to find one with the blood of both lands running through their veins? Once the gates between our world and the world of men were closed, I thought such a being would never again exist. Now I know the foretelling to be true."

"Such a being is destined to *take* life not save it," I said hating that was part of what I was, part of the blood running through my veins.

"Aye, the halflings took life. They used their power just as we use ours. The offspring of Danaan and human were gifted with a power we'd never seen before or expected. And some of them used it against us in the Old War. How one uses their power is up to them, a choice. We aren't ruled by it. And I don't believe your kind was either."

"They were outlawed, put to death, the gates closed against them. Whatever they did, they caused the law today." I stared at the water rushing over the rocks. "I don't want to become the monster they say I am."

"Then don't." He put his hands on my shoulders and turned me around. "I don't see the heart of a monster. I know what you are, Deira. Your grandfather told me. I know you have the power to steal the life force from any living thing you desire." I cringed, but he just smiled. "So you learn how to control it and you choose what to do with it."

"You speak of choices and yet you will walk down the path your mother set as if you have no choice at all."

He shrugged. "Such is the nature of fate. Sometimes we come right back around to it, no matter all the other choices we've made." Confidence and utter conviction blazed in his eyes. "Together we will set right to the wrong, Deira."

He thought fate and foretelling would drive us, make us succeed at an impossible task. How many warriors had gone through the Deadlands and the Void in search of our Light? No one had ever returned.

"You put too much faith in words, Balen." I headed back to the camp.

Where most Danaans believed their fate was set in stone before their births, humans possessed a strong sense of will, a belief that they could change their lot, make a better life, rise above fate and make their own way—or so my Father often said. I didn't believe in fate.

I couldn't.

Otherwise I'd be admitting to myself that I was simply a puppet, that I made no real decisions or choices of my own. I'd been forced to live that way in Murias for too many years. I wasn't about to do so again.

Finding my mount where I'd left him, I busied myself preparing the saddle and tack to ride once again. I was angry. I didn't want to be part of his quest. I didn't want to save the world.

I didn't want to save the world.

It was a hard, terrible truth to swallow, and I hated myself for thinking it, for feeling it.

Balen approached with his horse. "How exactly do you propose we find the Lia Fail anyway?" I asked, as he tightened the girth on my mount.

"Travel across the Deadlands, through the Void and into Éire."

"Éire?" My father's homeland. The world of men.

"It must be you, Deira. You alone know things, things learned from him that will aid us. So much was destroyed after the war; anything having to do with mankind was put to the flames."

Balen finished with my mount and went back to his. A tiny spark of . . . something blossomed in my chest. My stomach somersaulted at the thought of Éire. Seeing my father's homeland had always been a dream, something I never thought possible.

I watched Balen. He worked with efficiency, his expression preoccupied. He paused suddenly, scowled and then shook his head. Was it me who put that scowl there?

A shrill familiar cry echoed through the grove. The War Raven had shifted into raven form and was circling above us in a wide arc. So beautiful and magical. So deadly and rare.

The whole of Innis Fail was the same. Not that I'd know

firsthand, but I knew some; I'd read enough books to know. Balen was one of those rarities, too. A great champion with the gift of fire. I'd seen that firsthand and it made me think of all the things still left to learn. Of course, any kind of future I might hope for would never be possible unless the Lia Fail was found and returned to our world.

I bit on my bottom lip, watching Balen from over the back of my horse as he tied his bedroll to the saddle.

I could go with him.

Try to do this thing he thought I could do, and in the process perhaps find out if my father made it back home. Balen picked up the scabbard that contained his broad sword. He fastened it over his back, the strap diagonal across his chest.

Guilt tightened around me. He wanted to save his world, was ready to give his life for it, and I was . . . unsure. I wasn't like him, not even close.

Travel across the Deadlands through the Void to find the Lia Fail in Éire—were near-impossible tasks. Time was different in the human world, my mother had once told me. It ran faster than here in Innis Fail. There would be no one left alive from the time when the Lia Fail was taken. Many generations would have passed. The known location of the Light might be lost forever.

And my father... Had he stayed here with me he'd be a man of fifty years now. But in the human realm, he'd be much, much older. Frail. Possibly gone. Probably gone...

"Deira."

Balen was mounted up and eyeing me impatiently. Quickly,

I gathered the reins, pulled myself onto the horse, and settled into the saddle. I urged him into a canter, passing Balen, not wanting the Fire Breather to see any hint of the pain and conflict my somber thoughts had brought me.

We rode until the light faded to a heavy, overcast gray. It would remain that way until nightfall.

Balen slowed his horse to a walk.

I noticed that the raven had kept pace with us. It perched on the limb of a tall tree, watching us, its dark feathers folded against its back.

"The creature," I gestured toward the tree. "The War Raven. What is it truly?"

Balen frowned as though surprised by the question. "Why do you ask?"

"Is it your companion?"

He hesitated and then answered carefully, "In a manner, aye."

"It speaks to you?"

"When it chooses."

"I read once that one must claim the heart of a War Raven to gain its powers. Is that true?" He shot me an incredulous look.

"You think I can claim a War Raven?" His grin deepened as he stared straight ahead, his body rocking easily with the motion of the horse. "That I have the strength and power?"

My eyes narrowed. "That *is* what I've read," I answered, holding back my smile. "I'm not sure if 'claiming a heart' is to be taken literally. Perhaps it means something else. Is that what you've done, claimed the creature?"

His laughter carried warm and rich on the cool air. His grin went deep, revealing straight white teeth, and dimples in the dark scruff of his cheeks—a startling change to the usual grim warrior's visage.

"I'm going to take that as a no," I said. He feigned a hurtful look. "How about breathing fire? Can you do that?"

His brows shot up. He thought for a moment. "I have many *strengths*. It might take some time to list them all, but if you're willing…"

A laugh slipped out and I shook my head at his teasing as he guided his mount between two mossy rocks. I went around the outside and joined up with him once again. For a long stretch of time, we were quiet. I enjoyed the sway of the horse's gait, the soft thud of their hooves on the packed earthen trail we rode. For once, I felt comfortable in my own skin and comfortable with someone other than Lidi.

"Perhaps one day I'll show you, Deira," he said with quiet amusement, "how well I can breathe fire."

He led the way, directing his horse down a slopping bank as I stared dumbly at his back, my stomach suddenly as light as air.

Single file we went down the narrow track and I was glad to concentrate on the trail. Though, at times, I found myself looking at Balen's wide chainmail-clad shoulders and the place where his short black hair met the back of his neck. Why such a small place captured my attention, I didn't know… Though I recognized the feelings it stirred in me.

I hadn't grown up so closeted that I wasn't familiar with attraction. I'd had my own obsessions with a few males from the palace. One, a messenger who'd often take his meals in the kitchen. Every time he'd enter, my heart would beat faster and my fingers would go clumsy. He only spared me notice when I'd dropped something or otherwise made a fool of myself. The other was a scribe in the Hall of Records. Smart, handsome, so talented. Sometimes we'd work together in the quiet of the hall. Sometimes, we'd even talk. And sometimes at night, I'd dream of love, of what it would be like to touch and be touched.

And I'd read. I'd read all those manuscripts and scrolls that a girl my age was forbidden to read. But no one ever cared what I read; they only cared if my veil was on and if I stayed away from the nobility of Murias. By fifteen, I was well-versed in love and sex. On paper. When it came to practice, however, I was severely lacking. Even at twenty-one.

Perhaps it was time to change that.

Chapter 7

We made camp at the edge of the Woodlands shortly after nightfall. Dense forest stretched out before us; thick, ancient, dark, and impossibly tall. The Woodlands were vast, said to contain lost cities, caves and lakes of legend, and creatures of lore. There were entire tribes who lived in isolation from the rest of Innis Fail, animals rarely ever seen, flowers of untold beauty and magical properties.

This was where I'd been raised, on the outskirts of one of the largest Woodland communities and the center of worship for the descendants of Dagda.

I'd finally come home.

I un-tacked my horse, placing the heavy saddle on the ground next to Balen's, then spreading the sweat-dampened saddle pad out to dry. With a clump of long dry weeds, I rubbed the brown beast down, removing as much sweat from his coat as I could and enjoying the work while Balen dumped a small pile of wood inside a ring of stones he'd already gathered.

Once I was done, I removed the bridle from my horse's mouth and set the animal free to eat whatever grass it could find just as Balen had instructed. Apparently, Sydhr mounts were trained to stay with the herd; the herd being us.

I made for the wood pile and dropped down in front of it to remove my shoes and rub my stiff ankles. "Do you think we've been followed?"

Balen crouched down on the other side of the pile, arms draped over his knees. "Nox would never expect me to run from a fight, from an attack on my people."

I grabbed my braid and shook it at him. "But what if they saw this and know of the foretelling?"

"The foretelling is known only to my people." He waved his hand over the wood and a small flame sprouted from the center.

Fascinated, I reached over the edge of the wood and caught his hand, turning it palm up. "How did you do that?" When I raised my head, it was to find him eye level with me, on his knees, one hand balancing himself on the ground. In my haste, I'd tugged him down, toward me.

It reminded me of that first time in the Great Hall. I tried to swallow, but my mouth had gone dry. The small flame in the wood began to grow, but not enough yet to make me back away.

I cleared my throat, feeling the need to say *something*. "It doesn't feel hot, your hand."

"Fire will not burn me because it's part of me. We exist together just as water exists in your people, the people of Anu."

In my people, I thought, releasing Balen's hand and sitting back down. Not, however, in me.

"Here." He moved to sit next to me and opened his hand. "I'll show you."

I didn't want to meet his gaze, so I concentrated on his hand, noticing every callous and scar, all the lines on his palm. He took my hand, making me hold his like I'd done when I reached across the fire. My first instinct was to pull away.

"Watch." He directed my attention downward. "You simply call it forth, like calling forth a thought or action."

It was so small, at first. But it grew until it danced as high as a candle flame.

"Brave enough to put your hand in the flame?" he challenged with a smile.

"Brave enough, aye, but smart enough not to."

That brought out a low chuckle. "The flame won't injure you, Deira."

My brow rose at that. He gestured toward the flame with a nod, urging me to see for myself. Tempted, I bit my lip, drew in a deep breath, and waved my hand over the flame. "It's hot."

"Of course it is."

I did it again, closer, slower, testing the flame and waiting to feel the first sign of a burn. Odd. "It's hot, but my skin doesn't burn. How is that possible?"

He closed his hand into a fist, extinguishing the flame, and

I let go. "I don't know how it's possible, only that it is. It's driven by intention. And thank Sydhr for the ability to control it or many a child would've burned down everything around them."

There was dry amusement in his voice. The growing campfire highlighted the lines that crinkled around his eyes, lines that should not have been there.

He was aging.

The realization struck me with more emotion than I would have guessed. To think of a larger than life champion, a Fire Breather, felled by old age . . . it didn't seem right or fair. But, as the Darkness grew, so did the aging process and our ability to heal most wounds. Innis Fail had been the land of youth. Once maturity was reached, we lived long, long lives, only cut short by violent acts, treachery and war, terrible accidents...

Some of our oldest citizens had chosen to roam other lands and times, or to release the ties of the body and journey on to the Place of Souls.

I drew my legs beneath me as Balen removed bread and cheese from the leather bag. He laid them on the linen cloth they'd been wrapped in and placed it between us.

"Why would Nox attack the camp? With three houses gathered, he was outnumbered to begin with."

Balen stretched out his legs and stuffed a chunk of bread into his mouth. "He grows bolder as the Darkness grows. What weakens us makes him stronger. He sees opportunity. The attack wasn't about winning the war, but a message. A message to say he's willing and able, that's he's not afraid or deterred by our numbers."

"If he knows about your quest to regain the Light, he'll put all of his resources into stopping you. He controls the Deadlands and the Void. The only gateway back into the human realm lies in his lands."

"Aye, it does. Nox was smart to argue for his gate's preservation."

Balen spoke of the other gateways into the human world and the decision to destroy them at the close of the Old War, a war where Nox had been an ally not an enemy. One gate, it was decided at Nox's urging, would remain. And that gate was in Nox's territory, for if a human was to come through, they'd find nothing but desolation and death—enough to propel them back into the safety of their own world.

And it had worked, until my father stumbled through the gate and miraculously found his way across the Deadlands and into the Woodlands where Mother found him and loved him.

"The Deadlands are beyond the Bren Cara Mountains," I noted quietly. "What's it like, your home?"

He smiled. "Jagged mountains. Green valleys. Hot springs and waterfalls from the snow caps." The harsh lines of his face softened, his eyes growing wistful as he spoke. "Fierce weather. Not perpetual summer like here in the Lowlands. It's wild and untamed like the eagles and ravens that fly overhead."

"And when this is over," I said. "You will give me a job, won't you?"

He nearly choked on a piece of cheese. He coughed so hard, that I leapt to my feet and into action, hitting him hard between the shoulder blades as Lidi had taught me to do.

All I received for my effort was a grunt, an exasperated glance over his shoulder, followed by a soft chuckle. "You are an unusual female, Deira D'Anu."

I stepped back, rattled. Embarrassed.

My heart knocked hard and painfully in my chest as I smoothed my hands down my leggings and sat back down, studying the fire. His words shouldn't have hurt, but they did. *Unusual* always meant something bad, something feared. I didn't want to be unusual. I wanted to be normal.

A finger touched lightly under my chin. I lifted my eyes, wondering why now, why must my damn tears start rising now, in front of him?

"I'm sorry. I have quickly forgotten the way it was for you." A hard glint came into his eyes and his jaw went tight. "My words were meant as a compliment."

He was angry. Angry for me. I didn't know what to say to that, since it was an altogether new experience. So I brushed it aside. "Well, you speak the truth. I am different, unusual. A Halfling. There's a blight on my soul and—"

"No," he said sharply. "There's not. That is not who you are. You are our hope, a blessing." He inhaled and exhaled deeply, looking into the darkness of the forest. "Perhaps that is my fault."

"You're fault?"

"We Sydhrs are a private people. Had I not kept the foretelling strictly within our own ranks, perhaps you would've been recognized for what you were from your birth and treated accordingly. We always believed the Light Bearer would be born to us since I'd be the one to lead her, and the foretelling came from one of our own."

"I'm not sure any of the other houses would have believed you, had you shared the foretelling. A halfling to save them? They would not have taken that kindly." I smiled. "Thanks, though, for the words. I'm not used to being seen as a good thing... It's good you didn't tell. Otherwise Nox would've been looking for me from the beginning."

Balen's expression grew serious. "I swear by the blood of Sydhr, you'll always be looked after by my house. Always accepted. Always regarded with great value, no matter the outcome of our journey." He handed me a chunk of bread. "You should eat more." He waited until I obliged.

It was hard to swallow the bread when a lump had formed in my throat.

The outcome of the journey, according to the foretelling, was Balen's death. Mine might not be told, but his—to him at least—was. "It doesn't have to be this way," I said after a spell. "You can fight. Sometimes it's possible to make your own destiny, to change things, to not give in."

"And how would you know, *seirnann*?"

"I just know. And what does *seirnann* mean?"

"It means Little Flame." He gestured to my hair. "For your hair and your..." He smiled. "Youthful optimism."

A very unladylike snort came out of me. He was teasing, the smile told me that, but I wasn't sure how to take it. He was distracting me from the subject of fate and death, avoiding it. And I guess I couldn't blame him. Who wanted to talk about their impending demise? But I wasn't a child. And optimism wasn't only for the young.

I left the fire and headed into the dark woods. "Stubborn," I muttered under my breath as I made for the stream nearby.

It *was* possible to change fate. But who would believe me? I had no proof. Just conviction. In that, Balen I were the same. We both had our beliefs and convictions, but neither of us had any proof—we just had faith.

The realization was frustrating and made the sense of helplessness I felt even greater.

The trees' long shadows stretched over the ground, cut by shafts of moonlight. The air had become cold and thin. I shivered, peering across the stream and into the black depths of the forest. The only thing that could stop Nox was the Lia Fail. If he discovered Balen and I intended to find it, he would come. He wouldn't stop. He'd be unmerciful.

Nox's misdeeds were legendary. He was King of Annwn, the Underworld. Of all the rulers of the five houses, he was the longest lived. He ruled over the territory of the Deadlands and the vast labyrinth of caves and hidden valleys of Annwn. It was whispered that while he committed terrible deeds, he also lavished wealth upon those who pleased him, mainly females. Females he'd stolen. Or tempted. Or enchanted. It was said that none could resist him. It was said that he was brutal and unforgiving in battle. That he was malevolent beyond compare. That his wealth and desires were decadent and obscene.

I crouched on the bank of the stream and drank, keeping my hearing trained to the sounds of the night. Then, I found a clump of bushes to relieve myself.

An Otherworldly, moonlit head craned over the bushes. "Fertilizing the forest are we?"

I yelped and nearly tumbled backwards.

With lightning speed, I righted myself and jerked up my leggings, my heart pounding. "Some things are meant to be private," I forced through gritted teeth, not bothering to move since the bushes provided a barrier between us.

"Why should privacy be reserved for such an inconsequential thing?" The War Raven cocked its head. Even with the close view, I still couldn't tell if it was male or female in its Danaan-like form. "*I* do not hide it."

I didn't know whether to laugh or congratulate it. "That is you're right," I said carefully. "Are you War Raven or Danaan?"

"Are you Danaan or human?"

"Both."

It shrugged. "Your tunic is stuck in your britches."

I bit back an angry retort and quickly fixed the tunic. "Is there something you want?"

Its luminous eyes blinked slowly. The long silver hair fell forward, framing its black face as it leaned forward to study me.

"Why are you here?" I asked. "What are you to Balen?"

"I am Balen's, that is why I'm here," it answered with a sing-song voice. "I am his and he is mine."

The snap of a branch cut our conversation short.

The creature straightened, lifting its chin. Its small nostrils flared and its eyes stared blankly ahead. My pulse quickened, but I remained still, poised to flee or fight.

The sound of running feet broke through the quiet.

Balen's dark form dashed through the trees, sword in hand, armor on.

The creature's eyes narrowed and glowed brightly. Its face stretched as its mouth opened to issue a vicious roar that rent the night air and sent the birds flying over head. I covered my ears, stumbling back, watching in horror as its teeth elongated and its body grew, dwarfing me as the dragon took shape.

Anger. So much anger swelled from it.

Then, a tremble began under my feet, building quickly. Through the shafts of moonlight, I saw them coming. Riders. The Fallen Warriors of Annwn. Nothing but sinister bones, tattered armor, and sharp swords. Sheer fright rooted me to the spot as Balen slid to a stop in front of me, shoving me behind him.

Dragon wings stretched skyward then swept down, pushing the air underneath them and sending debris mushrooming off the forest floor as it lifted off, tucking sharp clawed feet against its belly.

"How many?" Balen shouted to the War Raven, pulling me back into the shadows. He shoved me down, his hand hard on my shoulder. Just as I looked up, dragon's breath lit up the night sky. Horses shrieked in terror, a sound that sent shivers up my spine.

I didn't hear an answer to Balen's question, but he must have heard because he cursed roughly before grabbing my hand and running through the forest, going deeper and deeper into the thick darkness where the moonlight couldn't penetrate the treetops.

He stopped beneath the limbs of a tall tree. "Up here. Hurry." He gripped my waist in both hands and launched me into the tree.

I gasped, my arms flailing as I flew upwards. I missed two branches, but managed to grab onto a third as I began to fall back down. Balen's hands shoved the soles of my feet, pushing me higher until I was able to pull myself up. When I gained my balance, straddling the limb, I reached for his hand.

He didn't take it.

Fire danced in his eyes, and in the darkness it was a bright and terrifying thing; they blazed with determination and a warrior's anticipation. "Climb, Deira. Don't come down until I return." His tone deepened with warning. "Whatever you do, don't make a sound. If they come, use your power. Let your instinct take over. Don't be afraid of it. Don't hold back."

My pulse thundered through my ears. "The Fallen have no life for me to take," I said desperately.

"They have a small spark. It's what reanimates them. You take it and they'll fall."

But I didn't know how…

"You do and you can," he said, reading my expression. "You can if your life depends on it. Remember what I said. Climb high. No sound."

He wouldn't leave until I promised. Unable to speak, I dipped my head sharply. He gave a curt nod and then jogged away, his tall, dark form swallowed up by the forest.

Chapter 8

I climbed, careful and slow, terrified of falling and trying not to think of just how high I was going. With each limb, my muscles tired, but still I went higher until the branches above me grew too thin to hold my weight. Finally, I settled against the rough bark, straddling a limb while looping my left arm around a smaller branch sticking out near my side. It was a good place to wait, a good place to keep my balance.

With the back of one hand, I wiped the sweat from my brow. Screams and steel echoed from the forest floor. From my vantage point, I could see flashes of the battle through the trees whenever the War Raven breathed its fire or Balen delivered a blow.

I prayed to Anu.

Since we had camped on the outer perimeter of the forest, I could still see the wide expanse of Grasslands to my left. It was there that Balen finally drew them. He'd found his mount and was galloping bareback until he was far enough away from my location before stopping and waiting.

At least thirty Fallen appeared.

My fingernails dug into the bark. "No. What are you doing?"

Balen's horse sidestepped, as anxious as Balen to fight. Then the dragon landed next to them and folded its great wings behind its back. It stuck out its neck and let out an angry roar.

Still, was it enough?

How did one kill the undead?

The Fallen charged. Balen dismounted and slapped his horse on the rump. Standing alone now with the dragon, he rolled one shoulder then the next, flexed his neck, and rotated his sword wrist a few times.

He was mad, crazy to dismount and face them like that.

Icy despair swept through my veins, gathering in my stomach and twisting into a tight frozen knot.

The enemy circled them.

I nearly lost my grip on the limb when the War Raven unfurled its wings and flew away, deserting Balen. A cry of protest rose, but I restrained it, knowing it would be foolish to call out now.

Denial after denial resounded in my mind.

The creature had just . . . left.

Rage melted the frozen knot in my gut as tears pricked my eyes. I'd kill that creature if I had the chance. I'd suck the life right out of it until it was nothing more than a husk of black leather.

A glint of metal caught my eye. Blue flame inched up Balen's sword. The Fallen closed in and the battle began. I did not blink. My heart, lungs, everything seemed to still.

There was beauty and grace in Balen's movements, and the end he brought to the Fallen was swift and confident. His sword flashed in a wide arc, sailing, slicing, separating, incinerating bone and turning it to ash. So fast, the movements. One after one.

They swamped him many times. And many times I thought it would be his last, his part of the foretelling fulfilled.

But he never tired. His movements never slowed.

Now I understood the difference between a soldier and a champion.

The chaotic scene grew hazy. I blinked, but the haze continued, the fight becoming slow, colors and movements blending together.

He will die for you.

It was not my voice, but another. Deep and haunting. Sorrow rippled through my body and a hot tear slid down my face.

Come now, Deira. The voice echoed in a tone both gentle and intimate. *Don't cry. You can save him.*

A low chuckle wrapped me in warmth. I squeezed my eyelids tight, trying to ignore the voice and bring back the clarity I had lost. My heart began a slow heavy beat.

So young... You desire so much yet understand so little. You have no power, no strength, Deira. You cannot save him on your own.

The words rang true. Another tear followed the path of the first. "Go away."

He laughed again. *This night, he will win, but he cannot stand against an army, for that is what I will send, day after day, night after night.*

There is nowhere to run that I will not follow.

Nox.

The King of Annwn's voice was inside my head.

I rested my forehead against the bark of the tree feeling drained and unbalance, and . . . shocked.

He comes, the voice said and immediately I swiped at my tears and searched the Grasslands, my vision becoming clearer.

I saw Balen mount up, saw armor and weapons and ash littering the ground around him. Relief surged from me with a great sob.

A low, knowing chuckle filled my mind. *The Lia Fail is lost, Deira. He will die for nothing, for a lost cause, unless you choose.*

"Choose," I rasped out. "Choose what?"

A cold, gentle wind rustled the leaves and blew the drowsiness away.

Nox was gone.

*   *   *

I climbed down the tree one painstaking limb at a time. My entire body shook like the brittle leaves that fell from the trees. My concentration kept wavering, kept returning to the voice, the words. Had it been real? Had the King of Annwn communicated with me?

But even as I questioned my sanity, I knew he had. I felt it in the way my mind's defenses had been waylaid; the warm, slumberous fog he'd created so that I couldn't repel him from my thoughts.

As I went down, my hands became scratched and raw against the cold, rough bark. How was I supposed to defend myself? How did I fight that kind of magic? He'd used me. He'd invaded my mind with such ease. How much had he seen there? Had he seen all my weakness, my thoughts, or could he only speak to me and guess at the rest?

By the time I reached the last limb, Balen approached on horseback at a slow canter, and I was fighting a full blown fit of rage. At Nox. At the War Raven. I threw a grim glance over my shoulder, blowing a strand of hair from my eyes, and seeing that Balen led my mount as well.

I dropped from the limb, brushed off my torn leggings and tunic, threw my braid over my shoulder, and waited. I squeezed my hands into fists, welcoming the burn of my raw and cut skin.

And where was that damned War Raven now? I thought, looking up at the night sky. The coward.

The horses slid to a stop in front of me. Balen held out the reins. "Hurry."

He was breathing heavily, his hair wet with sweat, his face dirty and hardened, streaked with blood that must've come from the Fallen's horses or perhaps a hound or two. Perhaps his own.

My legs were shaky as I stepped forward and took the reins. I clutched a fistful of the horse's mane and hauled myself into the saddle. "Are you hurt?"

"No." He kicked his horse ahead of mine and headed into the forest.

I adjusted the strap to my satchel, which hung diagonally across my chest, and followed him.

For nearly an hour we rode in silence, save for the hooves thudding rhythmically on the soft forest floor, and the jingle of tack and Balen's armor. We picked up a path that eventually paralleled a wide river, and passed tall oak trees so old and massive it would take eight or nine grown males holding hands to circle the great trunks. The hoot of owls sounded occasionally and, hovering in the darkness, tiny fireflies blinked their soft yellow light.

These were things I remembered, things which should've brought back pleasant memories. But I was still angry over Nox's invasion, the raven's desertion, and I was worried about Balen. I knew why he had drawn the Fallen away, but I didn't like it. I didn't like that he would've sacrificed himself for me.

A splash brought me out of my thoughts. Balen's horse was crossing the river. I guided my horse across the knee-deep water, went up the opposite bank, then settled into a slow walk beside Balen, searching for something to say.

"We'll make camp soon and then head for Falias," he told me, exhaustion staining his words.

"Is it safe to stop?"

"Aye. That attack was simply a warning."

"Why do you say that?"

"If he wanted us dead, he would've sent more. He's toying with us."

I thought of Nox's words, his threat to hunt us down. "Even so, are you certain we should stop?"

"There are some places the undead cannot go. This forest is one of them. There used to be markers at the edge of forest, preventing the Fallen from entering. They've been moved farther inland. We passed one shortly before we crossed the river." He glanced over and saw my question before I could ask it. "The markers are wards, protections against Nox's dark power. But they must be weakening. It must be why they were moved inward, closer to Falias, to regain strength over a smaller area of the forest."

Immediately I thought of the War Raven. "Where's the raven? I saw it from the tree. I saw it leave you." My ire returned in a flash. "You could've been killed."

"I've faced far worse." He ran a hand over his face.

"How do we even know the Lia Fail still exists?" I asked, remembering Nox's words. "For all we know it was lost."

Balen dragged his fingers through his sweat-soaked hair, making it stay back off his head. "It exists. The foretelling—"

"Oh, aye, the *foretelling*," I echoed, angry that his fate and mine, apparently, rested with a mad queen. "And you'll just ride to your doom because your prophet said so."

A fiery glare struck me as he snagged the reins, pulling my horse and his to a halt. "I don't want to die, but I will if it means saving our world. What would you have me do, Deira? What?"

I shook my head and tried to pull the reins from his hand but they didn't budge. He wouldn't let me retreat so easily. "I would rather die trying," he said, his expression grim, his eyes glittering with the force of his convictions, "than to grow old and watch my land, my people, those I love perish. I would lay down my life this very moment if it meant turning back the frost."

And that, I thought to myself, *is what makes you a hero and me a coward.*

Tears stung my dry eyes. I kicked my horse ahead of him, wishing the darkness would close in and swallow me up.

Would that I'd grown up with people who loved me, in a land where I felt such loyalty. Would that I felt such strong convictions. My people had tried to kill me and when they couldn't, they shunned me. I'd grown up an outcast, an embarrassment, things that did little to inspire loyalty like Balen's.

All the confusion, all the uncertainty and inadequacies sat like a heavy weight upon my shoulders. I was not the one in Balen's foretelling.

Unless I could defeat Nox with my pen and notebook, I was useless.

Chapter 9

Finally, we halted in a small area protected by trees on one side and the river on the other. We worked silently, stripping the horse's tack, rubbing them down, before preparing a spot to rest.

Balen gathered wood and started a small fire as I spread out our blankets and then rooted in the sack for the remaining bread and cheese. After we ate, Balen headed to the water, sat down on the bank, and began removing his armor, slowly and stiffly.

The sight of him doing something so domestic and natural, held my attention for a long time until I began to feel uncomfortable spying on him. I focused on the campfire, but the flames only held my attention for so long before my gaze returned to him.

It was obvious by his movements that he needed help.

I bit the inside of my cheek, caught by indecision. Any warrior could remove his armor; it was designed that way. Unless one was injured... Balen had said no when I'd asked him earlier if he'd been injured. He'd never appeared in pain, but then he had his pride. He wouldn't show it if he was.

His fingers attempted to undo the buckles along his side that would allow the chest plate to be removed.

I'd been a servant for so long that helping him should be a simple task, but it was not. I rolled my eyes to the starry night sky, and took a deep breath before saying, "I can do that for you."

Balen glanced over his shoulder, one eyebrow cocked and his body still. I thought he wasn't going to answer, but then he inclined his head and I set to work.

"The War Raven did not desert me," he said at length.

My fingers worked less-than-deftly at the buckles. "It left you to fend for yourself. I call that desertion."

His deep sigh sounded resigned. "I told it to leave."

I fumbled a buckle. Balen looked back at me with a half-hearted smile. "It's complicated . . . our relationship."

"And what," I said, "you thought you could take thirty Fallen on your own is that it?"

"Aye." I was a simple, honest answer.

I stared in astonishment, not understanding why he wouldn't want the help, and why he'd risk it. *Males.* That was an oath I'd often heard in the palace, and I found myself using it now as I finished the buckles and pulled off the chest plate off;

surprised the weight of it. Balen's shoulders sagged in relief as I set it on the ground.

He removed the sword belt that held his short sword and then undid his leg guards. After those, came the black chain mail tunic, which caught on his hair when he tried to pull it over his head.

"Here, let me…" I said.

The chain mail was surprisingly warm to the touch. My finger brushed the back of his neck and his skin was hot. As I worked the damp strands of hair free from the link, I tried to ignore how intimate the moment felt. "There," I said tightly.

"Thank you." He set the mail atop the pile of armor, then removed his boots and socks, wiggling his toes in the cool air. I noticed a sword nick on his neck and one long slice just above his elbow.

"You're wounded."

"No matter. It'll heal. It just takes longer these days…"

The Lia Fail was the heartbeat of our world, the thing that sustained and healed, the thing that fed the light and kept our land in perpetual summer and warmth. Wounds, both in the land and in our people had become tougher and tougher to heal.

Balen stood, grabbed the ends of the padded black tunic, and began to pull it up. I watched, riveted by the play of muscles in his back and then his bare arms as the tunic went over his head. He let it drop to the ground.

He was muscular but not bulky, not an ounce of idleness anywhere. He looked . . . dangerous with the blood streaks and dirt on his neck and hands. No wonder he could move and strike so fast, was as strong and unwavering as the trees that towered over us; he was built for war.

What fascinated me most, besides his form, was the intricate marking that coiled from beneath the waistband of his leggings up the left side of his torso to cover the shoulder, neck, the tip of his ear and temple, and then down over the bicep and forearm. It depicted a War Raven in dragon form entwined with flame, as though they were one and the same. I couldn't tell where one began and the other left off.

"You may want to cover your eyes, Deira," he said, obviously feeling my stare.

Realizing he was unlacing his leggings, I spun around, his soft chuckle ringing in my ears and my cheeks blazing.

A splash sounded.

I doubted Balen's women reacted so innocently. I wanted to groan but didn't dare. At least *I* did not cavort with a tent full of females. And, really, did he need that many?

I turned back toward the stream. Moonlight lit up the water so that his head and shoulders were clearly visible, the water just coming to his armpits. He dunked under and then broke the surface, his hands smoothing back his hair.

"Get a hold of yourself," I muttered under my breath, before stalking back to the fire.

He behaved like no leader I knew or read about. Not that I knew so many, but I knew my grandfather and the other royals of

our house. I settled on my blanket before the fire and finished
gnawing on a tasteless chunk of bread.

"Deira," he called. "Would you bring me my bag please?"

I grabbed his bag and tossed it toward the river bank then
sat back down, trying not to hear him moving around.

Eventually the bag dropped next to me. I looked up to see
him in a fresh shirt and leggings, his feet bare and his hair wet.

He sat down. "There's clothing in there for you as well."

Curious, I grabbed the bag. Inside was the red tunic
trimmed in gold and the sheer gown. Neither one was suitable for
the journey, and I sure as Dagda was not going to take a swim like
he'd just done. I closed the bag, set it aside, and then arranged
myself on the blanket to sleep, facing the fire, one hand tucked
beneath my head.

From my prone position, I watched Balen take a long
drink from the water bag. He stretched his arms high, worked his
neck a little from side to side, and then reclined on the blanket.

The ground wasn't hard, but it was still cold and
uncomfortable. I imagined what it would be like to sleep, entwined
in arms that could generate heat...

I rolled over, annoyed with the direction of my thoughts
and forced myself to sleep.

* * *

I dreamt that I walked through a long, black corridor, finding my way by my hands alone. The wall was smooth and cold under my palms. And cold. So cold.

The sheer gown I wore did little to keep me warm. My feet were bare and frozen. My hair fell loose down my back. The only sound was my uneasy breathing and the shuffling of my feet.

I stopped and glanced over my shoulder. No light behind me.

No light ahead of me.

Just darkness.

Still, I continued as though I knew something must lie ahead.

I heard whispers beyond the walls. Moans. Grunts.

Urgency. Pleasure. Pain.

An unwelcome tremble went through me. My face and skin grew hot. The voices, both male and female, became louder, echoing through the corridor and wafting over me as I moved. I covered my ears, wanting it to stop, wanting to end the flood of awareness flowing through me.

But it didn't help.

My body was the enemy. It was changing, becoming warm and languid and achy. I knew those sounds. I understood what I was walking toward.

Why couldn't I stop and turn around?

A low, wicked laughter caressed my mind. I faltered and shook my head, trying to keep it clear. "Go away," I whispered, feeling the wall again.

My hair moved. Warm breath bathed my neck. A hot shiver ran down my spine. I whirled around, but no one was there.

I had to keep moving. *Don't stop*, I chanted to myself. *Don't stop whatever you do.*

Again the laughter.

"Leave me be!" I yelled. "Get out of my head!"

My words echoed down the corridor. As they dissipated, the moans took over, growing louder, more demanding and deafening. Intense and needful. I kept moving in the blackness, taking each step carefully, never knowing where my feet might land.

"Deira!" A voice called.

"Go away!"

"Deira!"

* * *

I bolted up. Pain shot into my skull. "Ow!" Immediately my hand went to my forehead. I heard a curse and saw Balen facing me, sprawled on his rump, holding his forehead.

My heart raced. My face was hot. I checked my body. No gown. My hair was still braided.

Heat still clung to me and my pulse continued to pound. I put both palms to my cheeks to cool them and took long even breaths, glancing at Balen only to feel a flush of shame, sure that he could see into my mind and body.

Balen's lips were drawn into a pained line. But his eyes blazed intensely and curiously as they swept over me.

I couldn't look away.

One of the horses snorted loudly, making me jump.

I jumped up and hurried to the cold stream on shaky legs. Balen followed. He paced back and forth along the bank as I cupped my hands in the water and drank deeply, the cold liquid sliding down my parched throat. I splashed the water on my cheeks, relieved when a chill replaced the heat.

Finally, I straightened and faced him. He'd stopped pacing, hands on his hips, his expression ferocious and bewildered. He dragged his fingers through his hair and frowned, seeming as confused as me. "Are you all right?"

No, I was not, but I nodded anyway.

How could I even began to explain what had happened? The Dream. The voice in my mind. The overwhelming feelings that flooded my body, both physically and mentally...

He took a step toward me and then halted mid-stride as though second-guessing his intention. "Deira."

I swallowed. "Aye?"

His look became frank, committed, and then it changed to frustration. He threw up his hands in a gesture of defeat. "We may as well ride now since we're both wide awake."

He stalked back to the glowing embers that had once been our fire.

"Good idea," I said to no one, following him back to camp at a much slower pace.

As I made my way to the fire to shake out my blanket, I felt as though I was becoming a stranger to myself. My emotions were at war, emotions I'd never dealt with before to this degree.

Balen saddled the horses and then donned his chainmail, tying the rest of the light plated armor onto the saddled while I packed the bags and then doused the embers with dirt, stamping the coals out with the soles of my shoes until none remained, leaving only the moonlight to guide our way.

The sound of my horse mouthing his bit, the rustle of their hooves and snorts made the quiet between Balen and I seem exaggerated. I took the reins as a guttural, high pitched scream echoed over the forest.

Chapter 10

"Stay close to me," Balen commanded as the scream died, leaving an eerie silence in its wake.

We waited.

The treetops rustled and bent, groaning in protest. Branches broke. I looked up, crouching down as I did. Balen shoved his horse's reins into my hand. "Move them toward the water."

Quickly, I led the horses away.

More screams.

The whoosh of giant wings. The thump of something on the ground, and a loud, angry grunt of pain.

Then silence.

I remained by the edge of the river for what seemed like an eternity until Balen called me back.

I brought the horses back to camp to a surprising sight. Ferryn, the one who had carried the buckets of water for my bath back at camp, was sprawled on the ground, Balen kneeling beside him.

Moonlight revealed the blood soaking Ferryn's chest, the paleness of his face, and the panic enlarging his pupils. He shivered all over and he was gaping, trying to catch his breath. When he spoke, his voice caught in a high pitch. "Drem caught me in its talons." He glanced at the wounds on his chest. "I came on horseback, but it . . . it grabbed me off." He covered one of the puncture wounds and tested the movement of his shoulder, but froze, gasping in pain.

"Drem was protecting us. We were attacked not too long ago," Balen said as I joined them.

Why was I not surprised? I might be in awe of the creature, but so far it had toyed with me, invaded my privacy, and while it might have been obeying Balen's order to leave the fight, I had yet to become a loyal supporter of the creature. And now it had nearly killed Ferryn.

Carefully, I peeled back the ripped tunic at Ferryn's shoulder to examine the wounds. "I won't touch. I just want to see," I assured him when he flinched. "Are you injured anywhere else?"

"I don't know. I don't think so."

The puncture wounds were deep. I was glad they hadn't gone through his lungs or shoulder blades. I wished I had spent more time learning healing in Murias. I turned to Balen. "What should we do?"

"We'll dress the wounds and then ride for Falias. The healers there will help us."

"Right." I smiled at Ferryn. "Falias is famous for its healers. You'll be all right. For now let's get you warmed up." I looked to Balen. "Will you start the fire?"

As Balen went to light the fire and add more wood, I helped Ferryn to our small ring of campfire stones. "We'll have to remove your tunic," I told him. "I promise to go slowly."

His eyes were still as wide as dinner plates, but he said, "There's a dagger in my boot. Cut it off."

I found the dagger and began cutting the tunic away from his body. He was wide shouldered and lithe like Balen, but didn't have quite the muscle mass. Yet. The puncture wounds bled profusely leaving bloody trails down the taut pale skin.

"It really plucked you right from the saddle?"

"Aye. Scary feeling, that."

Balen crouched next to us and inspected the wounds. "We can pack it with Noden moss to stop the bleeding and then we'll need bandages."

"We can use the gown," I suggested.

I set to work using Ferryn's dagger to cut the beautiful gown into strips while Balen collected Noden moss from the rocks near the river. The moss was known far and wide for its antiseptic properties. We worked together, using the cool water to cleanse the wounds and wipe away the dirt and other debris with the extra strips I'd cut.

Ferryn winced and gasped, but he never cried out. I admired his courage. His skin had paled, and a greenish tint filled the shadows of his face. Several times Balen and I exchanged looks of concern.

"What of the battle?" Balen asked Ferryn as we tended him.

"Easily routed. From their numbers I don't think it was meant to be won." He winced again as I placed moss against one of the wounds. I held it while Balen wrapped it. "Ixia is gone."

Startled, I glanced at Balen. His expression didn't change save for the slight intake of breath that suggested more anger than shock. "Orin sent me as soon as we realized. It wasn't long after you and Deira rode out. We think they were after you—" he gave me a sorry glance— "Orin thinks Nox knows. How could they have known so quickly that we found our Light Bearer?"

A dark frown overtook Balen's face as he tied off the bandage. "We've been betrayed by one of our own," he said quietly.

Ferryn dipped his head in agreement, but I wasn't so sure. "How can you be certain?"

"Under my command, all Sydhrs were forbidden to speak of the foretelling," Balen answered. "One of our own spoke of it. Either directly to Nox's forces or indirectly." He motioned for me to continue with the moss. "Either way it's treason."

The crackle of the fire filled the silence. Sparks shot into the sky. It would have been the perfect time to confide in them that I'd heard Nox's voice in my mind. And yet I couldn't seem to form the words.

"He won't stop, will he? Now that he knows." Ferryn's eyes were wide with worry.

"No," Balen answered. "He won't. His focus will be on us now."

On me, I thought darkly.

The memory of Nox's voice lingered in my mind along with the disturbing certainty that the King of the Underworld had only just begun his assault. Part of me wanted to tell Balen everything, but I couldn't seem to get it out. It had been such an intimate thing, and I didn't want Balen to think I was weak-willed, easily swayed, or . . . tainted in some way by Nox.

I'd have to tell him, and soon. Once we made it to Falias. Once Ferryn was taken care of. Once we were alone. Then I'd tell him.

After we finished dressing the wounds, Balen began repacking the bags as I helped Ferryn to his feet. A lock of his hair fell, covering his eye. He went to shove it back, but the movement caused pain and stopped him cold. I held onto him tightly as he swayed. Then, I reached up with a small smile and tucked the hair behind his ear for him. "There you go."

His cheeks flushed red. "Thank you," he said, clearly embarrassed.

"You're welcome. I can help you to the horses, but I think Balen will have to lift you up."

Balen finished with the bag, picked it up, then bent down for his short sword, strapping to his waist, and then his broad sword, which he slung over his back.

Then, he stepped to the fire and stared at the flames, his profile illuminated by the light. Tiny reflections danced in the black mail and plate he wore. His jaw was covered in a heavy dusting of black scruff. He looked like a king to me then. Weary and weighted by responsibility, one who'd been at war far too long.

He lifted his hand, holding it palm down above the flames. And then he withdrew the flames from the wood into his hand.

All my life I'd watched the people of Anu manipulate water. To summon it at will. But witnessing Balen withdrawing flame from wood... I would not have guessed such a thing was possible. He spoke no words nor made a great show of it. From wood to hand. Just like that.

"He's the only one of us able to do that," Ferryn commented quietly, also watching him. I felt unsteady inside, my emotions chaotic and confusing.

"This must be a shock to you," he said, his voice stammering through the pain, "to learn you're to save our world."

I tried a smile, but it failed.

"Balen will see you through." Ferryn's eyes shone with belief.

How could I even begin to explain my true feelings? That I was uncertain and angry this burden had been thrust upon me. I wanted to tell him that Balen was wrong.

"You love him. Respect him," I noted.

"We all do. He is more than a king; he is one of us. He'll die for us. How can you not love someone like that?"

How indeed.

* * *

The scent of wood and moss and dead leaves hung thick in the night air. The frost hadn't penetrated as far into the deep woods, so it was warmer, much warmer than Murias. Falias would be a welcome sight.

The city was close to my mother's estate. I remembered going there as a little girl to shop in the market or play in the fountain while Mother talked with the Keepers of the Cauldron—the priests of Dagda and protectors of her gift, the Cauldron of Plenty.

The Danaans of the House of Dagda were the most tolerant of humans. Before the Old War, many humans had come through the gate within the forest. Many had lived there, choosing never to go home again. And eventually they'd died there. Although that was long ago, the House of Dagda still held humans in slightly better regard than the rest of the Danaan population. They didn't blame the entire race of men on the betrayal of a few.

Despite all that, Mother and I always went to the city without Father. And she always wrapped my hair in a tight veil and used her colored powders to darken my eyebrows and lighten my skin. Still, my nature was known to the priest class and many of the shop-keeps. Mother had been well loved in Falias, so the mystery of my birth and differences remained hushed, never mentioned aloud.

At least to Mother and me.

But Father had been like a prisoner. And he'd been so unhappy. I could see that now.

I studied Balen's back as we rode in single file. The words he'd spoken before, about loyalty and his desire to save his people no matter the cost, sprang to mind. As well as my own negative response. But, perhaps my loyalty and purpose resided with the people of the Woodlands who had once sheltered me.

If the darkness and frost could be stopped, wasn't it my responsibility to try? Mother would have wanted me to; she wouldn't have expected me to, but she would have hoped…

The rhythmic cadence of the horse's gait lulled me into deeper thoughts. We traveled in silence, me on my mount and Balen riding tandem behind Ferryn so that he could support the young Sydhr with one arm around his waist.

Somewhere along the way, a subtle trickle of wariness began to creep in, making me sit straighter and scan the dense black forest. I strained to listen, eventually hearing the rustle of leaves, of soft thuds on the ground. My horse heard it too, his ears flicking, his head higher, more alert.

Ahead, large, silent shadows appeared on either side of us, falling in step with our party.

The Great Bears of Falias.

Their slumberous gate was just an illusion. They were so large they covered as much ground at a walk as our horses could at a trot.

I glanced behind me and saw that a third had fallen in behind us. When I returned to the trail it was to find Balen looking at me over his shoulder, his head dipping in a slight nod, telling me everything would be all right. I nodded back and then thought of the War Raven, hoping it didn't choose that moment to make another unfortunate appearance.

The Great Bears of Dagda were no stranger to me. They'd ruled this part of the forest for as long as anyone could remember. They were vicious protectors of their territory and, like Sydhrs, slow to involve themselves in politics. They were made by Dagda, just as the War Raven was made by Sydhr, from magic and bear and Danaan. They were protectors of her land, able to take the shape of Danaan or the Great Bear at will, though they most often chose the predominate form of the bear. Unlike the War Raven, which, until now had been thought extinct, Great Bears flourished in the Woodlands.

I'd been gone for so long that I'd forgotten so much. I shouldn't have been surprised that they knew about our arrival, nor that they'd escort us through their territory.

Ferryn leaned heavily against Balen's arm, his head hanging tiredly. Champion or not, Balen had to be weakening. At this pace, we'd never get to Falias.

For two days, we traveled with the Great Bears.

They never shape-shifted into their Danaan form, and when we camped, they remained on the perimeter, lying down in the cushion of leaves and pine needles. Balen and I cared for Ferryn, too tired to handle anything but the basic necessities.

Ferryn had developed an infection. His body wasn't regenerating as well as it should. This, Balen explained, was most likely the result of the War Raven's blood or saliva mixing with Ferryn's wounds. A bite or blood from the creature could be deadly, yet another reason they were so feared by Danaans.

And why so few remained.

It was midday when the Great Bears escorted us through the city gate, a wide arching tunnel carved into the trunk of a massive oak tree. The entire city of Falias was surrounded by a vast ring of oaks, their trunks pressed tightly together, forming a natural protective wall against invasion.

Light shone at the end of the tunnel, much brighter within the city than under the deep canopy of the crowded forest trees. The thick scent of bark and earth filled my nostrils as the faint sounds of city life echoed through the tunnel.

I nudged my horse next to Balen's. "We should take Ferryn to the priests."

Ferryn raised the back of his head from Balen's shoulder. "I'm fine." His glassy eyes couldn't even focus on me.

"Aye, we know," Balen said dryly.

We exited the tunnel into the market square. The scent of freshly baked bread made my stomach rumble. Faint music from flutes and a lyre drifted from a nearby tavern. I remembered the smells and sounds, remembered looking up as a child at the high bridges that spanned from tree to tree and the low arched bridges spanning the river, which meandered through the city.

I expected the Great Bears to leave, but they continued to lead us through the city, down winding streets and main thoroughfares.

The descendants of Dagda varied in form, which made them unusual compared to those of other houses. With large round eyes the color of every flower one could imagine and hair in every shade of brown, their coloring allowing them to blend effortlessly into the forest.

The city was also a haven for other Danaans who preferred the quiet, relaxation and solitude of the forest. The Woodland estates beyond the city were a popular place to unwind and vacation. And the libraries and apprentice schools were some of the most respected in all of Innis Fail, which reminded me that I needed to restock my ink and paper supplies as soon as we were settled.

The Great Bears led us beneath a wide arch supporting the city's main aqueduct, the faint sound of running water echoing in the space. The aqueduct fed the public bath houses and fountains, as well as many private dwellings and public establishments.

I recognized many things as we entered a quieter area of the city. The high stone wall covered in sweet aromatic wisteria, the fountain I used to play in as a child, the stone steps leading into the Hall of Records, and opposite that, the same steps that led into the public temple with its great wooden columns.

We rode the horses between buildings and down a well-worn dirt path, thick on either side with trees and bushes and vines that hung overhead on low arching branches. The path went downward then leveled out into a vast green park filled with ancient Hawthorne and apple trees. In the middle of the park was the sacred lake of Dagda, so serene and quiet that its surface appeared to be made of glass.

A campus of temples, dormitories, and teaching halls had been built in the park. The main temple was an enormous rotunda, built on low stilts in the center of the lake, accessible by the bridge that spanned the entire length of the lake and ran right through the first floor of the rotunda.

The park was home to the Cauldron and its Keepers, a race of Danaans unlike any other. They were tall and willowy like the reeds that ringed the far edge of the lake. Mother had always told me that Dagda herself had created them long ago from the reeds, the lake water, and her own blood so that they'd always protect her sacred waters and the cauldron that lay somewhere within.

I breathed in deeply and then let out a shaky breath, the memories of my mother so vivid in this place that they brought tears to my eyes.

As a child, I'd never really noticed the beauty around me. But now I saw it. I *felt* it. I glanced over to see if Balen felt it too. But he remained alert and grim, always on guard. Ferryn had lost consciousness again. We were a weary, ragged bunch, at odds with

our surroundings and the priests who passed by in their robes of
finely spun linen and wool.

The Great Bears left us at a tall building covered in vines.

Now that we were here and safe, every ache, every tired
muscle, every hunger pang multiplied. I dismounted carefully,
holding onto the saddle for a moment to let my weight settle into
my legs, and then I hurried over to help Balen with Ferryn.

"I can do it," Ferryn mumbled, coming to. "I'm not a
child."

Balen slid off the horse first, his hands remaining on
Ferryn's waist so he wouldn't fall. Once Balen was down, the
young Sydhr leaned into waiting arms and Balen dragged him
carefully off the horse.

Ferryn's knees buckled. His head tipped back, his throat
working as he tried to focus, but couldn't. "What of Ixia? We must
save her. We must..."

The wide doors to the building creaked open.

A priest glided down the three steps to meet us. I thought
Balen was the tallest male I'd ever seen, but the priest towered over
us. His long robes swirled around slippered feet and his hood
framed a face with grayish brown skin, big, slanted green eyes, a
small nose, and a wide, thin mouth. His serene, elongated features
stirred my memory.

He dipped his head to Balen. "The healers will take him
now."

Three healers appeared, coming around the priest. Ferryn
protested their help, but one of the healers touched him,

whispering something soothing and kind. Ferryn went limp. They took him easily from Balen and carried him into the building.

The priest's attention fell to me. "Welcome daughter of Ariannon. You have grown."

"Eburacon." The name came unbidden from my lips and, with it, memories came flooding back.

Immediately, I knelt in respect to the High Priest of Dagda. I felt a light pressure on my shoulder as though he had placed his hand there and bid me to rise, but he hadn't touched me. Such was the power of his mind.

He shifted his serene expression to Balen, bowing his head. "Welcome to Falias, Balen, Champion of Sydhr. Please, come. We have much to discuss. But first—" he cast a distasteful eye to our state— "let us see you bathed and fed."

We followed him into the main hall of the building then down a long, narrow hallway. Everything was built slender and tall, like the priests themselves. Tall ceilings, tall doors, tall iron candle stands, which held tall candles... Their buildings were beautiful, made of varying kinds of wood, all polished, all carved with intricate scenes of nature and Dagda's life. It was quiet too, the shuffle of our footsteps loud against the polished wooden floor.

Eburacon stopped near the end of the hallway. Two doors were on either side of us with another larger one at the end. "Your chambers will be here." He indicated the two doors, but he stepped to the larger door. "First, you must bathe."

He knocked. It opened to reveal two servants. "Jensine and Alsa will assist you. You must be cleansed and anointed to enter the main temple. Plus," he added with a faint flash of humor, "you both smell." He bowed curtly before leaving.

"Well, that was uncalled for," I mumbled. He should try fleeing from battle with less than a change of clothes and days of travel ahead him and see how he smelled afterward.

"But true," Balen said with a shrug.

I cast him a glare and he grinned at me. It was the first time in two days that I'd seen him smile and mean it. "Speak for yourself," I said, lifting my chin and entering what was another long hallway, only this one went down into the earth.

"You've been here before?" Balen asked as we followed the servants.

"Aye. When I was a child with my mother. She raised me at her estate not far from here. But I was never permitted inside the buildings or the temple." I met his gaze. "You?"

"I've been here many times, but never to the temple or the baths. We always stayed in the city."

The air grew hot and damp. Torches burned in ornate brassieres on the wall, sending shafts of golden light upwards in long arcs. Sweat beaded on my forehead and back. Mint and herbs scented the air. The farther we went, the thicker the scent.

Jensine and Alsa opened a set of high double doors, and we stepped into a vaulted chamber over an underground spring. Large rocks made natural separations, creating large pools and smaller secluded ones. Steam floated up from the surface. Rooms had been carved into the rock walls and torches blazed everywhere. A priest exited one room and passed us, nodding serenely.

"This way," Alsa said.

In a dressing chamber, Balen and I exchanged questioning looks. Surely they didn't expect us to strip down and bathe together.

Balen's eyebrow arched. He could tell exactly what I was thinking and a wide childish grin appeared, the transformation stealing my breath. I arched my brow at him and crossed my arms over my chest, trying to force my pulse back to normal as Alsa waved a hand to another room and said to Balen, "This way."

Ha! I shot him a superior smirk as he was led from the room with a quick parting leer at me.

Chapter 11

Alone in the chamber with Jensine, I began to undress. "Please, this is my task," she said with a hesitant smile.

I wasn't sure I'd ever become accustomed to being waited upon. I dropped my hands from the tie at my waist, allowing her to untie the sash and then pull the dirty tunic over my head. The thin blouse underneath came next, and I stood there bare to the waist in the warm chamber, holding my hands over my breasts.

"It's rare that we have visitors here," she said in a soft steady voice. "Your servants don't undress you?"

I shook my head as she stepped closer and reached out to my waist. Her fingers undid the laces to my leggings, brushing against the bare skin just below my navel. "I have no servants. I am one," I said, my voice choked.

I wanted to perish right then and there. My cheeks burned and grew hotter as she tugged my leggings down, then waited for me to step out of them.

Once I did, she set to work unbraiding my hair.

She sighed. "Your hair is so different. So many shades of red and orange... It's really rather pretty."

"Thank you."

"Come," she said after my hair was undone.

We moved into another room where Jensine selected a sheer, filmy gown, and pulled it over my head. "Most prefer to go without, but I believe you would prefer a covering, no?"

"Aye, I would, thank you."

It wasn't exactly a covering in my mind. It was so thin that once wet, I might as well be naked anyway. She smiled at me. "We celebrate the form as all Danaans do. You don't bathe like this in your city?"

"We do." I lifted my hair from the neck of the gown and let it fall over the material. I didn't bother explaining that I bathed with Lidi and the other servants of my house.

"This way."

She led me into the cavern.

"I'll wait in the dressing room to anoint you when you're finished. Please take your time in Dagda's waters for they are healing and rejuvenate the mind and body."

I thanked her and then stepped across the warm rock to the water's edge. I glanced over my shoulder to see her retreating into the dressing chamber.

I put one toe in the hot water and sighed.

I inched my way in, the gown billowing around me until I had to press it into the water to weigh the material down.

Herbs and mint sprigs bobbed on the surface, and floating trays with lit scented candles made the chamber relaxing just as Jensine had said. I waded in until the water reached my breasts, then I pushed off the rocky bottom to swim.

The weightless feeling was a welcome relief after the hard journey on horseback. I rolled onto my back, letting my arms float in a wide arc.

Placed in baskets around the area, were sponges and soaps. And more servants who I guessed would gladly give me a good washing if I asked. As I swam around a large outcropping of rocks, I saw a naked priest prone on his stomach as a servant rubbed oil into his skin.

I went still.

Apparently, males and females bathed together.

Quietly, I swam back the way I'd come not wanting to be seen. I spied a basket and hurried to it, hoping to wash quickly and then hurry back to the dressing chamber, but as I swam around the rock, I choked on a startled gasp of part air, part water.

Balen strode naked to the pool's edge and waded in until the water closed over his shoulders.

My heart pounded wildly. I couldn't seem to move, shocked just as much by my reaction as by the sight of him. It was undeniable, the flood of attraction I felt, an attraction that had been building all this time.

I had two choices. Swim back to the naked priest, or face Balen.

The priest was much safer. I turned to go, but I'd waited too long. A splash of water hit me in the back of the head. I whipped around to see Balen, treading water in front of me, chin deep and grinning like a damned fool. His black hair glistened in the candlelight, his brows like two slashes of devilry, and his smile rugged and beautiful.

"You find this amusing?" I asked, annoyed at the restless energy surging through me.

"Aye. Highly." He stopped treading and stood on the bottom, rising a bit higher, the water reaching his chest. "Your people don't bathe like this?"

"Of course *they* do. We *servants* don't have such luxury. Just a small tub by a kitchen fire." A tray of scented candles floated by, and I directed it in front of me. As a barrier it was pathetic, but it was something at least.

He studied me, those amber eyes taking on a thoughtful glint. "You have never lain with a male, have you?"

I groaned, utterly humiliated. I wanted to sink under the water and never come up.

"There's no shame in it. You are well of age. Beyond it, in fact."

With every word, my anger mounted. "Thank you. I'm well aware."

"No male servants or guards then?"

I let out a pent up breath and rolled my eyes to the vaulted rock ceiling. "Who would have me, Balen?"

He'd seen how I was treated in Murias. How most Danaans regarded me. No need to explain it further and doing so was just an exercise in pity.

And the last thing I wanted was for Balen to pity me.

His smile died, and the playful light vanished from his eyes, turning him back into the stoic, grim leader I'd seen so much of already.

"Then were idiots, Deira. Ruled by their fear and not worthy of you."

I stared down at the tray, moving it back and forth between my hands. Nice words, but they did nothing to ease the growing ache in my chest. "Thanks," I managed with a small shrug.

"Deira." He waited until I looked at him. A boyish smile tugged at the corner of his mouth. "Would you like to lay with me?"

His eyebrows were raised. And his eyes, lit with laughter, said he was goading me. Nothing more.

"You are not amusing. And the answer is no," I said, just to be clear.

"Are you certain?"

"Aye, very."

"Aye, you're certain? Or, aye, you wish to lay with me?"

My mouth gaped like a fish plucked from the river. Embarrassed, I snapped my lips together. "Why are you doing this? You're a king. I'm blighted, a halfling. What you suggest, whether in jest or truth, isn't possible."

His expression blazed with sincerity. "I never jest, Deira." He lowered his body into the water, so that it lapped at his chin. He fanned his arms through the hot liquid. "Though I admit, for some odd reason, I feel the need to goad you. Perhaps it's simply to make you smile."

"Then your goading has failed. I'm not smiling."

"I can see I've lost that battle. How *are* you feeling then?"

"Annoyed," I answered. "You behave like no king I know."

"Where I come from, a king is not raised above his people. He's a servant to them, instated by Challenge, and his ability to lead and fight. I am no different than any Sydhr warrior otherwise."

"And do other Sydhr warriors have a tent full of wives?"

His eyes narrowed. "A tent full of wives? Who told you this?"

"No one. I saw them with my own eyes. Ixia and the others."

An astonished look crossed his face and then he burst out laughing, a deep sound that echoed in the cavern. I wanted out of this conversation, out of this underground lake, and away from him. Suddenly, I didn't much care for my state of near undress. As I let go of the tray to leave, he spoke.

"I forget you know so little of our culture. While I'm quite capable of satisfying a tent full of women," he boasted, swimming in a small circle around me. "They are not my wives. Ixia is my sister and the others are my cousins."

Of course. My mistake was more humiliating than anything else so far, and it was painfully apparent that conversing was not my strong suit.

I gave up and swam away, intending to go back to the dressing chamber, but Balen caught my hand in his.

I didn't turn, but closed my eyes and inhaled deeply, refusing to say anything more and embarrass myself again. He tugged. His hand was warm and strong, and it felt good around mine. I drew in a deep breath and faced him.

"Please. Don't go."

He said nothing else, made no move, but something vulnerable passed through his eyes. Loneliness, I thought. Weariness, too. He might claim to be a simple Sydhr warrior, but the responsibility to lead his people did, no matter what he claimed, set him apart. We were so different, and yet our vulnerability and loneliness, in that moment, connected us.

"One thing a Sydhr male often does for his female," Balen said, "is wash her hair."

A jolt rippled beneath my skin. Swallowing took effort. I wanted to point out that I wasn't his female, but I couldn't get the words out. His big hand dwarfed mine. He squeezed gently.

"No more goading," he promised.

I gave a quick nod, unable to do much of anything else.

He guided me to one of the baskets on the rock ledge where he rooted inside, smelling each bar of soap until finding one he approved of. Then, he placed his hands on my shoulders, turning my back to him. "Lean back into the water, so I can wet your hair."

I was sure my heart had never pounded as fast as it did then. His hands smoothed the hair back from my head, his touch sure, yet gentle. My mouth went dry and I stayed tense until he finished. Then, he stood me up. I faced the ledge as he began soaping my hair, gently massaging my scalp.

"Relax, Deira. Close your eyes and enjoy it."

That was the problem. I was afraid I'd enjoy it too much. No one had ever touched me this way. I rested both elbows on the ledge in front of me, my chin on my overlapped hands, letting my legs dangly freely in the water. I concentrated on easing the tension from my body, breathing slow even breaths and letting his big hands work the soap into my hair.

His fingers massage my scalp in slow circles until I was drowsy. He gathered the length of my hair and threaded it through his fingers. Then, his hands went to the back of my neck and kneaded the soapy, slippery flesh.

"How do you feel now?" Hs voice was low and rough.

"Good. Sleepy." His fingers kneaded the base of my skull. "Very good."

He chuckled softly. My thigh brushed his, and all I wanted was to get closer, for his hands to glide over my shoulder and cover every part of me. The thought tensed me up again. I lifted my chin from my hands and glanced over my shoulder.

He was so close. I couldn't breathe. His fingers stilled.

The hot water rocked against us. He leaned in until his lips brushed my temple. Heat surged through me. I leaned back against him, feeling his solid chest against my back. His left arm slipped around my waist. His lips moved to my ear. Instinctively, I tilted my face more toward him, and he leaned over and captured my lips with his own.

I gasped against his mouth, my eyelids sliding closed as heat flooded me. They were so soft and warm, his lips. I didn't want it to stop. I turned in his arms.

His hand splayed against my back, holding me against him, the other hand still cupping the back of my neck. My hands found their way to his back, the muscles hard and solid under my palms.

"Open your mouth," he whispered, his lips against mine, his tone husky and unsteady.

I did, and his tongue swept inside my mouth. Again, that bolt shot through me. We moaned together. He pressed me back against the ledge. I felt restless, tormented. Urgent and achy. His kiss was slow and consuming. Tongue against tongue, in a torturous rhythm that I returned with earnest.

Balen ended the kiss by pulling my bottom lip into his mouth and between his teeth, biting it gently before letting go and kissing me softly. His lips spread into a grin as he moved a strand of wet hair from my neck and licked the place where it had been. My head dropped back and my eyes opened to the ceiling. I couldn't focus on anything but the sensations coursing through me, the feel of him, his skin, his scent, his taste.

He will die for you, Deira.

My hands on his back stilled.

He wants you because you are different and rare. He is but bored.

"No," I breathed, suddenly assaulted by too many emotions at once.

He will die and you will be left with nothing. But I know you. I know what you are. I can give you everything you've ever wanted.

I tried to close my mind, to force him out, but he'd already snaked his way inside.

He will use you. 'Tis nothing but lust you feel swelling against your belly, nothing but lust you feel pooling between your legs, nothing but-

"Leave me alone!" I shoved at him, my heart pounding too fast.

Balen froze.

Slowly, he straightened, the amber blaze in his eyes going cloudy and confused.

He braced one hand on the ledge behind me and scrubbed the other down his face, taking a moment to calm his ragged breathing. Then his hand dropped from the ledge and he stepped back, lips grim, jaw tight. He appeared as though he was about to speak, but then thought better of it. Instead, he simply turned and left me.

"No, wait!"

I swam after him. He stopped, but did not turn around.

"I didn't mean... You don't understand."

He dragged his fingers through his hair, facing me with a heavy exhale. "I do," he said. "I never should have . . . you are young, just a child . . . and not my kind..." He paused before swimming away.

A silent scream welled inside me, tasting of bitterness and rage. The drowsy warmth that had clung to me was now a boiling, wide-awake fury.

I was not his *kind*. Not Sydhr or not full-blooded Danaan? Not good enough for him. Pure enough. And I was *not* too young. I'd had to grow up after my mother had died. I'd never had a childhood beyond my sixth year.

How dare he say that I was too young, that I was not his kind. I was. I *was* a Danaan.

I slapped the water with my hands and let out an angry groan. Damn him. And damn Nox!

I stayed in the pool, trying to regain some control over my emotions and give myself time to think.

After a while, I ducked under the water to make sure all the soap was gone from my hair. Then I washed quickly before making my way back to the dressing chamber where Jensine removed the wet gown, dried my skin and hair, and then rubbed rare hysop oil into my skin. Hysop was used to anoint those wishing to visit Dagda's temple on the lake.

As I lay on the table, Jensine working the aromatic oil into my skin, my muscles relaxed and my mind drifted. Thoughts of Balen and Nox began to filter in, but I shut them out—they'd taken up enough of my time for one day. Instead, I focused on the massage, the expert way Jensine pushed and kneaded my sore muscles.

Once she finished, she placed a warm linen sheet over me and left me alone for several minutes while she went for my clothes. The warmth seeped into my skin. I closed my eyes and let out a content sigh.

"Are you ready to dress?" she asked upon her return.

I blinked awake and rose onto my elbows to see her carrying a bundle. "Aye. And if you tell me dinner is next, I might just forgo the dress and run for the food."

She laughed. "You must be starving after your trek. I hear you only had one loaf of bread between you."

"And some cheese." I swung my legs over the table as she held up a gown the color of the night sky, a deep inky blue that hung over one shoulder and left the other bare. The edges were trimmed with a thick band of silver thread.

"This color will look nice with your hair."

I hopped off the table, clutching the sheet against me. The dress was beautiful. "Are you sure I should wear this?"

"Eburacon had it sent down for you, so aye, you should wear it. You don't like it?"

"I do. It's very beautiful."

"I think so, as well." She stepped behind me. "Lift your arms." I did and she slipped a sheer under garment fabric over my head followed by the gown. It slid down my body like a cool rush of water, pooling around my bare feet.

Jensine began brushing the tangles from my hair. "Aye, I was right. The color is good." She arranged my hair loosely atop my head, showing off my bare shoulders and neck.

"Shouldn't I wear a veil?" I asked.

"Oh, Dear Dagda, no. We shouldn't cover this up. Unless," she hesitated, "you would like one. I didn't mean to direct you. I'd be happy to get you a veil..."

"No, it's fine." And I supposed it was. I wasn't in Murias anymore. I wasn't in hiding. If people didn't like it, if it reminded them of war and heartache, they could choose to look the other way. I could take it. Question was, could they?

"Here, have a look." Jensine directed me to the long oval mirror in the corner, standing behind me with a small smile of satisfaction at her work. "What do you think?"

I stared at my reflection.

Seeing myself dressed as my mother had once dressed, as a daughter of the noble House of Anu should've been dressed... I had no words. I never thought to see myself so. For the first time, I didn't look with depression or regret at the things which made me different. My hair looked nice. My skin was smooth. My brown eyes looked soft and pretty.

For the first time, I *liked* what I saw.

Tears stung my throat. I should have liked this person all along. No matter what clothes I wore, no matter what anyone said or did to me.

Pride was something I hadn't felt very often, but now it blossomed like one of the struggling flowers in the frost, finally breaking through the surface of the earth and finding the sun. It was there in the eyes that stared back at me. I was becoming proud of who I was.

I lifted my chin ever so slightly. Jensine's eyes met mine in the mirror. "I love it," I answered.

Alsa appeared in the doorway. "The table is ready."

Chapter 12

I picked up my satchel and followed Alsa from the caverns and into the main building. The gown flowed lightly around my ankles, the faint sound it made like reverent whispers in the quiet corridors.

Alsa opened an arched set of double doors and ushered me into a private chamber where Eburacon waited near the window with his back to me, his long fingers clasped behind his deep green robe.

"Enjoy your supper," Alsa whispered before closing the door softly behind her.

The chamber was cozy with its carved wall panels and thick timber beams overhead. A fire burned in the large hearth. There was seating before the fire. Book shelves lined the walls and were stocked with manuscripts and scrolls. A dining table had been set in the center of the room.

I smoothed the front of my gown, drew in a deep breath, and approached Eburacon.

He motioned to the table, so I did as bade and seated myself, staying silent as he served me from three platters, one of sliced meat, one of wild carrots and onions, and another of sweet breads. He filled his own plate then sat opposite from me.

"Nox of Annwn speaks to you," he said without accusation just simple fact.

An instant denial flew to my lips and hung there unvoiced.

"His power clings to you like faint perfume."

A tremble went through me. Suddenly the room wasn't so cozy anymore. In fact, I felt rather caged.

"Dagda is strong in me still. But that, too, fades with the frost," he said, explaining how he knew my secret. I should have known he'd be able to see the truth, fading power or not.

I thought of the boundary markers that surrounded the Woodlands. "That's why your markers were moved closer to Falias. Balen was right. The darkness and frost weaken not only the light from our skies, but the power of the priests as well."

"But that is a secret no one wants revealed, Deira," he said, carefully slicing his carrots. "Why concern the people?"

"Why?" I asked, surprised. "Because they need to know they're in danger. They need to know their power is affected, too."

"They will soon realize." Eburacon picked up a jug. "Drink?"

Absently, I nodded and waited for him to fill my cup. My stomach rumbled, reminding me there was food on the table. Food for the taking. I dug in.

"The time has not yet come to reveal all of our weaknesses. There is still time to set things right."

I glanced at the door, but couldn't bring myself to ask about Balen. He should be here, but I was glad he wasn't. I still didn't have the courage to tell him about Nox.

"If Nox is able to connect with you, Deira, he grows stronger." Eburacon paused, piercing me with those mesmerizing green eyes. "He will do anything to keep his growing power for it means his victory."

The food was delicious and I had to make myself slow down or I'd be sick. "How can I stop him from entering my thoughts?"

"I will think on this tonight. But you must not listen to him. He will confuse you; use your emotions against you. Be a force against his words. Your will alone is the only thing that can keep him from seeing into your heart."

As I considered his words, the truth seemed to bubble right up my throat and out of my mouth. "I don't want this—Nox after me, going to the Deadlands, finding the Light—any of it." Admitting my cowardice made my shame grow by leaps and bounds. I found I could no longer eat or look Eburacon in the eye.

"Indeed. No one asks for such a burden, do they?"

His gentle words were unexpected. I lifted my gaze to see him smiling at me. He gave a small shrug, adding, "You have come this far…"

Aye, I had. But the length I'd come was insignificant in comparison to the journey left ahead. It seemed impossible. "I don't even know what the Lia Fail looks like."

"It is all things Danaan, the source of power of the Ageless Ones from which we all descend. The very heart and soul of our land. Once, long ago, this power was captured in stone—the Lia Fail, we call it. But it is simply an essence, Deira. An essence that feeds this world. It could reside anywhere now."

"How does one look for an essence? How does one without the power of the Ageless Ones running through her veins detect such a power?"

"Ah, but you *do* have power. Do you know that if you steal the life force from another, for a brief amount of time, you will possess his power as well? You are a great conduit. You can capture energy and wield it as your own. That is why your mother was so afraid to leave you. That is why the other halflings before you were so feared. They posed too much of a threat, you see."

I toyed with my fork. "It doesn't feel like a gift. It's something that must be taken from another. I'd be a thief, a parasite, stealing life, or stealing a day or a year from another's life. It's too . . . horrible to consider. Besides, I don't even know how to control it."

He acknowledged my words with a somber, thoughtful nod. A deep sigh escaped my lips as I stared at my cleared plate.

"Balen dines with Ferryn," Eburacon said, reaching over to spoon another helping of the baked dessert onto my plate. "Sydhrs are a strong, unique people, Deira. You must let their leader be your guide. You must trust him to aid and protect you."

"You know of the foretelling?"

"Aye, I know of it."

I pushed at the dessert with my fork. "How can he do this when it means his death?"

"How can he not? It is for the good of us all."

"You must think me selfish then. A true coward." The complete opposite of Balen.

Eburacon chuckled softly then brought his cup to his lips. After he drank, he said, "Balen has had many years of this knowledge. He has always known his fate. He accepts it. You have not had the luxury of time. Your feelings are only natural." He sat back in his chair and regarded me for a long moment. "There is a gate deep below the temple."

A wave of shock spread through me.

"It will take you to the land of your father, to our lost Lia Fail. At dusk tomorrow, I will take you there. Until then, you must eat and prepare."

* * *

I made my way out of the building, taking the time to appreciate the wood carvings on the walls and doors as I went by. Polished for thousands of moons, they shone in the light of the tall lanterns that lit my way. Eburacon's words still rang in my head. A gate. There was a gate here in Falias. Apparently not all of them had been destroyed after the Old War.

It was night, the air cool welcome against my bare skin as I strolled over the spongy grass to the bridge. The entire grove was quiet and still. Soft orange lights blinked through the trees, coming from the temples and dormitories around the lake. A faint breeze carried the scent of the water and the crisp, clean smell of grass and the blooming wisteria, which grew from ancient roots at each end of the lake. It had long ago wound its way over the railings toward the center rotunda.

Inside, the rotunda was lit by thousands of candles of all shapes and sizes. The center altar sat below the feet of a thirty-foot-tall wooden rendering of Dagda, her arms outstretched in a loving gesture, a rendering of the Cauldron of Plenty balancing on one palm and a Danaan couple, male and female, on the other. At the points of the four directions, steps led straight from the rotunda into the lake.

I had nothing to give, nothing to place on the altar, no flowers to throw in the lake, so I kept going, crossing through and onto the bridge and finally to the far side of the lake where Eburacon had said I'd find a building with a pointed roof and tall, narrow windows framed with pale green curtains.

A stone path led to the open door. The windows were open too, the curtains billowing gently in the breeze. Soft voices and male laughter came from inside.

The hall was small. There was a hearth at the far end and padded benches and tables and sitting areas. Herbs hung from the rafters and over the hearth. To my right, a wide archway led to a large kitchen and work area for making medicines. Every inch of wall space had been dedicated to labeled jars and supplies.

I'd found the healers hall.

I smiled at a male at a nearby table who picked dried leaves from a stem, which he placed in a pile on a work table. Farther into the hall, I heard the laughter again and approached a set of couches by the hearth.

The fabric of my gown had grown cool from the night air and it gave me a shiver as it moved against me. Ferryn reclined on a long couch, his color better, and a smile on his face. He noticed me and his eyes widened.

I resisted the urge to look down and check the gown, to make sure everything was where it should be. Being dressed like a lady with my hair uncovered was enough to make my nerves fly, but then a dark head appeared over the back of the second couch.

Balen.

My belly took an airy turn as he rose easily from the couch, his form and size impressive as ever. He regarded me with an intensity that shot straight to my soul.

Ferryn held out his hand and beckoned me to join them. "Deira, I'd hoped you'd come." He patted the space on the couch next to him, moving his legs to make room. "Look at you," he said, his cheeks turning pink. "If ever there was a lady fitting for our god of fire, it is you."

Which was appropriate give the fact that I was about to go up in flames of embarrassment. I was truly grateful for the breeze that trickled through the open windows.

Ferryn patted the couch again. I sat down.

Balen returned to his seat on the couch opposite us. He leaned back casually, his black-clad legs spread out before him. He wore a clean tunic, and the chain mail was gone, though it made him no less intimidating.

"You look well," I told Ferryn, finding my voice at last.

"I feel well." He flexed his shoulder to show me. "I've been trying to convince Balen to let me come with you on your journey."

Balen and I refused at the same time, causing Ferryn to laugh out loud.

"Bah. My fever is gone. I am fine."

"I'm sure your mother misses you," I said. "She'll want you back. And she'll need you if we fail." I hadn't meant to say that last part, to bring to the forefront the thing no one wanted to think about.

Ferryn pushed himself up higher on the couch, drew in a deep breath, lifted his chin, and stared straight at Balen. "I intend to Challenge."

The statement didn't seem to surprise Balen. He leaned forward, rested his elbows on his knees and rubbed his face with both hands. "You're not ready, Ferryn. Let Orin or Gorsedd Challenge."

"Anyone can try. That's the law."

Tension flashed between them; Ferryn like an angry child and Balen like a father at his limits.

"You will speak of my passing before it even happens? Already thinking of ruling the people. When did you become so ambitious?"

Ferryn's fists clenched and his face became red. "I would follow you to the ends of the world if you let me. But someone must think of what's to come once you pass. Someone must take up the Challenge. I have always been in your shadow, learned from you, watched you, trained with you. I would be a good leader."

Balen scrubbed his face again and his shoulders slumped as he let out a heavy sigh. "I know you would. I know."

For a time, no one spoke.

Though I wanted to learn more of this Challenge, I didn't break the silence. I couldn't look at Balen without envisioning his end. How could we sit here and speak of it as though it was fact? How could a warrior people not believe in a fighting chance? Eburacon had said Balen accepted his fate, had known for a long time that he'd die to protect his people, but there had to be a way to rewrite his fate.

"My letters are retched," Ferryn changed the subject. "If I'm to spend time here mending, would you scribe a letter for me, Deira?"

"Aye," I said, grabbing onto the opportunity like it was a lifeline. "Gladly."

Balen rose. "Then I will leave you both to it." He gave a curt nod and left.

When he was gone, Ferryn's shoulders slumped. He leaned closer to me, the errant lock of black hair falling in front of his eyes once again. He pushed it back and smiled, but the sadness remained in his eyes. "You do look very pretty, Deira."

I glanced down at the gown I wore. "Thank you. I'm not used to looking like way…"

"Well," he said, leaning back, "the look suits you."

I wasn't sure what to say other than thank you. Ferryn was so different than Balen; open, warm, friendly, not at all intense and formidable like his leader.

"It's all right," he said with a shrug. "I make females speechless all the time."

I laughed. "I'm glad you're feeling better."

"As am I."

"So what is this Challenge you spoke of?"

"It's the right to be king and champion of our house. One must travel to the very top of the world where the eagles soar, to the highest peak of our land, Bren Cara, the mountain of fire, where Sydhr forged the War Raven. There, the Challenger must become one with the creature."

The excitement in his eyes made me smile. "How does one do that?"

"I have no idea. That is part of the Challenge."

"It explains the creature that shadows Balen."

"Drem Cara, we call it," Ferryn said. "Cara in our ancient tongue means fire."

"And Drem?"

"No one knows but Balen."

I imagined what Balen had gone through to become the leader of his people, facing the War Raven, becoming one with it…

"Now about that letter," Ferryn said.

"Right." I reached for my satchel.

"We shall begin. *Dearest Mother…*"

* * *

After scribing a letter from Ferryn to Nuallan, I bid him a goodnight's rest then left the building for my quarters, crossing once more the bridge over the black lake.

Part way across, I paused to admire the wide expanse of moonlit water and to listen to the litany of prayers sung by the priests in the center rotunda. They appeared on the steps going into the lake, making offerings—flowers, precious gems and metals, carvings of wood and bone, all fashioned for the goddess. Candles were set on floating trays made from braided reeds and then pushed gently onto the lake's surface, reminding me of the underground bathing cavern.

It was beautiful, the sight. Peaceful. Serene.

I couldn't believe there was a gate in the grove. I thought I'd have more time. To choose. To come to terms with the quest thrust upon me. My thoughts shifted to the land of my father. It was so close. No longer a dream or impossibility.

Mother's last words came back to me. *One day you'll be accepted, Deira, by every being of this darkening land. You'll see. Even the creatures, big and small, will love you. You'll see...* She'd always believed in me. And now I questioned if she hadn't known all along the path I would take.

Would it be the same as he described? I'd memorized his writings and everything he told me of his homeland, the details, customs, history, and language. Would he still be alive? Had too much time passed? I dragged a long breath into my lungs, surprised to find that it stung—the air had grown much colder.

Had I any true Danaan power, the chill would seep into my soul and diminish my magic. It would make me weak and tired. And that was only the beginning. The lake would freeze. The fragrant wisteria would die. The reeds would turn to shafts of ice.

One day, our land would be like the Deadlands. Cold. Barren. Void of any light or life.

The song of the priests continued, growing stronger and deeper. Eburacon proceeded down the rotunda steps and into the water. He stopped knee deep in the lake, his arms open wide, his mouth moving in prayer. At his presence, an energy stirred in the air as though the whole of the grove awakened. The grass, the leaves, the trees, the night blooms, everything seemed more alive. A soft green glow lit the depths of the lake.

Goosebumps rose on my arms. I could see my breath in the air. Wariness threaded through me like the thin layer of frost that began creeping over the railing, the moon's glow lighting the small icy crystals. Immediately I thought of Nox, and shut the door to my mind as Eburacon had advised. I would not let him in again.

No sooner than I'd been about the task, a hot wave of energy flowed through me so suddenly that I gasped.

The strength in my legs gave out and my knees hit the bridge, both of my hands still gripping the railing. My head hung heavy between my stretched arms. Smells came to me clear and strong. Sounds were more acute, as though a veil on the world had been lifted and everything was clear and known.

The feelings and emotions within me were so strong. So overwhelming. Light surrounded me, nurtured me. So much light...

Remember this power, for this is what you seek.

The voice was so beautiful it took my breath. A mother's voice, strong and powerful, loving and kind. Peace and acceptance embraced me. A warm line of tears trailed down my cheeks.

"Deira?"

My name seemed lost amid the senses that battered me.

Large hands gripped my rib cage and lifted me to my feet. The scent of clean skin, and rich aromatic hysop oil filled the air. I steadied myself, removing my hands from the railing, and placed them on Balen's forearms.

"What's wrong? Are you ill?"

His scent, his words, everything was more vivid to my enhanced senses.

I shook my head, trying to clear it and finding it difficult to speak.

He captured my chin gently in an effort to determine what was wrong. I tried to look at him, but couldn't focus. Then he swept me up. My head fell against his shoulder. My free arm fell limp, dangling in the cold air. I drifted as he began walking.

Chapter 13

I was on a bed, still wearing the gown, and Balen was nearby, which was at once comforting and disconcerting.

Whatever had happened on the bridge hadn't made me tired or groggy. In fact, I felt better than I had in days. I opened my eyes and pushed myself up against the headboard.

Balen pulled his chair closer to the bed. He reached to the bedside table, poured me a cup of water from the pitcher then handed it to me.

I emptied it quickly. "What happened? Did you bring my satchel? I was on the bridge—" It came back in a rush. The frost. The voice. And then Balen… After that, I couldn't remember.

But I remembered what happened before and it had been incredible.

Unable to contain the slow smile spreading across my face, I remembered the goddess. For the first time in my life, I'd heard. Albeit, a small thing for any Danaan to feel the blessings of the gods, but for me it was monumental.

"I felt her," I said through a burgeoning smile. "Dagda, she spoke to me."

"You've never felt the gods before?"

"No, never." And then I was struck with something else equally as shocking. "She showed me… Balen—" I grabbed his arm— "I know what the Lia Fail feels like. I know what to seek."

We were one step closer, thanks to Dagda.

Balen didn't move, didn't speak, but emotion swam in his eyes. All this time he'd known his fate. But this was the first time I'd seen the stark realization of it reflected in his eyes; his time in this world would soon come to an end. A bleak understanding that perhaps hadn't hit him so bluntly before. Or if it had, he'd hidden it well.

A jagged ache took hold, sadness and denial settling like a heavy weight, pinning me to the bed. In a need to comfort, I cupped his cheek, wanting him to know it mattered. "I'm sorry."

He caught my hand. "Don't be. I've lived long, Deira."

I let my hand fall to the coverlet, but he held onto it, his large calloused one dwarfing my own. I studied our hands for a spell as the ache grew, causing a great well of despair. "I don't want you to die."

One black eyebrow arched, and his lips curved up a shade. "Nor do I." He glanced down at our hands. "Would that we had more time… I was wrong before to call you a child."

Regret pierced my chest, mingled with the vivid memory of our encounter in the baths when he'd called me a child. We had very little chance of exploring a future between us, and less of a chance at surviving the next few weeks. "Promise me." I squeezed his hand. "Promise you'll not give in, but fight. Fight until the very end."

"I could do no less, though it won't change the outcome."

I wanted to argue, to convince him otherwise, but he saw my intention, leaned forward, and kissed my forehead.

When he straightened, he said, "All that is mine will be yours. I would see you taken care of."

I didn't know what to say.

"You'll have the freedom to do what you will. Scribe books to your heart's content. Build your own Hall of Records. Whatever you like. Whether we succeed or not, you will have earned whatever measure of comfort I can give you."

He assumed I'd go, that I'd ride out with him and save the world. I didn't trust myself to speak, afraid I'd blurt out my cowardly indecision.

"Rest." He rose. "Your satchel is by the bed."

After he closed the door, I stared at it for some time until my heart didn't hurt so much. I drank more of the cold water then swung my legs over the bed, needing to move, to get up and do something because lying in the bed with sad thoughts would do me little good.

I noticed that the clothes I'd worn upon arriving in Falias had been cleaned, mended, and folded neatly atop a chest of drawers. My cloak had also been cleaned, so I shook it out then swept it around my shoulders, clasping it at my neck, covering the beautiful blue and silver gown.

Quickly, I grabbed my satchel, eased open the door and slipped from the bedchamber.

Hallway lanterns still burned, but otherwise it was quiet and empty, most of the priests and students having retired for the night. Soft voices drifted from another corridor along with the scent of recently eaten meal, but I saw no one as I made my way to the main hall.

The tall double doors opened easily as I pushed my way outside and moved quickly down the narrow path that led away from the grove and into the public city square where the people's temple and the Hall of Records stood.

The Hall would not be closed; being a scribe often meant late nights writing by the light of a single candle. The scribes here were no different than in any other city.

I took the steps two at a time and slipped inside, closing the doors behind me. I rubbed my cold hands together smiling at the familiar smells of parchment paper, candle wax, and ink. This was where I felt most at home, surrounded by shelves upon shelves of manuscripts.

Soft light illuminated the long center hall furnished with work tables. Each table had a lantern and larger lights burned at intervals along the sides of the hall where, rising to the high ceilings, were the records, scrolls, books, and maps of Falias.

Six scribes worked diligently, few glancing at me briefly before returning to their tasks. I moved to one of the tables nearest the door, not wanting to disturb anyone. I removed my notebook and writing instruments from the satchel. I only had a few blank sheets left. I set one flat on the table, smoothing the surface, before opening my vial of ink and placing several drops into the hollow shaft of my pen.

The tip of my pen stayed poised over the paper for a long stretch of time. I bit the inside of my cheek, unsure of how to begin a letter to Balen.

Scribing my feelings on paper was harder than I'd thought it'd be. But I had to do it; I couldn't allow myself to go through the rest of my life without telling him what I thought about his sacrifice. His courage and the care he had for his people and land was extraordinary. And if Balen was indeed meant to die protecting me, he had to know how much that meant to me, and how much I thought of him.

Scribing it to paper was the only way I knew how.

As the night progressed so did my ability to open up. Once I started, the words poured from me and before I knew it, I had used two sheets of my paper, and was satisfied with the outcome.

I set each piece aside to dry then got up to stretch my legs, working the kinks from my back and fingers. My hood kept my face hidden as I strolled around the edges of the hall, skimming over the manuscripts on the shelves as I went.

A warning pricked my conscious just before I heard the potent voice.

Hello, Deira.

I flinched and my step faltered, making me grab onto the shelf beside me as the languid, mocking tone spread through me in a slow wave.

I glanced from beneath the hood, wondering if anyone else could hear the pounding of my heart or the voice in my head. I straightened, swallowed, and calmed myself, trying to do as Eburacon had said. Block my mind to the voice.

But there was only laughter, a deep, intimate sound that made my legs weaken, and my stomach turn. I squeezed my eyes closed and pinched the bridge of my nose. No, I would not let him in. I didn't want to hear.

Oh, you want to hear. Even if your mind denies it. Your body wants it, wants me, Deira, and only me. You and I, we are the same.

A soft indulgent sigh, like a breeze, caressed my mind.

"No, you're wrong," I whispered through clenched teeth. I forced myself to move, back to the table to gather my things.

Soon, we shall meet.

"Never."

I reached the table and began to gather my supplies. I knocked over the ink. The vial broke on the floor and shattered the silence of the Hall. The scribes looked up as I bent to pick up the pieces, ink staining my fingers as I shoved the broken vial into my cloak pocket.

Once I had everything in my satchel, I hurried to the door.

The cold air blew around me, almost mockingly, as I ran outside and down the steps. I stumbled in the empty square, trying to shake off the sensations Nox's voice caused in my mind and body.

You will come to me.

I ignored the voice and raced away from the Hall of Records to the path that would take me back to the sanctuary.

You will come to me for the Lia Fail.

I skidded around the back corner of the Hall. My pulse surged so fast through my veins that it drowned out everything around me except Nox's voice. I braced my hand against the wall.

"You lie," I barely managed to get out. "You don't have it."

Oh, but I do. I have everything you seek, Deira. Everything.

"You have nothing I want."

He laughed, not hiding the trickery and manipulation in his tone. His arrogance pushed me to anger. I focused on that feeling, drawing it together, envisioning a blast of hot fire against Nox's cold shadowy form. It might be in my mind, but it was a battle nonetheless.

I tapped into a pool of rage I didn't know existed in me, and I used it. I let it flow and burst forth in an enormous shove of energy against the mental image I'd formed of Nox.

A white flash erupted behind my closed eyelids.

He was gone.

I leaned over, gasping for breath, amazed that I'd done it. But my victory was short-lived.

"No." I dropped to my knees, stunned. "Oh, no."

A small tree squirrel lay dead on the ground, its body still warm.

I'd called upon the power inside of me as Eburacon had instructed, and as a result I'd drawn the life from this small innocent animal simply by virtue of it being close by.

Bile rose in the back of my throat. I stumbled up and retched in the bushes.

A cold sweat pricked my forehead. I straightened, unsteady on my feet, swiped my sleeve over my mouth and then sucked the chilly air into my lungs.

In the soft soil beneath a nearby tree, I dug a small grave with my ink-stained fingers, barely able to see through my tears as I placed the body inside and said a small prayer.

How was I to fight Nox now?

I couldn't resist him in my mind without hurting another. How would I resist him in the flesh?

Wanting Eburacon's advice, I hurried back to the main complex and to the priest's door, hoping he'd be there in the private chamber where we'd eaten, where he kept his books and ancient scrolls.

I knocked insistently. The door opened. He didn't seem surprised to see me. In fact, he looked as if he was expecting me. "I'm sorry to bother you." My words tumbled out. "I heard him again, and I tried to stop it, and I did, but I…"

It was then that I noticed the two others in the room.

Balen stood by the corner of the hearth.

The War Raven, Drem Cara, in Danaan form was seated by the fire. A broad smile stretched its lips, its yellow eyes glittering with interest. Its thin pale hands were folded in its lap, and it wore the same blue cloak as it had the first time I'd seen it in the Grasslands.

Eburacon closed the door and went to the table in the center of the room where he poured me a cup of water. It was the same table we'd dined at earlier, though now it held stacks of books and scrolls. I took the water, wondering how he knew I needed it, and drank the contents.

He held out a hand to an empty chair by the fire. "Please, sit. Warm yourself by the fire. Your face is dirty and red with cold, child. What happened to your hands?"

I looked down. In the light, they were much dirtier and ink-stained. "Nothing . . . I . . ." I stared at the three Danaans, all so different from each other. My mind floundered. They'd heard my words and now I'd have to find a way to explain them.

I set my satchel on a side table and walked woodenly to an empty chair by the fire—the chair farthest from the unnerving creature. Its eyes followed my movements. So did Balen's, but I couldn't bring myself to face him.

Eburacon joined me in the companion chair near mine, carefully arranging the folds of his green robe. I held my hands out to the flames and took my time warming myself; anything to put off explaining.

Balen pulled a chair away from the table and sat as well. He studied me hard before he asked the question I waited for. "Who do you speak of, Deira? And why were you at the Hall of Records?"

"The Lord of Annwn speaks in her mind," Eburacon answered for me.

I flinched at the truth and finally chanced a look at Balen. "How long?" he asked, his tone flat, his expression dark and deadly calm.

"Since we entered the forest. Since that first attack." Quickly, I tried to explain. "I didn't know how to tell you, or how you'd react. I should have said something…"

Drem laughed, the sound gleeful and, at the same time, cryptic. Then, it ceased suddenly and returned to its former expression. Balen shot it an annoyed glance.

I should've told him. I had waited too long.

"And what did the Lord of Annwn have to say on this cold night?" he asked rigidly.

"He claims to have the Lia Fail," I answered. "He claims I will come to him for it."

I didn't share the rest, the more intimate details. Embarrassment colored my cheeks. I switched my attention to the fire, concentrating on the way the flames danced, and the pop and crack of splitting wood.

"She will go to him." This from Drem, who seemed to take immense pleasure in saying so.

I ignored the creature. "Is it true? Does Nox have the Lia Fail?" No one spoke. I turned to the priest. "But it's in the land of my father. That's what I was told."

"Aye. The Light is there. And Nox travels freely between worlds."

"But who rules the Deadlands if he's gone? Who rules the House of Annwn?"

Eburacon leaned forward. "The question you should ask is who would *want* to rule the Deadlands."

"Nox could have moved the House of Annwn to Éire," Balen said.

"Bah. All this talk. Destroy the gate," Drem said so petulantly that it was clear this was an old argument. "Leave him to rot in the land of man, and then I will pick the flesh from his bones when he dies."

Balen ignored the comment. "Why were you in the Hall of Records?"

The letter I'd written seemed silly now. "I was reading my father's books." My face heated with the lie. "I seem to concentrate better in the Hall..." A miserable sigh welled inside me.

"It would seem Conlainn prepared you well for this journey," Eburacon said.

"You think my father knew I'd journey to Éire one day?" I asked, surprised.

The priest chuckled softly, shaking his head. "No, I don't believe your father knew, Deira. But sometimes we are compelled to do things for reasons unknown to us at the time. Sometimes we are guided with a gentle nudge or thought, never understanding or aware that we are being led."

I shifted uncomfortably in the chair, asking the question that had always haunted me. "How much time passes there? Would he still be alive?"

The priest's brow rose with gentle concern. "Men do not live long like we do, but there is a small chance, for the glow of our immortality would've clung to him for some time after he left our land."

"Unless he tripped on his sword," Drem spoke up; its eyes alight with the possibilities. "He could have fallen off his horse," it began listing, "or met with foul deeds, or been attacked by hounds, or even drowned in—"

"Enough!" Balen's deep voice rang with warning.

Drem froze, its mouth still open. Hostile glares shot between the two. Sparks flared in Balen's eyes. Drem's mouth gradually closed. Its face became expressionless, but its eyes held hurt. It tipped its chin high and then turned to stare at the wall beyond Balen's shoulder.

I glanced at Eburacon, releasing my breath, so sure that violence would erupt. He seemed unaffected by the outburst as though he understood the odd relationship existing between the Fire Breather and the War Raven.

Eburacon rose, causing Balen to rise out of respect and me as well. Drem remained in its seat, sulking. "We have much to prepare for," he said. "Rest will do you all good."

Seeing my escape, I snatched my satchel from the table and managed a fumbled goodnight before hurrying from the room.

I didn't look back as I rushed down the hall to my bedchamber. Once inside, I locked the door and leaned against it with an enormous sigh of relief. Lifting my eyes to the tall ceiling, I said a quick prayer to Anu and Dagda to help get me through this.

After unpinning my hair and removing my clothes, I
washed my face and hands, scrubbing as hard as I could. At the
mirror, I studied my reflection and thought of the tiny life I'd taken
tonight. Never again. I'd never do that again.

I slid underneath the green coverlet in the sheer slip,
finding a small measure of comfort in the cool, clean bed linens
and the soft pillow that cushioned my head.

Eburacon was right. The rest would do me well.
Tomorrow would come soon enough.

Chapter 14

For many, tomorrow in Innis Fail never came.

Sometime during the night, I woke from my sleep and rolled onto my back. No dream or noise had caused my eyes to open, but I was wide awake and possessed with the urge to get up.

As my eyes adjusted to the darkness, the vague shape of the ceiling's timber beams came into view. Under the coverlet, it was warm—the last thing I should've wanted was to leave. But the urge wouldn't go away; neither would the feeling that something was wrong.

I slid from beneath the coverlet, hugging myself for warmth, and padded barefoot to the tall, paned window. The chill in the room was far greater than I'd expected; the floor frigid under my feet. I pushed the curtain aside and peeked out, my breath fogging the windowpane.

I rubbed it away. Outside, the grove appeared dark and quiet. The large shapes of trees and buildings cast elongated shadows in the moonlight. I saw nothing out of the ordinary and was about to turn away when movement caught my eye.

But there was nothing.

The sound of a closing door and muffled voices echoed from far off down the hallway. My door was thrown open and light poured inside.

"Deira! Get up!"

I spun around, instantly covering myself with my hands for the slip left little to the imagination.

Balen's eyes went wide, his mouth open on words he'd been meaning to speak. As my eyes adjusted to the light, I noticed he wore his battle gear, and a hand rested on the hilt of the short sword at his waist.

As if poked, he turned around to give me privacy. He saw my clothes on the dresser and tossed them behind him. "Get dressed. Quickly."

I caught the pile before it hit me in the face. "What's happening?"

Hurried footsteps echoed down the hall, accompanied by low, urgent voices. I donned the leggings and tunic then sat on the bed to pull on the socks and shoes.

"We must go," he, said impatiently as soon as the last shoe was on. He had my cloak in his hand and took my upper arm, directing me ahead out the door and into the hallway.

Priests, disciples, students, and servants hurried in both directions. Balen used his large body to weave a path through.

My satchel.

"Wait—" I yanked against him, looking back toward my room. "My books…" Fully alert, completely in warrior mode, Balen barely paid attention. "You don't underst—"

"Leave it," he tossed over his shoulder. "There isn't time."

"But—"

I couldn't leave my father's writings and Mother's pendant. I dug in my heels, prepared to fight until Jensine's body was carried by in a sling. One of her arms dangled freely. Lifeless. A small line of blood made a jagged path down the skin and then dripped from the tip of her finger.

My mouth dropped open.

"Damn it, Deira. Move." Balen's harsh command spurred me into action. Dazed, I moved, not knowing where I was going or what had happened.

We came into the hall where more of the wounded lay amid a flurry of activity.

No, I realized, not wounded. Dead.

My stomach clenched. The laments, the shouts, and the frantic searches for loved ones meshed into a dizzying chaos. As we passed a line of bodies and mourners, I was glad Balen moved quickly and without hesitation. I kept my eyes straight ahead.

Finally we pushed our way outside. I stumbled down the steps overwhelmed and disoriented, but Balen was there to right me, his confident voice diminishing some of my panic.

"Arms over your head. Breathe." He lifted my arms.

I did what he said, dragging deep quantities of air into my lungs. He released me and I leaned forward, resting both hands on my knees until my heart calmed and the panic didn't seem so consuming.

And Balen, he just stood there, still as could be, exuding impatience, energy, alertness, showing no signs he was affected by the sights inside, by the dead, by the blood...

"What happened? Are we under attack?"

"No. They've come and gone." He caught my hand, and we began hurrying down the path to the bridge.

I understood at once where we went—to the healer's building to get Ferryn. I had no trouble keeping pace as we broke into a run across the bridge. We nearly ran right by him within the darkness of the center rotunda.

"Balen!"

Ferryn rushed to us, clasping Balen's shoulder and then nodding to me. He was out of breath, his face pale, but his eyes bright.

"Assassins," Ferryn said out of breath. "A number of them, struck and then gone."

"Aye," Balen confirmed.

Footsteps echoed on the bridge. We turned. Eburacon made his way swiftly toward us, his long face ashen and his expression grim. Several priests followed behind him, the concern and dismay on their faces evident. Some had tears streaming down their cheeks.

"You must go now," he said never pausing as he glided toward the main altar.

As he passed, I sucked in a quiet gasp. Blood stained the back of his robe. *His* blood. He'd been stabbed in the back.

"Hurry," he called over his shoulder, skirting the altar and going down the steps leading into the lake.

I hurried down the steps after him, darting in front of Balen. I touched Eburacon's shoulder gently. "You're wounded," I said as he paused and canted his head toward me. "Let the healers care for you."

Warmth came into his eyes. "You sound like your mother. You have inside you a great capacity for love, Deira. Never doubt your heart." His words stunned me. "I live now only by the will of Dagda. Tending to my wounds will do little good. We must open the gate, for there is no tomorrow for me. Your path lies ahead in the waters of the goddess." His expression softened. "I know it is not the path you want. It is not the path your warrior wants either. But the time has come for you to accept it."

I stared at him, unable to speak, argue, or agree. Now that the time had come, fear washed through me. I thought I'd have time to prepare myself, to read Father's books and come to terms with the foretelling. There was so much I still needed to learn. The rush, the urgency . . . I never got to choose.

"You *have* chosen," Eburacon, reading me so easily. "You chose days ago. You just don't like it." He kissed my forehead and then smiled. "A reluctant savior, but one all the same."

I squeezed my eyes closed.

"Come. The gate awaits in the water below." Eburacon continued down the steps.

Surprised, I stared at the water but saw only blackness. The wet air dampened my skin like a cold sweat. Water lapped gently against the steps as the priests began to chant, the same chant I'd heard before. Their words, a steady cadence of praise to the goddess, seemed to strengthen Eburacon. Energy swarmed around him.

Balen leaned close, his voice dry. "Looks like we're about to get wet. Are you ready?"

"No."

Eburacon raised his arms. His head tipped back and a low hum began in his throat. That same energy, that same sense of peace and acceptance filled me, though this time it was not so overwhelming.

A smoky green glow appeared within the depths of the lake, and the water receded from the first few steps as though giant hands held it at bay.

"Go now," Eburacon whispered, his eyes closed, his face still raised in prayer.

Down. Into the depths. Into that gaping hole surrounded by water.

I swallowed as Balen slipped his large, warm hand in mine. He gave me a confidant nod, a warrior's nod, that ready acceptance of whatever was to come.

As we stepped around Eburacon, he broke concentration to say, "When I see your mother in the Place of Souls, I shall tell her of the courage of her daughter."

Forbidding myself to cry, and unable to speak, I nodded.

"Blessings of the goddess go with you. Your sacrifice," he said to Balen, "will not be forgotten."

We continued one step and then two, the water receding as we went. I glanced back at Eburacon and then at Ferryn who raised his hand in salute.

And then down we went.

I held Balen's hand so tightly, my knuckles hurt. Shadows moved within the wall of water around us, darting like fish, but those shadowed swimmers were nothing as simple as fish. Farther and farther we went until we came to the rocky lake bed and a round shimmering pool of liquid green.

Balen glanced back, and I foolishly followed his gaze. The water was gradually closing us in, forcing us forward. The only place to go was into the pool.

We looked at each other, rousing our nerve. "This is it," I said, trying to rally my courage. "We must go."

"Aye, this is it." His voice was strong and steady. "Deep breath."

I glanced one more time at the water coming closer, and then drew in an enormous breath. We jumped hand in hand into the shimmering pool of green.

* * *

I tensed, ready for the shock of cold liquid, but the shock never came.

With my eyes closed and my breath held, my senses heightened. Coolness passed over my body. It was thicker than water, a liquid that did not get us wet.

Then even that sensation was gone. No wind. No sound or movement. Just a weightless, empty space.

The absence of life, of time and energy, was distinct and terrifying.

In the blink of an eye, we were out, but within that blink there was a sense of eternal nothingness. I never wanted to experience that feeling again, of being so lost and cut off from life. Thank Dagda for Balen's strength for he never let go of my hand, and when our feet hit the ground as though we'd simply taken small jump, he grabbed my elbow in case I faltered.

I didn't falter, but it took some time to reorient myself.

Before long, I detected the unmistakable scent of rich, damp soil, and heard the drip, drip, drip of water against rock.

Ahead of me, everywhere I looked, was darkness. Then a flame flickered from Balen's open palm, burning brightly in the darkness.

I faced the direction in which we came, my eyes adjusting to the light. There was no luminous green pool behind us or above us. I stepped forward, searching, but Balen snatched me back, and as he did I felt the wind sucking me, pulling me towards the Void.

"No, not that way," he said, his voice echoing in the vast cavern.

I froze as the ends of my hair lifted toward the nothingness. My cloak billowed in the same direction. I stumbled away, away from the blackness.

"How will we get back? How will they know to part the water?"

His face remained grim. "Perhaps the water parts on its own," he said so flatly it was clear he had no idea what would happen if we tried to go back.

But then Balen didn't need to know how to get back. He wasn't going home.

"This way." He took my hand once again and began the trek upward along the uneven floor of the vast cavern.

I tried not to dwell on the possibility that we might be stuck in Éire with no way home. Instead, I focused on picking my way over the rubble of loose rocks and jagged ground. There were carvings on the walls, more and more of them as we progressed—spirals, symbols of the sun and moon, strange figures that looked like man and beast. The shuffle, slide, and step of our footsteps, and our breathing, echoed in the cave.

Light appeared up ahead. Balen extinguished his flame. The floor had become flatter and finally we reached stone pavement. The walls were also made of stone, and the path to the light had become tall and narrow, so narrow that Balen's shoulders nearly brushed the walls.

"Stop here." He rested against the wall. "Let our eyes become accustomed to the daylight."

I rested against the opposite wall, but I couldn't tear my attention away from that light. "Dear Dagda. We're in Éire. That's Éire out there."

"And in here." He smiled.

"What should we do?"

"You're the one most versed in the land of Éire, not I."

I gave him a flat look. Father's books on the subject had been left back in Falias. Perfect. Thrust into a new world, and *I* was to be the expert. I raised my brow. "And what does that make you?"

His mouth quirked. "Your sword."

Fighting a smile, I turned back to the rectangle of light, drew in a deep breath and pushed away from the wall, slipping by Balen to lead the way, knowing my 'sword' would follow. Knowing the sooner we began, hopefully the sooner we could return.

Chapter 15

I paused in the narrow stone archway, my heart, my breath, everything still and waiting. With one step, I'd be in the land of my father. Despite the dangers that faced us and the impossibility of our task, I couldn't deny my excitement.

My heart swelled with memories of him, of the stories he told of the people and his land. I smelled the sweet fragrance of grass, heard the rustle of leaves beyond. I'd finally come to the place I often thought of when I'd stand on the ramparts and let my hair fly free in the wind.

Balen waited behind me, still and quiet, allowing me this moment without interruption.

This land was my dream, but I knew, with a sinking heart, it would also be the land of my nightmares. One or both of us might not return home. Once I stepped into the daylight, I'd never be the same.

"Deira let me go first."

Sober, I flattened my back against the wall to let him pass, but he paused in front of me, the front of our clothes touching in the narrow space.

"You'll tell me if Nox speaks to you."

It wasn't a request. I meet his steady gaze and agreed. It was the first he'd mentioned it after finding out in Eburacon's chamber.

The air around him stirred, and I knew he was prepared for anything.

We stepped into the daylight.

I shielded my eyes, squinting at the rolling, grassy field and the edge of a forest in the distance. There was no shelter there, nowhere to hide unless we went back. I looked over my shoulder to see the passage. It was a built into a high mound covered in grass.

Balen caught my hand. "This way. To the trees."

My heart raced. The light was so warm on my face. I stumbled a few times, my attention on the land, the flowers in the field, the blue sky, and the bright golden light that bathed everything in wonderful warmth.

Once we reached the shelter of the forest, Balen scanned the surroundings. The breeze stirred his black hair. He stood so straight and tall, imposing in his black chain mail and tunic. He must've felt my stare because he looked my way. And I was struck by the sight. "Your skin . . . it's . . ." I didn't know the word. It wasn't a glow, but there was a luminous quality to it.

And then I remembered something my father had once told me. When the Sí—mankind's name for all Danaans—came into the human realm, their skin took on a faint, Otherworldly glow. They said it was the light of their immortality shining through.

His watchful eyes took on an amused glint.

"Is mine?" I touched my face.

The corners of his mouth twitched. "Aye. It is. Faintly."

I laughed. Desperate to hold onto the moment, needing to feel happy like this, if only for a short time, I put both hands on Balen's shoulders and rose onto the tips of my toes. A look of surprise filled his eyes as I kissed him softly on the mouth, closing my eyes, breathing in deeply as though I could draw him inside me. The scent of fire and leather, of salt and skin, flew through me and burst like a million sparks in my stomach.

His hands gripped my hips and pulled me closer. One of his hands went to my hair, twisting it as he cupped the back of my head. Our lips parted. Our tongues touched, and I had the sensation of leaping into a bright empty sky and soaring.

We kissed long and deep and slow, learning each other, taking our time. With each moment, heat grew in and around me. The memory of his hand on my skin in the underground lake made me want that again.

I broke away, staggering back, shaken, feeling too full, too heavy.

Balen dragged unsteady fingers through his hair and let out a shaky breath. He glanced around, worried about our open position, worried about protecting me, but wanting more from me. "This isn't finished," he promised.

Suddenly, I didn't feel quite so bold. "I know," I said, then followed him into the woods.

After several minutes, my desire subsided and my thoughts turned to the task at hand.

"We should find the fathá. They are—"

"Priests and lawgivers. My father spoke of them often. He said the fathá worship variations of the Ageless Ones. Their temple will be in or near a grove of oaks in the forest, hidden and old."

"You are well informed then. We should pick up a trail at some point. Stay close."

The ground was cushioned by layers of pine needles and leaves. The dense canopy of ancient trees inhibited new growth, so we had little to bar our way as we searched for a path. For a long time we followed animal trails.

My father had told me that we shared many things with Innis Fail. We worshipped our ancestors as gods, the four Ageless Ones, and mankind worshipped them as well. Before the Old War, when the gates had been open, we traded freely. We shared a similar language, shared animals, livestock, flora, grains, and vegetables. I recognized plants and trees. Saw small shrubs and forest flowers that I'd seen many times over.

My father's people had held Danaans in awe. To them we, too, were like gods, wielding magic and controlling the elements, possessing Otherworldly beauty and knowledge, and living forever.

I wanted to share my thoughts with Balen, but knew we must travel quietly.

Birds rustled the leaves. Animals scurried as we went by. There were no signs of man about, but still I felt watched. When the caw of the raven reverberated through the forest, my blood ran cold.

It landed on a branch in front of us, cocked its head, and stared at me.

Balen held out his arm. "Come, Drem." The raven flew from its perch and onto Balen's arm, which dipped from the weight of the large creature. The wings stretched wide then folded against its back.

"It followed us," I said, bewildered and surprised by its presence.

"Ravens travel unencumbered between our lands. But here in Éire, Drem can only take the form of the simple raven."

I didn't trust the creature and didn't like *not* knowing how it was connected to Balen. And what the creature's words had meant. *He is mine and I am his.*

* * *

As night fell, we made camp. I washed my face and hands in a stream nearby then returned to see Balen sitting quietly near the campfire, chin resting on the tips of his fingers.

I settled across from him. "Where's Drem?"

He shrugged.

I gathered my hair over one shoulder and began braiding it to keep it from tangling as I slept. "Is it male or female?"

"Neither. Both."

Firelight reflected in Balen's eyes as he studied me quietly. "When the god of fire created the War Ravens, it was not to procreate. It was to serve him. They cannot breed."

"And what is your relationship with the War Raven? Does it serve you?"

He scrubbed a hand along his jaw, staring at the flames for a time before answering. "We share souls."

I blinked, the words not quite settling like they should.

"When the Ageless Ones moved on from Innis Fail," Balen explained, "the custody of the War Ravens fell to Sydhr's descendants by right. He created them, used, and trained them. Only those who pass Challenge can join with the creature. Those leaders who came before me, and I myself, only passed Challenge because the creature recognized the blood of Sydhr in our veins. If it runs strong enough, if our power is strong enough, we are joined. If not, we die."

"But you don't control Drem. It comes and goes as it pleases."

"I don't control Drem any more than it controls me. But we protect each other. We must. Drem took a part of my soul, as I took a part of its."

The idea that Balen did not possess his complete soul unnerved me. It didn't seem natural or possible. I stared hard at him, trying to see a part of the creature within him, but I only saw him; the same fiery eyes, the same black hair, the same aura of relentless strength and conviction.

"How can one live like that? Are you not empty without all of your soul?"

"I was born to this. Within Drem is the breath of Sydhr. I don't feel empty but full." His head titled, eyes going narrow. "You don't like Drem."

I couldn't lie. Besides, my expression told him exactly what I thought of the creature. But Balen only chuckled. "Drem takes some getting used to."

I shared a smile at his understatement. "So it can't change form here in Éire?"

"No. But I am privy to its eyes and ears, and soon we'll find our path to the Lia Fail."

"And to Ixia. You've not mentioned her since Ferryn came to us with the news."

He picked up a stone and rolled it in his hands. "What would you have me say?"

"Something. She was taken by Nox. She is your sister."

"If I have the chance to free her, I will. But my path has been written, Deira. And my path is to see you to the Lia Fail."

I couldn't keep the surliness from my tone. "Your path has only been uttered."

"This is an argument neither one of us can win," Balen said with resignation. "I don't deny your belief, Deira, but neither must you deny me mine."

I let my braid fall. "You're right." I let out a heavy exhale. "I'm sorry. My father's ideals and views have always struck a louder cord in me than the ways of my mother."

He angled to stretch out his legs, crossing one ankle over the other. "In many ways, you are like Drem and I."

"How so?"

"There are two sides to you. The Danaan side, the blood of Anu, and the legacy of your mother. And the human side, the side that conflicts so sharply with the other, the one which you embrace even though you have never lived it."

"The blood of my father is stronger in me most of the time," I admitted. "I have dreamt of coming here all my life."

For a moment, he didn't respond. "And what will you do once you've returned the Lia Fail? Will you return here or will you stay in Innis Fail? What does your future hold?"

My chest tightened. He asked a question I could not answer. "I don't know. I guess that's the difference between us."

His head cocked to the side, a wry smile pulling at his lips. "True."

* * *

That night, I dreamt of my father. Flashes of our short time together. The deep ring of his laughter. The smiles. His love for me that brightened his brown eyes. The red of his hair. The way he would wiggle his thick eyebrows at me to make me laugh. Our walks through the garden of Mother's estate, he with a book tucked under his arm, me with plucked flowers in my hand and a skip in my step.

For a short time, my life had been perfect. When Mother heard her calling to the Place of Souls, it had been so hard to let her go. But Father had been there for me, had taken me into his arms and claimed I'd never be alone. Yet he'd left me too.

In my dream, I was that little girl again.

I ambled past the open arches that spanned the long length of the main corridor of our house. The curtains billowed softly. Gray daylight dimmed the colors around me, the mosaics at my feet, and the flowers beyond in the garden. A chill was in the air. Dead leaves fluttered in from the garden and skipped across the floor as I headed toward the study.

My heart beat quickened.

The house began to shift, becoming old and ruined. Cracks appeared in the walls. As I went, paintings disappeared. The curtains became torn and stained. Outside, the garden shriveled, the crackling of stems as they shrunk echoed in the silence.

I glanced down at my feet and saw they weren't those of a child, but of mine as a mature female. Yet I still wore the sheer white nightgown I'd worn the morning I discovered Father had gone.

You should stop walking, my voice warned. *Turn around. Don't go into the study. You know how much it hurts to go in there.*

But I couldn't listen, couldn't turn back.

Even though I tried, my steps continued forward until I was at the open door. Dread coiled around me like a serpent, threading through my legs, around my torso and neck. I shivered.

Father sat at his desk, his profile to me, shoulders hunched over, furiously writing as he often did by the light of the tall window by the desk.

I'd seen this image many times, the way he'd pause, bite the inside of his cheek, then stare longingly out the window. He was a tall man, with wide shoulders and a bulky build. He had the look of a warrior and the eyes of a scholar.

He paused in his writing as though sensing a presence and then he glanced my way. I held my breath. My skin tingled and went cold as a frigid breeze swept inside. I wanted to shiver or hug myself but I couldn't move.

"Ah, Deira, come in, come in," he beckoned with ink-stained fingers.

My mind balked, insisting I not go into the study. But I stepped inside the room.

"You see this," he said, gazing down at the page while dipping the tip of his pen into the inkbottle. "This is your history. All about your ancestors. Your heritage. I should be done soon." He nodded to himself and began writing again. "Very soon, I shall be done."

I braced my palm on the corner of the desk and glanced out the window to the sound of Father's pen scratching on parchment. The garden was dying, life being sucked from every living thing. A current of wind swirled through the garden, picking up leaves and bursting the dried flowers that had once been vibrant and full.

This wasn't right. This wasn't how I remembered our home.

This was nothing but a horrible dream.

Father's hand suddenly closed around my wrist. He stared up at me, his eyes burning with intensity. His skin appeared ashen. Gray shadows curved under his eyes. Pain shot through my wrist, his grasp hard and cold and unwavering. "Deira," he whispered urgently.

"Aye, Father, I'm here. I'm right here."

He blinked then looked up, as though seeing me clearly for the first time. His expression turned vehement, blotches of red staining his cheeks. "I will never leave you." His voice, always so gentle and fun, was angry and rushed. "*Never.*"

His grip tightened. I cried out, pulling away from him, but he didn't budge.

My throat closed. Tears stung my eyes. Dear Dagda, I wanted out. Out of this nightmare.

Suddenly he released me, and his face became normal again. He smiled gently, the singular smile he'd always reserved for me, and only me. "Now, go on and play in the garden until supper."

Chapter 16

I woke at a snail's pace, my eyes eventually adjusting to the hazy, muted slice of daylight through the trees. From the angle, I could tell it was just after dawn. I lay on my side on my cloak, facing the burned-out campfire.

Balen was not across from me.

I sat up, finding Drem perched atop a rock peering at me with that maddening calm. I got the impression it enjoyed the affect it had on me. As I pushed to my feet, I shot it a hostile glare, refusing to let it frighten me, and shook the leaves and pine needles from my cloak.

The morning light made the dew on the ground sparkle, leaves, and rocks, shadows and light everywhere I looked. It was magical. I breathed in deeply, the air wet and fresh.

And then the shadows moved.

Drem pushed off from the rock. Its shiny black wings caught the light as it flew into the air, its caw echoing through the forest, pricking the fine hairs on the back of my neck. I whirled in a slow circle, realizing I was surrounded. I clutched the cloak to my chest, eyeing the ground for a weapon. A rock. A branch. Anything to protect myself.

Hands landed on each of my shoulders. I screamed, spinning around, and kicking.

"Deira."

"Balen!" I kicked him in the leg.

It was too late to stop it. Pain shot up my foot, but from the grunt that issued from Balen, I'd say it hurt him worse than it hurt me.

"Damn it. What did you kick me for?"

"You were gone when I woke up, and then I thought I saw..."

But I hadn't been mistaken, the shadows within the forest *had* moved. Men and women gathered in a circle around us. Cloaks of faded green trimmed with red covered their shoulders and beneath they wore white tunics and brown leggings.

"These are the fathá," Balen said.

One came forward, the only one with colorful stripes on his robe. He lowered his hood, revealing thick red hair shot with gray. It was long and hung in braids over his shoulders. His eyebrows were white and the lower part of his face was covered in a beard the same color as his hair. He had shinny blue eyes that stared at me with wonder.

He bowed at my feet. And when he did, so did the others.

Confused, I looked to Balen. He shrugged. "They did the same to me," he said under his breath.

And I knew to them we were like gods.

Would that Lidi could see me now. She, like me, would be highly amused by the notion.

The man in the colorful cloak straightened. "I am called Liath Airgid. We're honored by your presence, Dia."

I smiled at the term Dia, the general term for god or goddess. I thanked him for his kind words.

"Please come. We have shelter, food, and a place to rest and bathe."

Liath led us deeper into the forest, the others filling in behind us. Someone began a soft song, and soon all the fathá joined in song as we journeyed through the sparkling forest.

I bumped Balen's shoulder. "Where are we going?"

"To their temple complex. They believe we've come for the festival of fire. I saw no reason to let them think otherwise."

"They are fortunate then," I said, smiling, "to have a god of fire in attendance."

"Fortunate indeed," came the amused reply.

I listened with a light heart to the sounds of the singing. For so long, all I'd wanted was to be accepted. And here, in Éire, I was more than a halfling, more than a servant, more than noble, more than a queen. I was divine. The novelty made me smile all the way to the center of the fathá faith where the trees gave way to a vast open grove.

In the center was a hill, Tlachtga, and atop it an enormous circle of stones. Around the base of the hill, circular wooden houses with thatched roofs had been built. There were several long rectangular wooden structures, and these, I guessed, were the lower temples, great hall, kitchen, and bathhouses. Smoke trickled from rooftops. Children played, and people went about their daily rituals.

I didn't feel as though we stood out from them, but we did.

As we proceeded, people noticed. Their eyes grew wide. They gathered around, bowing and reaching out to touch our hands, our clothes… I looked back at Balen in his black chain mail and tunic, the light glinting off his black hair. Aye, I suppose to them, seeing him was like seeing a divine being. He was taller, stronger, and more beautiful than anyone I'd seen even in my own land. He moved with a dark, predator's grace, and a noble, powerful presence.

I wondered what they saw when they looked at me. Self-consciously, I smoothed my tunic. My chin dropped a notch. I felt the heat in my cheeks.

"Chin up, Dia," Balen said, mildly, leaning close. "You are a goddess, after all."

I kept my eyes trained on the back of Liath's cloak. The irony did not escape me. If there was anyone in my world less equipped to be mistaken for a goddess, it was me.

Word of our arrival spread quickly. I studied the women lining the path. I was taller than most of them, but not by much. Many had red hair, braided or left loose to hang over their shoulders. It occurred to me that these were my people, too. The idea was dizzying.

Liath led us to the doors of the largest wooden structure. It reminded me of the temples in Falias, though not nearly as tall or ornate. In everything around me, I saw the influence of our society—the symbols, the art, the carvings on the great wooden doors.

"This way," he held open one side of the door.

Our feet scraped softly against the stone floor. Thick wooden columns held up the timber roof, their surfaces carved to resemble idols. Ahead, at the main altar, a wooden idol stood in grand attendance over everything else. Its head touched the ceiling, its face lost in the shadows above. At its feet, a tiny spring bubbled up from the ground, the water contained by large blocks of stone.

A woman knelt there, her back to us as we approached. Her soft whispers drifted in the space, her voice melodious. Liath stopped behind her and then stood aside, waiting. I glanced behind me and saw that the others had stayed behind. It was only Balen, Liath, and me.

Thick, wavy hair, a combination of brown and red, hung past her waist. Her gown was white, a color reserved only for the most important occasions. As she rose, I saw it hung loose on her frame and pooled at her feet. She stared at us, and I stifled a gasp for her eyes were opaque, glazed white over blue. I held my breath, wondering if she did indeed *see* us.

She gathered her gown at the hips then stepped forward, toward me. Her skin was pale and unblemished, her lips full and pink, and her nose straight and strong. She drew up close to me, so close I smelled the herbal scent of her skin.

"The bridge between us," she mumbled, peering so closely her nose almost touched mine. "Aye, and you." She turned her head sharply to Balen and smiled. A beautiful smile, but unnerving. She appeared youthful, womanly, yet as old as time. "You carry inside you the deep magic of your ancestors."

She bowed her head. The white glaze over her eyes cleared to a dull blue and her smile became serene and genuine. "We are honored at your presence. I am Deirdre."

"You know much, priestess," Balen remarked.

"I only know what my goddess reveals."

"And who is your goddess?"

"I am Anu's chosen."

Her words didn't surprise me. The Ageless Ones existed beyond the lands of Innis Fail. They spoke only through prophets and those they chose. It was the same here in Éire.

"And you are Deira," she said. "Descendant of Anu and child of Conlainn Mac Roich."

My heart leapt. "You know of my father?"

"Everyone in Éire knows of your father. His story is myth, told to children and in the halls of kings. He was crowned king of Emain Macha on the eve of Lairgnennasadh, and then, by the next sunrise, he vanished. Generations passed, and suddenly he returns to lay claim to his land. But no one believed him. So much time had passed. They thought him mad. Conlainn the Mad, they called him."

I stepped back as though a great force had struck me hard in the stomach. I couldn't breathe. Balen's hand slid into mine and squeezed, but it didn't comfort me. Nothing could.

Father had never told me who he was, only that he came from Éire for the love of my mother. And look what it had brought him; loneliness and grief. He'd lost his crown, lost my mother... Lost me.

"He went mad?" I barely choked out. "Did anyone believe him, that he was who he claimed? Was it true?"

She shrugged. "There were many who believed, for he returned with a treasure unlike any other, but 'tis a dangerous thing to lay claim to a kingdom that already has a king."

He was gone. My father was gone.

Despair, the same grief and overwhelming desolation, I'd felt when my mother had passed, squeezed my chest tighter and tighter, constricting my heart.

Balen squeezed my hand again and this time a surge of his heat climbed up my arm and spread into my chest, warming my entire body, an easing some of the ache. He smiled down at me, a trace of pity in his amber eyes. "Don't lose yourself in the past, Deira. It has come and gone, and can do no good to you now."

How easy it was to say such things. I wanted to snap at him and tell him so, but I bit my tongue. Balen wasn't trying to make light of things; he was trying to help. Aye, my father's death happened ages ago, but to me it was brutally new and raw, not something that had simply 'come and gone'.

Deirdre ushered us toward the inner chamber of the temple. I released Balen's hand and followed numbly behind her, wondering how she could appear so chaste and demure one moment and provocative the next. It was a mix that grated on my already stricken nerves. Perhaps she should wear a cloak or an overcoat over her thin, white sheath of a gown. She'd been rather blunt telling me of my father, almost as though wanting to see how I'd react, wanting to see my shock.

By the time we entered the inner temple, my anger and grief had mixed into a bitter concoction. My father hadn't deserved to die like that, alone and mad. He hadn't deserved that at all.

We were led into a courtyard, a garden similar to the one I'd played in as a child, with stone-tiled floors, flowers, vines, and fountains, then into a room like the main temple but smaller. The open spaces between the large wooden columns framed a landscape beyond of green valleys, hills and forests.

The next chamber was large, with walls of dark, polished wood covered with carvings and heavy curtains to retain heat. There were low couches and pillows, fur rugs on the floor, and a wide stone hearth.

I saw it all through a hollow daze.

Deirdre left us with a few softly spoken words to Balen, none of which I paid attention to, though I envied the ease at which she interacted with Balen.

Deirdre exhibited the confidence of a Danaan. She fit better in that role than I did, and she was human through and through. She had the confidence of one blessed by the goddess; she had that intimate connection I'd never had with Anu.

Balen led me to a low couch. I dropped onto the cushion, numb in body and agitated in mind. He knelt in front of me, capturing my attention, drawing me in so I couldn't look away, so

I'd listen. But I was already closed off. As he went to speak, I cut him off. "Did you know? Did you already know about my father?" His face didn't change but I saw a flicker of guilt in his eyes. "You *knew*. How could you have known?" Though it didn't really matter how he'd come across the information; it mattered that he hadn't shared it with the one person who had a right to know.

I jumped up, unable to sit still, and stomped to one of the great columns that supported the roof, my hand braced against the wood. I stared at the garden, seeing my childhood flash before my eyes, seeing everything in the flowers, and the grass, and the leaves…

My heart raced and the blood rushed through me so quickly that it hummed in my ears. I swung around. Why hadn't he told me? Prepared me to soften the blow? "What else do you know? What else does everyone know that I don't?"

My fingernails dug into my palms.

He straightened then dragged his fingers through his hair as he considered my questions, looking as though he was caught in a predicament of sharing what he knew or continuing to keep me in the dark. The expression added fuel to the growing storm.

No one had told me anything. Not Balen. Not my mother. My father. Eburacon. They all must've known where he'd come from, his station in life, what had happened to him. Why did they keep it from me? Why hadn't Balen prepared me for this . . . grief?

The heat of my anger stung my cheeks and spread throughout my body. "They all knew. You," I pointed at him, "knew." I couldn't take in enough air. My nostrils flared. Hot tears

slid from my eyes. I thought of Father leaving me, of my life
serving my Danaan family. "Why?"

Balen grabbed my shoulders, his expression fierce, his
black brows reminding me of Drem's dark wings. "You are a royal
heir of our enemy, Deira. Those who stole everything from us."

"And that was a long time ago, Balen."

"Do you think it matters? Our land, our people are dying.
Had your mother or Eburacon shared that your father had been
king of Eire, you would have been used. Revenge for the loss of
the Lia Fail, an example to show mankind how cruel we can be.
They kept the truth to protect you. Eburacon only shared it with
me the night of the attack."

I jerked from his hold and marched to the open arches to
stare once again at the garden. Everything made sense now. Why
my grandmother had hated me so much. Why my grandfather
seemed torn between loving me and shunning me. Why Mother
had been so adamant that I grow up in the Woodlands, away from
everyone else, away from those who might discover the truth. And
why Mother kept my father a prisoner. But it still didn't answer the
question that haunted me. Why he left me. Why he left me there in
the very arms of the enemy.

I heard the rustle of Balen's movement behind me. I
stiffened. He didn't touch me.

"Were you going to tell me?" My question sounded cold
and hard. I felt betrayed by him; the one I'd allowed into my heart,
the one I'd trusted.

"It wasn't for me to tell," he said, so close so that my hair moved with his breath.

"It was for a *stranger* to tell then?" A heartless laugh escaped me. "Well, that makes perfect sense."

"Eburacon said you'd learn the truth when it was the right time to learn it. He said Anu would guide you in Eire."

"I need not her guidance! She has ignored me my whole life. I'm tired of being *guided*. Tired of my life being decided by others, sharing information only when they want, pushing me into a fate I never chose..."

I backed away from him. My fingernails dug harder into my palms, but the pain felt good. My anger felt good. "I'm tired of being a *thing* to others." Tears pricked my eyes. "No one will decide for me ever again."

My heart hammered fast. Goosebumps traveled up my arms and to the back of my neck.

Energy hovered around Balen; I saw it in the air, like pinpricks of glowing light, and I wanted it for my own. Within my mind, I lured it as one would when tempting a child or frightened animal. But this power, Balen's power, was steadfast and strong; it needed to be lured, like a lover. Aye, like seduction. My thoughts changed. I smiled.

It came, and danced before me, swirling, gathering, and then it flowed through my body.

Dark whispers surged into my mind. I recoiled, suddenly bereft of Balen's warm power and filled with a terrible black emptiness.

You've had the power all along. Take it.

Soft laughter came with Nox's voice.

It was but a whisper, nothing more. And then it was gone and the power I'd lured from Balen encircled me once more.

I took it. I pulled it in, gathering it, using it. The loose strands of my hair moved. My cloak billowed around my feet and legs. I burned all over.

My gaze collided with Balen's. He stood with his feet apart, a glint of fierce readiness shone in his eyes. Damn him for all he knew. For making me feel for him. Damn him for everything.

I tunneled all my focus at him, gathering the power until it bloated, threatening to spill out. I cocked an eyebrow at him and smirked. Because I had power. I was Danaan, too. I had something to prove. And I *had* to let it out.

The release of energy, of fire, flew from me like a great whoosh of air, sending me staggering back. It slammed into Balen sending him off his feet and into one of the carved wooden columns. It splintered from the impact, the echo carrying to every corner of the chamber.

I could barely catch my breath.

A strange sense of emptiness swept inside me where his power had been. And weakness, so much weakness. I squeezed my eyes shut and tried to shake away the dizziness.

Breathe in, breathe out, I told myself, struck by what I'd done. I'd taken his power from him and wielded it as my own. *Dear Dagda.*

I swiped away a few sweat-dampened strands of hair that stuck to my forehead and cheeks as Balen got to his feet.

We faced each other again. I couldn't read his expression, but I saw his chest rising and falling, the slight flaring of his nostrils. He swiped a hand over his mouth, set his jaw, and crossed the distance between us in long, angry strides.

Instinctively, I backed up.

"Don't ever do that again." His voice came out ragged, but still forceful. He didn't stop until my back pressed against the wall. "I did not betray you. I did what I was advised to do, what I thought best."

"You should have told me." I swallowed hard. "What else have you been *advised* to keep from me? What other lies and half truths?" I couldn't shake the feeling there was more; I'd seen it in his look earlier.

My question angered him, for his eyes shifted from amber to flame in a blink. His body leaned into mine. I had nowhere to run. "Nothing, Deira," he said, on a regretful exhale. "There is nothing else."

The hurt in his voice told me he lied, but it also told me it pained him—whatever this lie was.

One of his hands braced flat on the wall near my head and the other came up to cup my cheek. I couldn't think when he was this close, when his scent surrounded me, and his breath warmed my cheek.

"This..." He kissed me gently then drew back just enough to say, "Isn't a lie."

Hurt squeezed my chest. I closed my eyes against the tears that rose from his gentleness, my grief, his secrets...

"Please, don't weep, Deira."

He gave me small kisses, excruciatingly slow and gentle. Each one lingered a fraction longer than the one before. His mouth was incredibly soft against mine, like the finest silk. My lips became wet and swollen from my tears and his kisses.

A fire lit in the pit of my stomach. I gripped his waist as the sound of hurried footsteps and an oath filled the room.

Balen withdrew. I colored fiercely. Liath fell to his knees. "Forgive the intrusion. We heard a crash and..."

I could only imagine what they must have thought when the column splintered. A quick glance at Balen's dark scowl told me he wasn't at all pleased with the sudden interruption. In fact, he looked ready to light fire to the entire temple.

Despite my embarrassment, I straightened my cloak, nudged Balen away then approached Liath.

"There's nothing to forgive," I told the quaking man. "Please stand."

Hesitantly, he lifted his head, his eyes unsure. He rose, glancing nervously from Balen to me.

"I'm sorry about the column," I said.

Stunned, he blinked and opened his mouth but no words came out. He shut it then tried again. "You are gracious, Dia. It is I who am sorry. For the interruption. It won't happen again."

"No, really—"

"Oh, for Dagda's sake," Balen breathed.

I glanced over my shoulder to see him looking very annoyed and impatient. His hands were on his hips and his scowl remained. "Next time you hear a crash, or screams," he gave me a pointed look even though he spoke to Liath, "don't come running."

"Of course. Apologies." Liath gave another bow and fled the room.

"That wasn't very *godly* of you. The poor man was frightened."

"As he should be."

Weariness settled over Balen's features and he let out a gruff sigh. "Perhaps we should save this for another time."

The draining feeling, which came from using my power, had returned. I hadn't taken time to come to terms with what I had done. Of what I now knew I was capable of.

I had power. And this time, praise be, I hadn't killed anything in the process. Balen's power was strong, strong enough to withstand my assault. And by the looks of him, he didn't *appear* harmed in anyway.

The whirlwind of my anger, my power, and my feelings for Balen all merged into exhaustion. It wound its way into my muscles and bones and mind. My eyelids became heavy, and I wanted nothing more than to sleep for a very long time. I gave in closing my eyes for a brief moment, but it must have been longer then I thought because Balen's arms slipped around me, lifting me off my feet. "Did I hurt you? Before?" I asked.

"Were you trying to?"

"No. Yes. Perhaps a little."

His chuckle rumbled through his chest as he carried me through the private temple to the bed chamber. My body sank into the mattress and the pillow cradled my head in softness.

Chapter 17

They lied to you, Deira. They always lie. How can you believe them now?

And Balen, he is the worst of all. Lying to you. Seducing you. Do you think he will want you, you whose power steals from his? Do you think he will want a child from you? A child with human blood?

He plays the champion. Ask him about his succession, Deira.

Ask of his honor on the battlefield.

Ask him...

I sat up slowly, Nox's words ringing in my mind and meandering through my body like a warm wind. Heavy sleep clung to me and made me more tired than I'd been before. Perhaps I'd slept too long . . . or not long enough.

A fire had been lit in the large hearth and night had fallen.

My muscles were stiff as I slid from the bed and padded barefoot across the stones to the woven rug in front of the fire to sit in the chair, wondering why Nox bothered with me at all.

Why tease and tempt me? Why distort my views?

He had to be incredibly powerful to project his thoughts into mine. It was unheard of. But then, most Danaans had no intimate knowledge of Nox of Annwn, his history, where he drew his power. Only that he had ruled the Deadlands and the Place of Souls longer than anyone could remember.

While I didn't believe Nox had my best interests in mind, his comments about Balen disturbed me.

I also knew that I had to be realistic with my emotions. Balen was the first male I'd kissed, the first to bring about intense feelings in me. I didn't want to be blinded by those feelings. I couldn't afford to be. Nox was laying the foundations of doubt, planting seeds that would grow and overtake the truth.

Balen *was* a champion. He didn't pretend. He was honorable, steady, and despite the fact he withheld the truth of my father along with the others, he'd done it for good and not out of maliciousness.

I stared at the flames for a long time, so lost in thought I didn't notice Deirdre until she cleared her throat to gain my attention.

She waited at the corner of the large rug, holding a tray laden with food. Her brow furrowed at my blank look. "Are you hungry?"

"Aye, I am. Thank you." I rose, and stepped forward to take the tray from her, but she moved to the side and set it on a table near the hearth. Unsure of what to do, I waited as she poured a cup of wine, removed the coverings on the plates and unwrapped the bread cloth.

"Would you like to join me?" I asked her.

She glanced over her shoulder, and I caught a brief flash of surprise before her face returned to the serene expression of before. After she finished arranging my supper, she turned and studied me. "You are different," she said frankly, her vivid blue eyes intent on my reaction.

"Aye, well, my father was not of Danaan blood, as you know."

She frowned and bit her lip. "No. 'Tis something else, I mean. There's a difference in you that isn't in Balen, or Anu, or those of this land."

"What kind of difference?"

She shrugged. Her blue eyes went cold and shrewd. I wasn't sure whether I liked this priestess of Anu or not. "I know not what it is," she muttered to herself more than to me as she pulled the wooden table between the two chairs. Her long hair fell to shield her face. "It is but a sense I have."

I motioned to the companion chair by the fire. "Please sit with me. I haven't had a female to talk to in quite a while."

There wasn't another cup or plate, so I took a drink of the wine then offered it to her as she sat down. She hesitated before taking the cup. My curiosity was stronger than my appetite, but I forced down a few bites of freshly baked bread and cheese.

"I know it was before your time," I said, "but would you have any other knowledge of my father? Did he live long?" The question pained me. "Did he find someone, a companion?" I held on to the hope that he hadn't died alone.

Deirdre chewed her food thoughtfully then drank deeply from the cup. "Conlainn had been gone for so long he couldn't find his place here among his own people. He knew no one for they'd all passed on. Out of time and out of place, he was. I have heard tell that he walked into the forest and never returned. That's all I know."

To hear of my father's isolation tore my heart in half. How he'd longed to return to his homeland; he'd left me, his desire so great. Yet when he'd risked his very life to leave Innis Fail, all he'd found on the other side was the same thing he'd left. He had no one. He was an outcast. I could only imagine what that did to him.

I buried my face in my hands and wept. I wept like I had when Mother passed to the Place of Souls. If only I could've been there. To have comforted him. To have held his hand and tempered the panic of death. I cried until there were no more tears left in me.

By the time I was done, my face was swollen and hot, and my head throbbed. Deirdre finished off the last bite of the entire meal she'd set out. She watched me, and I wondered if she'd ever taken her eyes off of me as I grieved. Not once had she offered sympathy, by words or touch.

Deirdre's coldness made it easier to check my emotions. I straightened in the chair and wiped my face with the sleeve of my tunic. "Do you know the place? The woods where he went?"

She lifted the tall wine jug, refilled the cup, and offered it to me. "I know, but it's a forbidden, dark place. No good comes from that forest. Why do you ask?"

After draining the cup, I set it on the tray and poured another. "Because it's where he died, is it not?"

"Aye, so they say. You wish to pay tribute."

"I do." I drank deeply, hoping the wine would dull my pain. "You'll tell me how to reach the place you speak of?"

Deirdre nodded. "Tomorrow, at nightfall, we begin the festival of fire to ensure a plentiful harvest season." She leaned forward. Cunning flashed in her eyes. "You and Balen attend the rites and I'll tell you where your father lies."

The wine slowed my response, but it didn't stop the flames that leapt to my cheeks. Deirdre stood and tossed her thick hair behind her shoulder. "It's a gift to be chosen. I've been chosen many times. Your joining will bless us with great fertility and good fortune."

I didn't want to *bless* her with anything. Especially with Balen. Not in that way. "I can't be with Balen."

I got up. I knew what the festival rites entailed, a chosen couple joining together, their coupling a symbol of fertility and the hopes of a blessed harvest. We held similar festivals in Innis Fail, but I rarely took part.

Her brow rose. "You have never lain with him. Or any male."

Her smug tone set me on fire. "And you have lain with many, I take it."

She grinned fully. "Only with the goddess's consent." She leaned back against the column by the bed, striking a wanton pose—to embarrass me. "Do you know I'm the most beautiful woman in Éire? Sought after by kings and champions alike. The goddess chose me for my beauty."

And not much else, I wanted to say. Aye, the goddess had chosen Deirdre—for her looks and her empty head. Empty head, meant empty vessel in which to fill. It wasn't fair of me, but Deirdre didn't inspire kindness.

She laughed, pushed off the column. "I could teach you."

I stepped back, horrified.

"You are naïve, daughter of Anu. I mean, I could teach you, tell you what to do and what to expect."

"I know what to expect."

"Do you really?"

"Aye, I do. And I won't join with Balen on anyone's terms but my own."

"Ah, so you would have him then."

Never before had a woman stirred such wrath in me. "Deirdre," I said, coldly. "Do you have a point, a purpose in all this?"

She walked around me to sit on the edge of the bed, crossing one leg over the other and leaning inward on one hip. The fire caught the red tones in her hair. Her gown stretched across her breasts. She knew exactly the image she posed.

I was wise enough to know I'd never understand Deirdre's motivations. I wasn't versed in female warfare. The double meanings, the wiles, the envy…

She thought on my question. "The world is a harsh place for a woman, Dia. It's a harsher place when one is lost and cannot find their way." She patted the mattress. "I'm not your enemy. I do what I feel the goddess wants of me."

"And she wants you to antagonize me?"

Deirdre laughed. Not contrived or devious. It was a genuine laugh. I surprised myself with my words and felt the bubble of laughter rise in me, too.

"Please come. Sit."

She patted the bed again and this time, I joined her, pulling one knee in and facing her. "I don't understand you."

"Good." She moved to sit cross legged, her hands folded in her lap. "You must always be on guard. Always question the intentions and sincerity of others."

Her words sent a shiver up my back. "Why are you telling me this?"

"To protect you. You must put your trust and your faith in yourself, Deira." She looked at the ceiling then sighed. "At least that's what I feel."

Immediately, I thought of Nox's words, the doubts he had planted about Balen. And now Deirdre warned me to trust only myself. It left me confused and feeling very much alone.

She took my hands. "You're not alone. You have the ear of Anu, and there are those who are genuine, who hope you succeed in saving your land."

"You know what I seek?"

"You are the Light Bearer. Aye, I know." She smiled. "I, too, have Anu's ear."

"And you have her blessing as well." Anu might hear me, but she'd never warmed me with her blessing as Dagda had done that night in Falias, never spoke to me, never cared for me. The goddess was in my blood, yet she'd rejected me.

"And Balen. Can I trust him?" I asked.

"With your life, this much I know."

"Deirdre, Innis Fail is dying. If the Lia Fail still exists, even a piece of it, it might help save us from the cold."

"Aye, Balen informed me and Liath while you slept," she said, sadness thick in her voice. "We told him all we knew. After the war between Éire and Innis Fail, all the pieces of the Lia Fail, save one, were brought back to Éire where they resided in the Hall of Warriors. The power within the pieces was great, but the fathá didn't possess the knowledge to mend the Lia Fail or to harness the power, so they pulled their magic and set the pieces into a sacred pillar stone within the forests of Cathair Crofin."

Hope rose. "The pillar stone, does it still exist?"

"This was ages past, Deira, so no one can say for certain. But . . . I will concede and tell you what I know. Many have tried to find the light and failed. Terrible deeds have happened in the woods of Cathair Crofin. Dark things exist there. 'Tis a burial place of lost souls, of the champions who have sought the prize and failed. No one goes beyond the tree line. And if they do, they don't return. Your father was one of them."

Goosebumps spread over my arms. I ran my hand over fur blanket. Thinking of Father brought another round of hurt. I pushed it aside, not wanting to feel that way again, not so soon.

"You know," she said at length, "the fertility rites can be performed here. They don't have to happen outside in the circle... You and Balen are descended from gods, and thus gods yourselves. That you are here now, with us, that you'll attend the festival is the highest of honors."

"Your offerings must be made. Your season must be blessed."

Deirdre winked at me. "'Tis either a virgin or a priestess. One of us must perform the fertility rite. Do you think Balen would be interested?"

I paled and then saw the merriment in her eyes.

"Like I said, you're far too naïve, Deira."

"I think the wine has gone to my head."

Deirdre got off the bed and put her hand on my shoulder. "Rest. I'll find a suitable male for the rite, and perhaps this year we'll have *two* blessings." She left the room laughing.

* * *

I woke the next sunrise to the aroma of fresh bread, meats, and fruits. Daylight bathed the chamber, its rays peeking through the curtains to warm the bed. Blessed warmth. Warmth I hadn't felt in so long. I threw back the fur blanket and soaked in the heat, letting it seep into my skin. After a long, luxurious moment, I rose to see a temple servant arranging the morning meal on the same table where Deirdre and I had eaten last night.

I lay down again, smiling. I hadn't seen much of Éire, but already I loved it; loved the rolling hills, the green meadows, and thick forests. My father had spoken of white cliffs and a fierce ocean. I longed to see all of those things.

How much my life had changed. Here I lay in luxury. A servant brought me food. There was no one to tell me when to get up, no royals to wait upon, no dishes to wash, no onions to chop. Just a world to save...

Once the servant left, I tossed my hair over my shoulders and slid out of the bed in the white sleeping gown, which had been set out for me last night. I braced for the impact of the cold stones on my bare feet, but there was no cold. I sighed aloud. The daylight had warmed the stones. How lovely.

Quickly, I completed my morning rituals and cleansings, intending to dress but easily distracted once more by Éire's wondrous light.

I stepped into one of the golden rays, lifting my face to the light, soaking it in with a grin on my face.

"Remind me to visit more often in the mornings."

Balen leaned against one side of the archway, arms folded across his chest, an amused grin on his face and laughter in his eyes. Daylight played over his form.

He was a beautiful warrior. My heart expanded seeing him standing there. The only thing lying between us were bright specs of dust hovering in the air. They floated in slow motion, and I felt frozen in time, frozen with a smile on my face and anticipation in my heart.

He pushed away from the archway, his smile becoming determined. All I could hear was the hard, eager pounding of my pulse. I forgot about the morning meal, the daylight, and the warm stones at my feet.

His form cut through the rays of light, a dark, powerful shadow intent on his destination. Without hesitation, he wrapped his arms around my waist and walked me backward until my legs hit the bed.

There, he paused, his gaze holding mine. And I knew. We both knew. Both accepted what was to come. There was no need to talk, no need to reassure. The time had come.

I rose onto the tips of my toes and pressed my lips to his. No more thoughts. Just feeling.

He kissed me back, rough palms sliding down over my hips, to my thighs where his fingers gathered the fabric of the gown and inched it up. The material skimmed against my skin like a whisper. I lifted my arms until the gown was over my head and gone.

The air on my bare skin gave me a moment of pause. But this quickly evaporated as Balen pressed me back onto the bed and settled his hips between my thighs. The weight of him was a surprising thrill.

Fire swirled in his eyes, another thing that gave me pause.

"I would never hurt you," he assured me, placing small kisses on my forehead, my eyelids, my temples. "It won't burn." He smiled against my skin. "Too much."

And he was right.

His heat seeped into me like a hot desert wind and I gave myself over, trusting him, accepting him, and leaving behind all the fears and worries. In that moment our duty to Innis Fail no longer mattered.

There was only him. Only me.

And when it was over, when my entire being had burst apart and come back together again, the sense of peace and contentment I felt was astounding.

Balen pushed onto his elbow. I stared at the intricate markings on his skin, the way they curled over his arm, his shoulder, the side of his neck. My hand ran down his hip and I knew it was there too, the marking...

A grin played upon his face. He brushed back my hair and placed a kiss on my forehead. His hair was damp, and his eyes had returned to their vibrant amber color.

"Did I hurt you?" he asked, trying to appear solemn.

I shook my head, unable to speak, for I was suddenly gripped with the desire to hold onto him forever. I wrapped my arms around his neck and drew him back down to me, holding him tight. My chest constricted and tears I refused to let fall stung my eyes.

He gathered me up, rolled over and took me with him until my head rested against his shoulder and the front of my body was pressed against his side. His hand idly stroked my hair.

Balen was going to die.

It was all I could think; those words over and over. Despair snuffed out the bliss of moments earlier.

"Deira," he said, resting his chin against the top of my head, "are you well?"

I couldn't let him see me like this. Not now. I raised my head and smiled. Once I'd thought his face brutal, hard, and dark, but now I only saw perfection. Even the tiny age lines around his eyes and mouth were beautiful to me. I traced them with my finger. "I'm all right. More than that. I'm blessed."

He lifted an eyebrow and a lop-sided grin appeared. "Blessed, eh?"

I laughed. "Aye, I am. By a god apparently."

He gave me with a quick kiss on the lips. "I am as well."

I let my head fall onto his shoulder just as my stomach rumbled.

"Breakfast?"

We sat up, eyeing the meal on the table. "Thank Dagda. I'm starving." I hurried from the bed, found my gown and yanked it over my head as Balen tugged on his leggings. We met at the table. I couldn't stop staring at him. Shirtless, his hair ruffled, the satisfied expression he wore... He scratched his jaw and caught me ogling him. He leaned across the table and kissed me, then filled my plate with food.

Chapter 18

The festival of fire marked the beginning of the harvest season. It was a time of celebration, of blessing, of ensuring the fertility of the land, the animals, and of man. The gods would be honored and, above all, Anu's tribute would be paid in the joining of man and woman.

I stood on the mossy bank of the sacred spring deep in the forest. The light had disappeared beneath the horizon, and the full moon rose in a darkening sky of purple and orange. Giant and full, it seemed too heavy for its journey tonight. The water at my feet reflected the sky above. With nightfall, the air cooled and became saturated with the scents of moss, woods, and water.

This was Anu's sacred water, a quiet spring and pool in a small grove of ancient oaks. A crude statue of the goddess had been placed at the fount of the spring. Flowers, garlands, and jewelry adorned her. Offerings lay at her feet.

I breathed in deeply and tipped my face to the moon,

feeling the power of the soil at my feet, the water, the woods; all that represented the goddess. A breeze blew through the thin white gown and caressed my skin. My hair flowed freely down my back.

There were no men here. Only I, Deirdre, and the priestesses of Anu gathered in a circle around the spring.

They sang to her, their eyes locked on the moon, their arms lifted as if embracing the power above them, a beautiful song; the words of which I didn't know. Deirdre had explained the proper tribute while my body had been bathed earlier in the day.

My bare feet pressed into the soft cushion of moss. Water seeped up and wet my feet. I released the ties to the gown. It fell over my shoulders then hips to pool on the forest floor. The cool air on my naked skin sent shivers up my arms.

Such an honor would never have been bestowed upon me in Innis Fail. I should be proud and grateful to be given this task. And I was. But I was terrified as well. I had searched my whole life for a relationship with the gods of my world, to have the kind of faith others had. Magic and religion happened all around me, yet never *to* me no matter how badly I'd begged and prayed to Anu.

Would she hear me? Would she acknowledge me as her daughter or turn her back on me once again.

As I glanced at the outstretched arms of Anu's believers, their trance-like songs of praise filling the air with importance. They were like me. Powerless. Human. Connected to the land beneath their feet and the sky above. And I was just another living thing amid a forest of living things. I belonged here; a part of life, a part of all the elements that sustained me.

I squared my shoulders and closed my eyes, breathing in deeply before stepping over the discarded gown into the spring. Cool water closed around my ankles as my feet sank in the sandy bottom. I moved forward until the water rose to the juncture of my thighs.

The singing continued, but it seemed as though it came from a distance. I cupped the water in my hands then lifted it skyward.

"Mother Anu, we stand under your moon, on your ground, in your sacred water." Water streamed through my fingers, down my arms, over my breasts and down to my stomach and thighs. "We, your children, sing your praise. Queen of Life, and Beauty, and Fertility. You give life to all things. You are all things."

While I spoke aloud, the words sounded distant, like an echo in my mind.

"Bless us with abundance. Oh, loving Mother, we invoke your life essence into our bodies."

My vision wavered. The sky bent in a wide arc of streaming stars. The moon hovered above me, so close I thought surely I could reach out and touch it. "Spread your abundant gifts over the land, and we shall honor you for all of our days, as we honor you now."

The sky moved in a slow circle, light and dark going faster and faster. My knees buckled. Time slowed as I sank into the water and into darkness.

My hair floated around me, waving in the gentle motion of the water, brushing against my skin like seaweed. The temple bed chamber flashed before my eyes. Balen and I lay there on the bed. My heart beat quickened.

Life, Deira, a wise female voice whispered in my mind, and I saw water and felt peace. *Life and Light are one.*

Another flash of my time spent with Balen.

Worlds die and new ones are built upon the remains. Life, death, rebirth. It is the cycle of everything. No one can stop it; though they might stay the inevitable for a time... If you fight it, it will destroy you.

Darkness. Looking up at gray, storm-filled skies. Rain streamed down, and with it the raven, its caw echoing like a terrible omen in my mind as it fell from the sky.

A sorrow so great gripped my heart. I curled into a ball.

The gift of life is yours. Blessings upon the land and children of Éire.

My lungs strained. Sharp pains shot through my chest. I twisted in the water, fighting. Panic. Fear. The water was too heavy to swim through. I flailed, getting nowhere, struggling.

Arms pulled me up. I gulped in breath after precious breath, sputtering and coughing as I did so.

Deirdre helped me to shore and knelt, pushing the wet strands of hair from my face. All around me were the bare feet of the priestesses. I raised my head. "The goddess has given her blessing."

She'd also given me a powerful omen, but that had been for me and me alone.

A cheer went up and beyond the woods on the hill of Tlachtga another cheer carried on the wind. Over the tree tops, sparks shot into the night sky.

The fires had been lit.

Deirdre helped me to stand and then pulled my gown over my head as the priestesses waded into the sacred spring to leave offerings of flowers, food, and tokens by the altar.

"Here, this will warm you," she said, drawing a thick fur blanket around my shoulders.

She didn't speak as we made the long trek back to the temple. Instead, she held me tight, her arm around my waist as we walked. I leaned into her, seeking comfort and warmth, welcoming the silence of the forest.

By the time we emerged from the black forest, the tremors had increased, my teeth clattering together. Everywhere, I saw villagers in their finest clothing. Flowers adorned the long, free flowing hair of all women of child bearing age. Men wore their finest. Most of the hearth fires in the village and temple had already been extinguished, and they'd be lit anew from the sacred fire atop the hill. The goats, cattle, and sheep had been brought in from the fields. Tonight they'd be driven between the fires to be blessed for another fruitful year.

Musician played drums, lutes, and harps, the lively melody mingling with talk and mirth. A great feast had been prepared, and my stomach grumbled at the aroma.

Children weaved their way through our procession, making me laugh at their antics and sweet, carefree laughter. Soon, they'd go to bed and leave the night to us.

"This way." Deirdre entered the main temple then led me back to the inner chambers where thankfully a fire still burned hot in the hearth.

Shaking, I stopped on the rug as she removed the fur, walked me closer to the fire, and the bathed the mud from my body with a soft towel and fresh water that had been waiting when we arrived.

"Is it like that for you as well?" I finally asked her when my teeth stopped clattering together.

"Sometimes." She placed each of my hands into a smaller basin and washed them. "I've never been pulled under," she said quietly, her hair shielding her face from view.

"Perhaps you're stronger than I and can stand on your own two feet when the goddess speaks."

She tilted her head to smile at me. "Perhaps. Or your vision was so strong it stole your strength to stand."

I sensed she wanted to ask what Anu had revealed, but I couldn't speak of it. It was too raw, and I didn't want to dwell upon what I'd seen and felt. Aye, I'd heard the voice of my goddess, the one whose blood ran through my veins, but her words were a warning as much as they were a blessing.

Deirdre finished washing my limbs and feet. "Come sit on the floor by the fire while I brush your hair. It will dry quicker that way."

She dropped onto the chair and tossed her thick hair behind her shoulders as I sat on the floor in front of her. Mother used to brush my hair. So had Lidi. I closed my eyes as Deirdre lifted my wet hair into her lap and began to separate the tangles, thinking of how far I'd come since the days of Lidi tugging and pinning my hair.

* * *

Deirdre and I proceeded up the hill, my clean white gown swishing around my ankles. A small chain of delicate white flowers had been placed upon my head. The light fragrance hovered around me like a gossamer veil. I was bare under the loose-fitting fabric, as were all the women who would give themselves tonight. My hair was dry now and it fell in unbound waves to the small of my back.

Here, I didn't have to hide. I lifted my chin a notch, feeling lightness in my soul, as I gathered the gown in my hands, climbing higher and higher.

So many smells and sounds, so much energy, greeted us at the top of the hill. The massive stones stood sentinel over the hill, watching in stoic silence. Several bonfires roared. Sparks shot into the air, popping or floating high into the night. Everywhere people danced, and ate, and sang.

We stepped onto a raised platform where Liath and Balen watched men and women link hands and skip in wide circles around the fires.

As I approached, Balen rose from his chair and pulled out the empty one next to him. His face was clean shaven, making the tattoo on his neck and jaw starker. His hair was wet and looked as though he'd recently swiped a few fingers through it.

But what struck me the most was the sense of lightness surrounding him; the darkness usually there had gone. A slow grin built on his face, creating a devastatingly handsome picture.

Heat and trepidation rushed through me as I met his amused eyes. He held out his hand. I slipped my in. And everything was better.

He tugged me forward until I bumped against him. "I've missed you," he whispered, his lips brushing my ear, his breath warm on my skin. Erotic shivers danced along my nerves. His scent filled me with fresh memories of our morning together. My chest went tight with emotion. Then the vision of the raven falling from the sky suddenly flashed in my mind.

"Deira," he said, feeling my sudden stiffness. "You have regrets."

"No, no," I assured him, trying to shake off the memory of Anu's omen. "No regrets."

His jaw clenched and his expression went somber. "There's much you don't know about me. Things you need to understand…" He squeezed my hand in reassurance. "Tonight, we'll talk."

"All right," I replied with a curt nod. Inside, confusion grew. I had much to tell him. And apparently he had much to tell me. The secrets between us were far from being over.

I shifted uneasily in my chair, half watching the festivities, my thoughts on Balen and I. I'd never had much opportunity to cultivate a good understanding of the opposite sex. I'd had some interaction, but it had been pounded into me from an early age that no Danaan would ever be interested in me or in passing along my human blood to his child. I'd come to accept that I'd never find a mate, never have a child of my own.

Until Balen began changing my views and giving me hope.

I drained my cup of wine then poured another. Before long the wine flowed like the river beyond the hill. Everyone was deep into their cups, the dancers, the priests and priestesses. Even Balen was drinking freely. He spoke and laughed with Liath, joined in with the songs and clapped as the herds were run between the flames.

He won't die if you leave him.

I froze, my cup halfway to my lips.

Do you hear? He won't die if you break from him now.

The resonating voice shook me to the bone. A tremor of fear crept up my spine, making the tiny hairs on the back of my neck stand straight. The music and talk fell to the background. The scenes around the great fire slowed.

I, too, know what it's like, Deira. We will never be good enough, pure enough, loved enough. They turned their backs on us, and they'll do it again.

I blinked hard several times, trying to clear my head of drink and regain control. Still, the scene before me moved too slow. Swept away by the magic of the festival, women pulled their loose gowns over their heads and danced naked in the arms of men, there before the fires, for all to witness.

The flames writhed and danced as if in a trance. Echoes of laughter, music, and moans flowed through me. Flowers trickled to the ground like snowflakes, fallen from the hair of women as they danced.

I've held you in my heart for so long. Too long. I grow tired of waiting...

My heart pounded in time with the drums. Desire flooded my body. I tried to shake the feeling away but I couldn't rouse enough effort.

Through the flames you sit, so innocent, so ripe... You've always been mine, Deira. Mine to love. Mine to touch.

His words made my body burn.

Mine to do with what I will. And I will do so many things to you.

I couldn't breathe. All I saw were bodies dancing before the flames.

We belong together.

Movement from the corner of my vision. A figure walking beyond the fires, studying me between the flames.

I knew. I knew it was Nox.

Thick straight hair, the color of molten gold, fell behind his shoulders and framed a strong face of immense beauty. His eyes were light, a pale color, and they held an expression of confidence, power, and seduction. He moved with his hands clasped behind his back and a half-grin tugging on the corners of full lips.

Balen's warm, rough palm slid over my thigh as I stared at the figure beyond the flames. Everywhere around me, couples lay together under the moon. I was rooted to the chair, unable to look away from Nox, as Balen moved my hair away from my neck then brushed his lips against my exposed skin.

Lust snaked through me. My head fell back a notch to allow him more access. His tongue flicked out and licked my skin.

I heard a moan and realized it was my own.

Nox smiled smugly through flames. My heart pounded harder and faster than the drums echoing through the night.

Chapter 19

I woke the next morning to the feel of the warm sun on my face and soreness in my back and thighs. The aftereffects of too much wine pounded through my head. I rolled over, away from the direct sunlight to find Balen sleeping soundly next to me. I didn't remember him getting into the bed with me. In fact, I remembered nothing after—

I sat up straight, clutching the blanket to my chest as the images came one after another. Balen and I . . . Nox watching. Heat seared my face. I slid off the bed, taking the blanket with me, and went to the garden.

The morning air was cool, but the sun had already begun warming the stone tiles under my bare feet. For a long time, I stared at the scene, the flowers opening themselves up to the sky, and the small brown birds flitting back and forth from tree limbs to the fountain.

I bit my lip. How could I have bared myself to everyone? To him? I wanted to leave, to run from all the new and overwhelming emotions. I wanted it to stop. I didn't want to feel so much for Balen.

I didn't want to hurt in the end.

I went back inside and nudged Balen's shoulder. "Balen. Wake up." He rolled onto his back, flung his arms wide, baring his magnificent nude form to my view. He squinted at me then dragged his fingers through his hair before scrubbing a hand down his face. "What is it?"

His rough voice jolted me out of the distraction he posed lying there. "The Lia Fail. Our search has not even begun."

"Drem searches for it." His eyes closed.

I drew back in surprise. He hadn't told me that. Why hadn't he said anything? The notion gave way to a small hurt. I gripped the blanket tighter around me unsure of how to feel about his admission. He didn't have to tell me everything. But we were in this quest together... I nudged his thigh. "Still, we should focus . . . not get lost in—" I made a sweeping gesture—"all this."

One eye popped open. "All this what?"

He stretched his big body, and I tried valiantly to avoid ogling him. "This . . . place. Getting too comfortable. I don't know..." I added lamely.

Confused lines appeared on his forehead. He pushed up onto his elbows. "We did agree to stay for the festival."

"Aye and the festival is over."

He fell back onto the bed and closed his eyes again. "You want to leave now? This morning?"

I busied myself with locating the clothes I had arrived in, biting back a smile at Balen's reluctance. I found my clothes cleaned and placed in the chest at the end of the bed. Under the canopy of the blanket, I donned my leggings, and then tossed the blanket over Balen to jerk my tunic over my head.

As I sat on the bed to pull on my shoes, Balen rose, placing a hand on my back. "There's no shame in what we did last night. Running away from here won't change anything."

How could I explain the turmoil I felt? That loving him and knowing what his fate might be, that there was nothing I could do to deter him from it…

With a heavy sigh, he got up and padded into the bathing chamber.

I braided my hair then went to the table by the hearth where breakfast awaited us. My appetite was tremendous. I ate a full plate of fish, bread, fruits, and cheese, washing it all down with cold water.

Balen joined me at the table, filling his plate silently, his expression somber.

"You've really been in contact with Drem?" I asked.

"Aye." He didn't touch his food. "Deira, the festival is something that's done every year here in this world, as in our own. But I should have realized, due to your upbringing you might not have taken part before, might not have witnessed what happens… In the light of day, things can tend to look coarser. But," his gaze stayed steady on me, "it was not coarse to me. I wanted you, needed you in a way I have never needed anyone."

A lump formed in my throat and my cheeks went warm. I tucked those words away, committing them to memory while it occurred to me that Balen was just as vulnerable to me as I was to him. The realization was humbling and empowering. I captured his face in both hands and kissed him. "I felt the same," I said.

We stared wordlessly at each other for a suspended moment before he broke contact and picked up his plate. "Drem has found a source of light in the forests of Cathair Crofin. It could be the Lia Fail..."

"Cathair Crofin?" A shiver went up my back. "Deirdre says the forest is home to lost souls. That those who enter rarely return." It was the same place my father had died.

"Aye, she told me as well. But we should remember mankind is not accustomed to such magic and darkness. Their legends and tales are things that might frighten them but not necessarily frighten us."

"Is the forest mentioned in the foretelling?"

He paused in his chewing, then resumed, not looking at me. "There is mention of a dark place, but that's all."

The flapping of wings and the scattering of other birds in the garden interrupted our conversation. I hurried to the gallery arch to see Drem settle onto the fountain then use its beak to pick at a spot under its large black wing.

The creature had spoken to me in Innis Fail, had breathed its fiery breath into the night sky, and now it was trapped in the form of a raven. That creature held part of Balen's soul. They were tied together by some ancient bond set by Sydhr himself, a bond that I could not begin to fathom. No matter how many times I saw Drem, wariness and misgivings followed.

Anu's omen came to mind and its vivid details added to my misgivings.

Drem continued to clean itself in the fountain. I leaned against the archway and watched it for a while, thinking of Cathair Crofin, my father, the Lia Fail, and how I would cope if something did happen to Balen.

The thought stirred all kinds of emotions in me. I cared deeply, much, much more than I wanted to admit. I had to protect myself in the event the foretelling was true, and in the event it was not. If we returned home, together, with the Lia Fail, Balen would return to his life, his kingdom, his family, those he cared for. And I wasn't sure I'd be counted among them.

And I couldn't help but wonder if I wasn't the Light Bearer, would he still want me?

His footsteps made me turn. Balen approached, wearing his black armor, buckling his sword to his waist as he headed into the garden. He said nothing to me, just passed by with a grim expression. Drem flew with four great flaps of its wings to land on Balen's outstretched forearm.

Balen glanced over his shoulder and gestured toward the exit. It was time to go. I cursed myself for reminding him of our quest. If the foretelling was true, we were one step closer to a horror I didn't want to face.

* * *

We left without a word to anyone, not even Deirdre or Liath. The rising sun warmed our path as we left the temple complex. Drem took flight, disappearing beyond the treetops.

"Shouldn't we have asked for horses?" I quickened my step to keep up with Balen's long stride.

"Horses will not go into Cathair Crofin."

"Couldn't you charm the animals?"

"Aye, I could. But my power will be better spent elsewhere."

I wondered if the power I had would serve me again when I needed it, for I had no doubts we'd confront Nox on our journey to Cathair Crofin. I had to gain control of my ability or else I had no weapon or protection should Balen fall.

"Balen?" I asked. "What do you know about Nox of Annwn? Have you seen him before?"

"Aye."

I waited for more, but he held on to his secrets. "Did you know him, when he was allied with the other houses? Did you meet him? Why do you think Nox is here in Éire?" I continued, stumbling over a clump of grass.

He stopped suddenly and I nearly plowed into him. "Nox is in Éire because he wants out of the Deadlands. And knowing him, he wants to rule both worlds. We have a long trek ahead, Deira." He moved by me. "Best to save our breath."

I lingered there, my jaw hanging open. His unwillingness to talk, to share his past and the things he knew about Nox, the quest, and even me started a slow-building anger. What was he hiding? And the fact that he didn't trust me, after the things we'd done together, stung.

"Balen!" I caught up quickly and blocked his path. "I think I deserve more than that. I'm a part of this. We're doing this together, yet you pull away, evade my questions, and know things I should probably know too."

He stood there like a pillar of dark stone, a scowl on his face. His expression told me he'd rather face another assault by the Fallen rather than share.

I laughed, my voice tired and hopeless when I spoke. "What in Dagda's name are we doing? I'm not your *Light Bearer*. We're heading into a battle that neither one of us can win, all on the chance that the Lia Fail exists, we can retrieve it, and carry it back to light Innis Fail."

I placed my hands on my hips and looked around at the vast, rolling landscape of Éire. "We're walking into Cathair Crofin alone with no legion behind us, all on a chance." I stared hard at him, his expression remaining unreadable and dark.

A muscle ticked in Balen's jaw. Unease fluttered in my stomach. There was something he wasn't telling me, something important. And suddenly I wasn't sure I wanted to know.

Guilt pricked my conscious. I'd withheld the truth from him as well. I hid Nox, his words, his appearance at the festival, the intimate way he entered my mind... I'd kept my secrets close to me. I'd asked Balen to be open and honest when I wasn't willing to do the same.

"Never mind," I muttered. "We have a long journey ahead." I took a few steps before Balen's hand on my arm stopped me.

"No, Deira, you're right. I've not been truthful or trusting. There are things; things which I meant to speak of earlier..." His black hair fell into his eyes as he looked at the ground. It had grown longer during our journey. A day old beard had begun to grow on his jaw.

"Nox and I have been enemies for a long time, even during the days of peace when his house was aligned with the rest of Innis Fail."

"Why did you become enemies?"

"Nox is one of two grandsons of Sydhr. He's very old, and chose not to retire to the Place of Souls with the other gods and their families. Just as the other children of the Ageless Ones were given dominion over Innis Fail—the beginning of the four houses—Nox was given dominion over the Place of Souls and the Deadlands. It was banishment, not a gift. For what, I don't know, but we both share the blood of Sydhr."

The male I'd seen through the flames had been painfully beautiful and incredibly powerful. He'd spoken in my mind not only here, but when I was in Innis Fail. That he could do so, from across the Void of two worlds, was a testament to his power and lineage.

"Sydhr gifted dominion over Bren Cara and the House of Sydhr to his favored grandson, my great, great, great grandfather, not to Nox."

I blinked. "So Nox is your great uncle, a few times removed."

"Aye. And he has hated my house from the beginning. We were also named wardens of the War Raven. Nox covets the creature, for it can traverse both worlds and the Place of Souls, and it's the only living being whose blood acts as a deadly poison to us. Its blood can also severely wound the Ageless Ones, which is why the War Ravens do not breed, and there are only a few left. Sydhr made it so that our souls bond with the War Raven, we *have* to protect it if we want to protect ourselves. If it bleeds, we bleed. If it dies, we die."

I just stood there, staring, those words like an icy slap. To have your life tied to another, to allow it to be free and not locked up safe, spoke volumes about Balen.

We continued across a meadow in silence. The wind whipped at our clothes and hair. The tips of the grass swayed beneath a blue sky heavy with white clouds.

"Balen?"

"Aye, Deira?"

"He's not tried to stop us. He wants us to come."

"I know."

I stopped and waited for him to halt his stride and face me. His brow rose. "It doesn't change things. The Lia Fail, or what's left of it, is in Cathair Crofin. Nox expects us, and we must face him."

"There's no plan. Just walk right into his territory and what? Let him kill us?"

And that idea was such at odds with the sight before me—
the sunlight glinting off Balen's black armor, his hand resting on
the hilt of the short sword at his waist, his cloak blowing behind
him, the pommel of his broad sword jutting up from behind his
shoulder. He looked calm and sure of what he was doing, and
utterly capable.

"The foretelling is the plan," he offered at length. "And
remember, all is not told. We might be successful. And we cannot
not try. The forest is over the next beinn."

I was terrified of what awaited us in the dark forest, of
what Nox and Balen would do to one another. Nox had wanted
this all along, to exact his revenge on Sydhr's favored bloodline.

I thought of the letter I'd written back at the Hall of
Records in Falias. He might never read it. There'd be no way now
for him to know how much I thought of him and how my feelings
had grown since. Unless I told him. The idea gnawed at me as we
journeyed to the top of the beinn.

The wind was fiercer there on the high hill, unprotected by
trees or landscape. My cloak flapped around me. In the distance the
dark line of woods that was Cathair Crofin spread out in the valley
below.

The sounds of the countryside had ceased. There was no
grass, no green near the woods. Like bleached bones, the limbs of
dead trees stuck out from the mists surrounded the forest.

The flap of Drem's wings broke the stillness. Balen lifted
his arm and the large raven landed there then folded its black
wings. He didn't caw, move, or blink, just stared at the forest as we

did.

An army of three.

A cold dread blew down my back as Balen's hand slide into mine and squeezed it. I glanced over to see him smiling down at me.

"Give me your other hand," he commanded.

Drem moved onto Balen's shoulder as I placed my other hand in his. Both studied me with quiet concentration. A surge of warmth came from Balen's hands and into mine, travelling up my arms and into my chest. "If I fall, go back to the fathá. They'll help you get home. Take my warmth and the power of Sydhr to strengthen and ward you against harm."

"All right," I said, taking a deep breath. I'd never been warded before. "What do I do?"

He grinned. "Nothing."

His smile brought out one of my own and, for that moment, it felt like there was only the two of us in all of Éire.

Surprising me, he leaned down and pressed his lips to mine. The most exquisite warmth and peace filled every space of my body. Energy and a sense of strength came with the warmth, setting me at ease and giving me courage.

When he withdrew, the protection ward remained in me and all around me. I stared at him in wonder.

"I take it no one has given you a protection ward before?"

"No." I licked my lips. They still tingled with his warmth. "Do you always ward people with a kiss?"

"You'd be the first, Deira," he answered, a smile hovering at the corners of his mouth. His attention returned to the forest. "Ready?"

"I was never ready for this," I said soberly.

Our fingers linked, we traveled down the beinn and crossed the valley toward the dreary forest of Cathair Crofin, my father's resting place.

A few steps into the forest and we were surrounded in darkness.

The pungent scent of wet earth, dead wood, and rotting carcass hung thick in the air. The ground was soft, a mattress of pine needles and decaying leaves. Twigs snapped and leaves rustled as though small animals scurried away at our passing.

Balen called forth flame onto a broken limb he'd plucked from the forest floor.

I followed closely behind him and Drem who remained on Balen's shoulder.

"How do we know which direction to go?" I whispered.

He held the torch high. "We go the way we are led." And then he commanded the torch brighter and waved it in a wide circle.

On both sides of us appeared the massive battle hounds of Annwn, their white fur stark in the darkness. Their eyes glowed red in the bright light. They stood still, three on both sides, though I sensed more.

I swallowed down my fear and found my voice. "What should we do?"

"They're here to direct us. They won't harm us until given the word."

I didn't need to ask where. We were going straight to Nox.

"It's the only way to get close to the light Drem saw," Balen said over his shoulder. "When Deirdre told me of the forest . . . I knew Nox was here. Death surrounds him. He cannot escape it even if he wanted to. It makes him easy to find." Balen slowed, waiting until I was beside him and he could hold the light to see my face. "It'll be up to you to regain the Lia Fail, Deira. He won't harm you."

I gave him an incredulous look. "Of course he will. He'll do anything to prevent the light from returning to Innis Fail."

"No. He needs you. He won't harm you."

I grabbed his arm. "Wait. What do you mean, *he needs me?*"

"You're the daughter of Ariannon, a princess of the House of Anu, and of Conlainn, once king of Emain Macha."

"And?"

Balen held the torch higher. "In you, Nox sees the royal blood of both worlds. Think, if he intends to overthrow us and rule both lands, who would further strengthen his rule? Who could provide an heir with a royal claim to both lands? No one, but you."

I drew back in surprise. "But he could take any daughter of a king of Éire. And the people of Innis Fail don't accept me now; they would never accept me."

"Taking a purely human queen would be far worse to our people. At least in you, he has the blood of the noble House of Anu. His heir would be noble on both sides." His words died for a short moment, before he said, "Nox wants you here, and there must be a reason. It's the only thing that makes sense."

And it was something Balen had known or suspected all along.

"You knew my father was a king. You knew my lineage and why Nox might want me here." My voice was strained as I struggled to make sense of it. A deep well of disappointment grew inside me. "You've led me straight to him. How will I be free of him when you die like you believe you will?"

"You are the Light Bearer, Deira. For the sake of Innis Fail, I had no other choice."

"Aye, you did. You chose a foretelling that has no final outcome! You followed a path someone else set out for you when you could've chosen your own path. How am I to retrieve the Light and escape him? How? When this is what he's wanted all along? When you fall, I am lost. The Light is lost. And I am condemned to a life of bearing children in the land of the dead."

"Deira. No…"

"Aye, Balen." I shook with rage, with a hurt so sharp it felt like a knife in my belly. "All this would've been nice to know beforehand. When I asked you if there was anything else I needed to know at the temple, remember what you said? *Nothing, Deira. There is nothing else.* You never allowed me to make the choice, to know what I was up against, and then decide for myself. You have kept me in the dark and directed my life just like everyone else."

Had Balen been honest with me, had he told me the true threat Nox posed to me, had he given me a choice, I still would have come to Cathair Crofin. I might have been slow in accepting the mantle of savior, but I would have chosen right. I would have helped him because I cared. About him. About the Light. But I was just a tool, a means to an end, a thing to bear the light home.

I fisted the folds of my cloak and lifted to keep it free from my ankles as I spun away from him only to draw up short. The battle hounds blocked my retreat, standing in a line, hair raised on the backs of their necks, lips pulled back to show their fangs.

"Step back, slowly."

I let out a frustrated groan, wanting to rail at them, fight them, make a stand.

"Deira."

With clenched teeth and fists, I moved back. Without a word or a look, I swept past Balen and continued down the small trail. As the hounds fell in around us, I realized that the only person I could truly rely on was me. The only person I could trust was me. The only one who had my best interests at heart was me.

I felt like a child again, the same child who'd stand atop the tower in Murias and stare out over the lake wishing for a mother and a father, wishing for someone to love me, to not leave me, or abandon me, or betray me.

Saving Innis Fail from darkness, the same darkness that enveloped this forest, was a noble quest. Balen was king, champion, and protector. The safety of his people came first. He loved Innis Fail. His was a true, abiding, desperate love, and while he was wrong for withholding the truth from me, he wasn't wrong about loving his people and land. He'd sacrifice us both for the tiniest chance at saving our world.

I reasoned it until my mind hurt. I understood Balen's motivation and even why he kept things from me—he didn't want me to run, to turn back. But it didn't make it right. I'd just wanted a *choice*. I'd let Balen into my heart and body. And after everything we'd been through, the intimacy we shared, the fact that I'd stayed on the quest thus far… I deserved better; I deserved his trust.

I was hurt, and that hurt was already turning into the hardest mettle. I'd use that; I'd do everything I could to find the Light and if Balen was right, if Nox of Annwn thought he could use me and manipulate me, he was in for a very big surprise.

Chapter 20

The forest was cold, the trek long and exhausting. Balen and I had not spoken a word, and somewhere along the way, I'd stopped glancing over my shoulder at the hounds.

The forest began to thin. The darkness and frost gave way to a silvery gray mist. Soon, we came to three wide steps, the stones blackened from decomposed leaves. The steps led to a long rectangular lawn of dead grass crowned by an ornate fountain in the center. And beyond, an immense, dark stone palace, its arched windows like sheets of black glass reflecting the forest around us.

Trees grew atop the palace, the roots winding down around the stones, finding crevices to latch onto and into. Behind the palace, rose an enormous hill, suggesting that the palace butted up against the hill or was part of it. Turrets soared past the trees, pointing skyward where crows circled and cawed. Small compared to Drem, but their cries were still disturbing.

A shaft of sunlight broke through the clouds and disappeared beyond the walls, as though it pierced the very heart of the palace.

Balen whispered softly to Drem as the raven began to fidget and flap its wings.

The hounds moved closer to us, three on each side, two at the back, and one—the biggest one—in front leading us. Their backs came to my chest. Their paws were the size of Balen's hand. They could easily take down a Danaan, or a human. Or a horse, for that matter.

Wind howled somewhere far in the distance of the dark woods, but here the quiet reigned, only broken by the brittle leaves and grass crunching beneath our feet. There was no water running from the fountain. It was dry, cracked and aged by time. The bowing female sculpture on top rested her forehead on her bent knee. One hand was palm up, against the ground, and the other was thrown over her knee and face, shielding her as she cried.

Even though it was a bit warmer than the woods, I shivered. The statue presented such anguish and hopelessness, a fitting warning to any arriving at the King of the Underworld's door. As we went by, I heard the slow drip, drip, drip—like tears falling into the dry basin below.

At the entrance to the palace, two of the hounds bent their heads and pushed at the massive front doors. Their hindquarters bunched and their nails scraped on stone. Slowly, the doors creaked open enough to allow us passage.

I was no stranger to opulence, to halls three stories high, and architecture that could make one's jaw drop. But this . . . it was cold and frightening. Leaves and debris littered the floor, our entrance sending them skittering down the black marble floor. Columns of the same material lined both sides of the long hall. There was nothing of warmth, no carpets or wall hangings, no great hearth with a raging fire, no candles.

The doors closed behind us, the echoing bang making me jump. I forced down my trepidation and moved down the hall toward a dais with three chairs—thrones that were in tatters. In the spaces between the marble columns stood stone sculpted warriors, larger than life, noble and fearsome. As I passed each sentinel, I felt eyes on my back.

Shaking off the eerie sensation, I focused my attention ahead of me. A figure appeared at the end of the dais, one hand resting on the back of a chair. A man, an old man with a dignified carriage and tears in his eyes.

My breath whooshed out of me and I staggered to a stop.

Those brown eyes... The look of regret and love directed at me, only me. I couldn't breathe, couldn't swallow. I reached toward Balen for support, but grabbed air. My vision wavered. My knees buckled. "Father?" the word slipped out on a whisper.

* * *

"Deira, wake up. Daughter, wake up."

The voice sounded far away, whispering words on the

wind—a dream—that couldn't be real. The blood vessels in my head pulsed painfully. Sickness roiled in my stomach. A moan rumbled from my throat, cut short by a cool, rough hand on my forehead.

I blinked until my vision cleared.

Above me a luxurious, deep blue canopy hung from the four posts of the bed. A fire burned in a massive marble hearth. The walls glittered with inlaid silver panels and sparkling gems.

I pushed onto my elbows, drew in a deep breath, and faced the man by my bedside, looking straight into the eyes of my father.

My *father*.

"No more fainting, child," he said with a smile.

He sat on the edge of the bed, a soft bed covered with the same blue material as the canopy above me, his old, withered hands folded in his lap. He was still striking, still handsome. And still my father.

"Are you real or spirit?"

"Aye, I am real. Old, but real."

I sat straighter, shoving my hair away from my face. "But…"

My mind was a chaos of questions. I couldn't take my eyes off him, couldn't believe he was there. With me. In Nox's realm. Alive. My father was alive. My arms were around him before I knew what I was doing.

Memories flooded back, the spicy scent of him, the breadth of his shoulders, the deep tone of his voice. I held him for a long time and sobbed like a child.

After, I released him and studied him, taking in every detail, noticing the yellow hue of his paper-thin skin and the blue veins underneath. His hands were the big hands I remembered, the same hands which held mine as we'd walk in Mother's garden. The veins and tendons were swollen and stark, but they were *his* hands. He wore a rich blue tunic trimmed in silver thread. His hair was long and white, a few stubborn strands of red remaining. His eyebrows had become bushier and white. His nose looked more prominent. And as he frowned, the wrinkles on his forehead deepened.

Happiness swelled my chest. I held his hands and inspected the ink-stained fingers. "You still write."

He smiled. "Aye. I can't seem to stop."

I showed him my own hands, the fingers still stained from the ink I'd overturned in Falias. We laughed together. "I have learned to scribe as well," I told him with pride, wanting so much to be like him, to make him proud. "I've kept all your books, everything you've written."

A warm glow softened his eyes and he hugged me. "I had hoped as much."

I continued to stare at him in wonder. "How can this be?" By all accounts, he should not have lived so long.

"The years I spent in Falias with your mother clung to me, extending my life." He glanced at my hands, which he held in both of his. He sighed heavily. Concern and trepidation swam in the brown depths of his eyes. "But I had help, Deira. I would not have lived to see this day, to see you again had it not been for Nox of Annwn."

I stilled. "What?"

"When I came into the woods searching for the power of the pillar stone to reclaim Emain Macha, he approached me. He promised me that one day you would rule in my stead, for my time had passed. And he extended my days so that I could see you grown, and see you secure in this world, a queen in both lands."

"No," I breathed, feeling as though I'd awoken into a nightmare. "No, this isn't right..." I looked around the sumptuous chamber.

"This is his home. He lives in great wealth and power. Everything you could ever want, he would give to you. He has promised me."

"And you believe the promise of one who has waged war on his own homeland?"

My father's lips thinned. He was troubled by his choice, I could tell. He shook his head sadly. "I have done what is best for you."

His words ripped open the tender wounds of my childhood. "Was leaving me for the best? Was leaving me alone, to Mother's family the *best* thing for me? Do you have any idea what they did to me? It was not the right thing."

He met my gaze. "Aye, it was."

I didn't know how to respond. The chaos, shock, hurt, all of it ballooned inside of me. I had to move, to escape the pain and joy of seeing him again, of the abandonment, and of knowing he'd aligned himself with Nox. I slid from the bed, nearly tripping on the fabric tangling around my ankles.

I righted myself, standing barefoot on a thick rug, gazing down in confusion at the deep, shimmering green gown I wore. It fell in soft folds around my feet, a straight line from the thick, jewel-encrusted band that wrapped around my chest just below my breasts. Above the band, the fabric had been gathered into tiny pleats that covered my breasts, but left a deep plunging space between them. Two gold clasps decorated the shoulder straps.

I scanned the room, seeing padded couches and low chairs, a dressing table with a gilded mirror, a table full of fruits, bread, cheese, and meats. Boxes and chests made of the finest wood and metals sat on thick, colorful rugs. This was a chamber fit for a queen.

My father was still on the bed, hands folded in his lap, his expression weary and sad.

"Oh, Father, what have you done?"

But I knew. I knew already what he'd done.

"I have promised you."

"You cannot. You haven't the right."

He stood. "I have every right. I am still your father."

"No, you gave away your say when you abandoned me in Innis Fail."

Tears filled his eyes and color filled his sunken cheeks. "I did not abandon you. Don't you understand?" He stepped forward and went to grab my hands, but I moved back. Hurt swam in his eyes. I searched the room for a way out.

"Where's Balen? What have you done to him?" Tears
stung my eyes. I was trapped, trapped in wealth and luxury I didn't
ask for or want.

"Deira, please, let me explain."

I ignored him, hurrying to the walls, trailing my hands over
the silver inlays, feeling the bumps of jewels and the intricate
designs carved into the metal. Where was the door? Where were
my clothes? I wanted out of this dress, out of this false place.

I found a door and pressed the latch. It opened easily. I
hurried into a hallway lit by the flames of candles in wall sconces.
The corridor seemed to go on forever in each direction. My
father's footsteps sounded from the room behind me. Hands
trembling, I gathered the gown so I wouldn't trip and then I ran
down the hall.

Tears streamed from my eyes, making it difficult to see.

"Deira!" my father called.

But I didn't listen, didn't stop running. All the old hurts
came back, threatening to steal the very breath from my lungs. Still,
I pressed on, passing door after door, but the hallway never
changed its appearance. It felt as though I was going in circles.

Slowing, I glanced back over my shoulder. No one was
behind me so I stopped, using the time to catch my breath and
figure out where to go from here. There was no sound in the
hallway, just the tall, dark shadows of the doors on either side of
me and the candles in between. The floor was made of polished
black marble and down the center was a long, woven rug.

My father had made a bargain with Nox of Annwn. Why? Why would he do such a thing? If only he had taken me with him when he'd left. My father, Balen, Nox... How could I trust them, any of them?

I started moving again. As I went, I listened intently for any noise, reminded of the dream I'd had when Balen and I first set out together from the encampment by the lake. But I heard no moans, no cries of passion, no voice in my mind.

I went down a wide set of curving stairs, coming to a long gallery and, beyond it, an enclosed courtyard full of lush flowers, plants, ornamental trees, and fountains. The songs of birds fluttered into the palace, and light spilled through the arches.

Gripping the sides of the gown, I crossed the marble floor.

This must be the place that received the ray of sunlight I'd seen earlier from outside the palace.

As I stepped into the courtyard, I saw no one. The steady flow of water and the birds' chirping seemed out of place in the middle of the dark woods of Cathair Crofin. The large paving stones were warm against my bare feet as I walked under the canopy of a long gallery, eyeing the vision before me. Before the cold, Murias had looked similar with its luxurious temples and gardens.

There were no doors along the gallery so I went into the garden, hoping to find an exit somewhere beyond. The palace walls surrounded the garden, balconies on the second, third, and fourth levels overlooking the scenery. The lower level of the far wall seemed to sink into the face of the hill.

In the middle of the garden, I stopped and my jaw went slack. *Dear Dagda.*

A tree surrounded by a circular patch of green grass. Long, bent limbs, so low I could touch them, stretched out from a gnarled trunk. Leaves like hammered gold sparkled in the shaft of sunlight poking through the clouds. A few round fruit hung from the branches, heavy and full, and as golden as the crown my grandfather had worn. A soft yellow hue glowed all around the tree.

I was at once struck by its beauty and how lonely it appeared in the small corner of the world. Drawing closer, I wanted to stand in its glow and feel its leaves. I wanted to hold the fruit in my hand and see if it was truly made of gold. A faint breeze stirred the gown around my legs and made the leaves on the tree dance in the light. I thought I heard the sound of tinkling as they brushed together.

Warmth emitted from the tree. I reached out to find the leaves were thin and leathery. Fascinated, I stepped closer under the branch to inspect the fruit. And then froze.

A male slept under the tree. He was on his back in the grass, hands under his head, one leg drawn up, the other stretched out.

He was golden like the tree.

Long golden hair. Thick lashes. His look reminded me of the great golden hawks that flew over Murias. Full lips that curved up at the corners. The shadow of a dark blond beard on his jaw.

Nox, King of Annwn.

His lips curved into a smile before he opened his eyes. Hands still tucked behind his head, he turned in my direction, opened one pale gray eye then the other.

"The gown fits you well," he noted.

I hardened myself against the deep, sensual voice. Hearing it in my mind had mesmerized me and brought about so many new emotions and feelings. Hearing it in the flesh was far more potent. If I didn't steel myself against him now, I'd never be free from this place.

He studied me, his eyes lingering for a spell before sitting up and patting the grass beside him. "Come, sit, Deira. We have much to discuss, you and I."

"We have nothing to discuss." I shoved my hair behind my shoulders and crossed my arms.

Nox's gaze went to my breasts, my movement causing their swell to become more visible in the gown's plunging neck line. I dropped my arms, heat stealing into my cheeks. "What have you done with Balen?"

"Nothing. Yet." He let out a sigh as he pushed to his feet.

I'd seen him once, through the flames of the fire festival. Up close, he was even more striking. And intimidating. He stood as tall as Balen and possessed wide shoulders and strength in his build, but there was something different about Nox, something I'd never noticed with anyone else before. No, I had. When I'd met Drem, the War Raven, with its low hum of energy.

Magic and power clung to Nox like a heady perfume. It altered his voice, his essence, even the air around him.

He is the grandson of an Ageless One, I reminded myself. *He has power unlike anyone you have ever known.*

He could take whatever he willed of me and be done with it. He hadn't yet, but sooner or later he would. "Is it true what my father says?" I asked as he straightened his plain white tunic.

"He has promised you to me, aye."

I stared beyond him; it was easier than looking at him directly. "Release Balen and Drem, return the Lia Fail, and I'll consent."

His laughter was expected. For a woman who had never been worth much, my demands were ridiculous.

"You have nothing to bargain with. I don't need your consent." He scratched his jaw, eyeing me thoughtfully, one corner of his mouth still turned up in amusement. "I've waited for you a long time, Deira. I want you to feel welcome here, to be happy and, perhaps one day to feel loved."

"Loved? By you?"

"Don't look so surprised. I *am* capable of the emotion. Because I rule the land of the dead, doesn't mean my heart is dead as well. You, more than anyone, should know what it's like to be misunderstood, to be betrayed, abandoned..."

He took a step toward me.

I held my ground, lifting my chin to meet his intelligent gaze.

"What have you to lose?" he asked. "Balen has thrown you to the wolves to save his precious house. You have no one back in Murias. No family. No friends. No one here in Éire, except your father. Why not me? Why *not* share the world with me? You'll have everything you've ever wanted and more."

Disbelief filled me; his words making a small impact, but an impact just the same. He captured my hands, his power sweeping through me with a wave of sensuality and euphoria. My breath hitched. The color of his eyes captivated me, the palest gray I'd ever seen.

"Think on it. You and I, we are the same. I was abandoned for my differences. I was cast out, driven away from those whose love I sought. Always alone. And now I have the power to regain what was lost to me, to prove my worth, and take my rightful place. I know what it's like, Deira. No one else can say that."

Nox seemed to understand my deepest hurts in a way no one else ever had. I swallowed. He confused me, clouded my judgment and made me feel things I didn't want to feel.

"Can your Balen say that?" he asked. "He has known nothing but acceptance and love from his family and his house. He will never understand what it means to watch a loving family from afar and wish to be part of it, wish to feel just one moment of it."

He squeezed my hands as he spoke. Tears pricked my eyes, for he spoke of me when he spoke of himself. I avoided the pain in his eyes. I didn't want to sympathize with him or relate to him. Nox of Annwn was manipulative and devious, I had to remember that.

Or was he?

He grabbed my chin and forced me to look at him. "We belong together. We are the same."

His eyes burned bright with conviction. I glared back at him, clenching my teeth, and hating that I understood him.

"The way we've been treated by others, aye, we have that in common," I said. "But you, along with my father, have trapped me, just as everyone has my whole life. Anything you want from me, I will not give it freely."

The muscle in his jaw flexed, and his pale eyes took on a glint of silver. "You sound like a petulant child, Deira. Have your tantrum, but it won't change your course or mine. Innis Fail will fall under my rule, and Éire will follow suit. It's up to you whether you live your life as a queen or as a prisoner, for there is no other path for you."

"Exactly my point," I shot back. "I want to choose my own path, not have it chose for me."

He sighed. "And that is a luxury none of us are given."

Two hounds appeared silently from the direction of the gallery. I stepped back, away from Nox. Anger rolled off him, surrounding him in a controlled, lethal force. "Take her to her room."

"No, wait—" Nox held up his hand. The hounds waited. "Let me see Balen. Please. Please, give me your word you won't harm him, and..." The walls closed in and I felt well and truly trapped. "And I will take my place by your side. I will . . . *try*." *To love you.* My heart thumped hard. It was the only thing I had to bargain with. The only thing Nox seemed to want from me.

His eyes narrowed as he studied me intently. Not wanting him to see the uncertainty on my face, I fell to my knees in front of

him and clutched his calf, pressing my forehead against the leather
of his boots. "Please. I beg this of you."

Nox remained rigid before laying a gentle hand on my
head. He stroked my hair, slipped his hand around the base of my
skull, and prodded me to look at him. When I did, tears slipped
down my cheeks.

He pulled me to my feet. His thumb wiped at my tears. He
shook his head as he tucked my hair behind my ear, searching my
face, seeming confounded. "Why do you matter so?" His hand
cupped my cheek, his wet thumb trailing along my bottom lip. "I
will indulge you on this," he said softly. "And I will give you a geás,
a binding oath. I'll not harm Balen. You may see him now and then
you'll return to me."

"Truly?" I asked, unable to hide the hope in my voice.

"Truly."

The fact that he'd yielded, stunned me. "But… Why would
you do this for me?"

His hand dropped from my face. "Because, Deira," he
answered, his voice tired and honest. "I don't want to be alone
anymore."

Chapter 21

I was supposed to hate Nox. He was the enemy; the enemy to everyone in my land. And yet his words . . . they gave me pause. His smile was bleak and cynical. I looked away, drew in a deep breath and tried to bring some clarity back to the situation.

"You'll give your geás, then?"

"As I've promised, aye."

It was more than I'd hoped for. A geás, once given, could not be broken. It might be the only way to save Balen's life. I searched for signs of untruth in the steady pale gray eyes, but all I saw was frost, cold, and unfathomable depths.

He motioned to the hounds. "They'll take you to Balen."

He left, disappearing into the darkness of the gallery.

I rubbed at my chest again, watching him go, knowing how he felt, his words echoing in my head. *"I don't want to be alone anymore."*

One hound went behind me and the other stepped in front of me. It glanced over its furry white shoulder and began moving beyond the golden tree. Woodenly, I followed, forcing

Nox from my thoughts and turning them to the problem at hand. I had no idea what to do next, but I knew, somehow, I must free Balen from Cathair Crofin.

We went deep into the palace, into the hillside where the smell of the earth was thick and pungent, so much so that the air became humid and difficult to breathe. The gray stone palace walls were replaced by crude rock, reminding me of the cavern where the Void had deposited me and Balen.

Torches burned at long intervals, lighting our way, yet creating dark shadows in between. There were small caves, chambers, and narrow corridors. Pools of hot water bubbled from the ground in some of the larger chambers. The hem of my gown became wet and dirty, and my bare feet were caked in dirt and scratched from the rough floor.

Occasionally, the echo of voices traveled through the underground labyrinth, but I didn't strain to hear the words or the sounds. There was nothing good there. No hope. No light.

Up ahead, a tall archway was lit with the remnants of daylight. The air had thinned and cooled, and as we left behind the massive hill, mist gathered around us outside, seeming to pull us into a vast field ringed by the dark forest of Cathair Crofin.

The hounds disappeared into the white fog, leaving me alone. I scanned the area, unsure of where to go. Balen was nowhere in sight. I turned in a circle. The mist was so thick it hid the archway that led back into the hill. This place, the forest, the palace in the hill, the courtyard, the field . . . it was a confusing labyrinth of indoor and outdoor places. One could lose themselves forever.

"Balen?" I called, keeping my voice low, unsure of what lurked in the mist.

Pain, hot and quick, lanced my foot. I bent down, inspecting a small cut on my heel and finding the culprit in an old sword poking through the wet ground.

The sword was held by a bony hand.

I went still, fear sliding icy-cold down my spine as my mind went back to the first attack at the encampment and the bony arms that had held me... Hesitantly, I scanned my surroundings, the mist thinning just enough for me to see and panic making my breathing fast and erratic. I was in the middle of a battle field.

A field littered with the dead.

Everywhere I looked were the bones and tattered remains of bodies; men, horses, and hounds. With my red hair, the only bright color in a sea of misty gray and white, I made an unmistakable target. Goosebumps flared along my skin. Nox might have made the geás not to harm Balen, but there was no promise when it came to me.

Shaken, I wrapped my arms around myself and moved, picking my way over and around rusted weapons and jagged bones. The field was wet and I tried not to think of what my bare feet truly stepped in as I went.

Ahead a dark mass loomed just beyond the mist. My steps slowed.

And then I saw him.

Chained to a pillar stone.

"Balen!" I ran to him, heedless of my path. His head hung low between his shoulders. His dark hair was damp from the mist and hid his face. Carefully, I lifted his chin. "Balen, it's me, Deira."

Save for a few bruises on his cheek and jaw he appeared unharmed. "Balen," I tried again. "Are you hurt? Talk to me, please."

I placed both hands on his face. His skin was ice cold, too cold for a Fire Breather. Shadows curved under his eyes. I hugged him, pressing my cheek against his, trying to give him some of my warmth, and wishing to Anu that I had power to give to him as he'd once given to me.

Desperate, I tried and tried, but there was nothing there, no power to give to him.

I prayed and pleaded and cursed the gods.

"Deira… You're smothering me."

Balen's ragged voice had me biting back a cry of relief. "Are you hurt? What did he do to you? I'm going to get us out of this, I—"

"It is but an illusion." Balen's throat worked as he tried to swallow. He glanced around with dull, haunted eyes. "All of this."

Illusions didn't cut into flesh, I thought, thinking of the wound on my foot.

"Where have you been?" He frowned, staring at me as though trying to see me clearly. "You've been gone so long."

"I haven't," I answered, confused, suddenly wondering which one of us was right. I had fainted in the hall and couldn't say how long I'd slept. But surely it had been no more than a few minutes. Yet Balen appeared gaunt and weak, as though he'd been chained, arms behind the stone, standing up, for many days. I tested the chains, finding the lock and then inspecting it. "These don't seem like an illusion," I muttered.

"No." He lifted his head as though the weight of it was very great. "All this around us, the battle field . . . it is an image of the past. Of my past."

"Your past?" I moved around the pillar to see if I could ease the tightness of the chains. "But why?"

"Revenge."

An iron peg had been driven through the open link in the chains, holding them up high. "Stand straighter," I told him so that there'd be enough slack to lift the chain over the peg. Once I accomplished the task, Balen slid to the ground. His arms were still chained behind the pillar, but at least he was off his feet. I came back around the stone and knelt next to him.

He looked at me. "Before I Challenged for leadership of my house, I led my father's legions against Nox. This, all you see around you, is the damage I wrought. I captured him and chained him, and then I left him."

"Left him," I echoed. "For how long?"

"I know not. It was my father's will and I did not question it. I never questioned him. Though at times I should have. I'm not proud of what I did, Deira." Pain filled his eyes, a deep disappointment in himself that I understood. Our rules of engagement afforded high nobility quarter in battle—

imprisonment, ransom, or, at the very least, offering a clean death. Things like torture, assassination, and so on were frowned upon. Due to his station, Nox should have been treated accordingly.

But then, Nox was never treated fairly, was he? He was never given the same acknowledgements and deference as the other leaders and aristocrats of the four houses.

"It was an old grudge. My father, his father before him, and so on, they constantly warred with each other… I should have ended it."

Sydhr choosing one son over the other had created eternal strife among his sons and their descendants forever. All this, the war against Innis Fail, the personal vendetta against Balen, stemmed from a father's choice.

I knew what that was like.

"Deira, I have done my part. You must find the Lia Fail and return home."

"I'm not leaving you here. Nox made a geás to me. No harm will come to you. You'll not die. I will see you home *with* the Lia Fail."

His eyes went wide. "You have bargained with him." He struggled against the chains. "No, Deira, no. He is the grandson of a god. He does not bargain."

I placed my hand on his shoulder, scared by his words and the horror that flitted through his eyes. "It's all right. I—"

"No, you don't understand. Don't let him into your head. You'll start to forget why you're here, where you're from, who you are… You must find the Light. Find it. That's all that matters now."

"But I don't know where to look," I replied hopelessly. Then, a rush of astonishment hit me. I *did* know. "I do know. I know where it is. The tree in the courtyard." The Lia Fail was part of or in that tree somehow. It had to be.

"Go then," Balen urged. "Waste no more time."

"But I—"

"You have to."

"I can't leave you . . . not like this." I cupped his face with my hands, my throat constricting with grief. "I'm supposed to save you." That had been my hope all along. How could I walk away and leave him alone in that place of coldness and gray? I couldn't. I hugged him, holding him tightly, hurting inside and filled with so many regrets. "I can't leave you."

I cried against his neck, knowing even as I said the words that there was no other choice.

"Drem flies free," he said, his voice choked. "As long as he lives, I live. When he no longer flies, you will know I am gone."

I drew back, seeing the grim determination in the warrior's eyes. He was too strong and powerful to be here, chained and brought low by his own blood, his own family.

"Why did you do this? Why did you walk into this?" But I didn't need an answer. He'd sacrificed himself, walked into Nox's realm in order to bring me here. From the looks of him, he'd put up a good fight. Though, I was beginning to understand that fight or not, the outcome would always be the same. Balen's purpose was done. He'd given me an opportunity to free our world from darkness and frost, to free it from Nox and give us a fighting chance.

"I have always known my path, Deira. I did the right thing for my people, my land. And I don't regret it . . . because in the process I found you." A bright flare flashed in his amber eyes. "I'm sorry I withheld the truth. I was afraid to risk it, afraid to trust in you." He smiled gently. "You can bear the Light, *seirnann*. I know you can. Innis Fail needs a new champion."

I stayed mute, biting the inside of my cheek so I wouldn't sob. Rigidly, I held back the tears, pressure building in my face. I had to show him I was strong, that I could do what he said. But inside desolation and grief was eating away at me.

I let my forehead rest against his and closed my eyes, the motion squeezing out several hot tears. "I will come back for you."

"I know." He kissed them from my cheeks. "Go, Deira."

For a long time I committed his face to memory, not wanting to forget a single detail. As long as Drem lived, I'd know Balen did too. I'd come back for him. I'd never stop until he was free. I kissed him hard on the mouth and then stood on trembling legs.

Being the one to leave hurt far worse than those times when others had left me.

One foot in front of the other, head held high, I strode through the macabre field of illusion. Mist would have swallowed him up by now and I tried not to look back, to let the image of him alone, lost in the mist, cripple me.

Leaving Balen broke something inside me. I felt a
hardening taking place, and I embraced it, closing myself off and
pushing Balen deep into a small protected pocket of my soul.

I had no idea where I went, but it didn't matter. Nox's
hounds would find me and lead me back to the palace.

Chapter 22

The hounds fell in with me, leading me back into the hillside, through the caverns, out into the courtyard, then inside of the palace to my chamber.

They left me alone in the opulent room. My feet ached, and I shivered despite the warmth emanating from the hearth. Beyond the bed chamber, a wide archway led to a private bath with steps leading into a rectangular pool of hot water. Columns ringed the outer edges. Candles burned in tall stands. Beyond the bath was a wide covered balcony with couches, flowering plants and a small fountain.

The echo of laughter wafted in through the open balcony. I followed the sounds, going through the bathing chamber and onto the balcony. The courtyard spread out below me, larger than I'd first imagined. The ray of sunlight still pierced the dull sky and bathed the golden tree in light. It was mesmerizing, like a dream of hope in a dark, gray world.

It was my chance at making everything right.

Across the expanse to the other balconies, movement caught my eye. Several women lounged on outdoor couches. I hadn't expected anyone else to be there in the palace, but of course there would be. Nox must have servants, family, females, attendants... In fact, the tales of the women he kept and the wealth he lavished upon those who pleased him was legendary, as was the brutality he exacted on those who did not.

I went back inside to find two female servants dressed in plain white gowns standing by the pool. One held towels and the other held a basket of soaps, oils and cloths. They bowed when I entered, but did not meet my eyes or say a word.

"Hello," I said.

"They do not speak, for they have no tongues." Ixia sauntered into the room in a regal gown of shimmering silver thread and beads. She looked down her perfect nose at me and her betrayal was at once clear.

Anger erupted so swiftly it took some effort to stay still and not launch myself at her. "You're the one who told Nox about me, about the foretelling." She had betrayed Balen and the entire House of Sydhr.

She smirked, strolling along the far wall, running her delicate fingers over the marble dresser and mirror, picking up items that had been placed there for me. "Light Bearer," she laughed. "You're not so special, you know. I only told him you were in the camp. He already knew the rest."

She was jealous, something that was both surprising and empowering. Ixia of Sydhr, one of the most beautiful Danaans I'd ever seen, was jealous of me. Though, now that I understood her heart, she was not so beautiful anymore.

"And you thought by betraying your house and all of Innis Fail that you would what, become powerful? Wealthy? Why would you betray your own brother?"

"Because he fights a losing battle. Innis Fail is dying and only Nox can save it. I won't fade away and grow old like the rest of them. Balen believes in a foretelling that spelled his death. Why should I follow a leader who plans to fall? Where is the hope in that? Were we to place our hopes on you?" She snorted. "You who cannot even call a drop of water?"

"Yet, you would live here when I am queen, under my rule." Somehow I doubted that.

She paused in her perusal of a trinket box on the dresser. "You'll not be queen in truth. Aye, you'll bear Nox's children, but you'll have no real power, no say, no freedom. He coddles you now, but that won't last beyond the next moon."

She picked up a gold ring set with a red stone from the trinket box, slipped it on her finger, admired it, then left the room, keeping the ring and dismissing me.

Oddly, I was not angry. Ixia had come here to put me in my place, to scare me, when in truth it was she who was afraid. Afraid of losing her place to me.

The servants approached and removed my soiled gown.

I went down the marble steps into the pool, the hot water closing in around my shoulders. Both servants followed me in still wearing their gowns. They washed my hair and body then left me to soak in the water.

The heat seeped gradually and luxuriously into my skin. I floated onto my back and closed my eyes, my thoughts turning to my mother. What would she have me do? How was I to bear the Light back to Innis Fail and keep Nox from stopping me or retrieving it again? Could I leave and abandon Father as he had abandoned me? How did I free Balen? Should I get close to Nox? Win his trust?

The servants returned some time later to dry me off and rub fragrant oil into my skin. My muscles became pliant under their skilled hands, making me sleepy and making my heartache and grief duller than before.

After the oil, my hair was brushed until it shined. The servants attached a pair of gold earrings with two small pearl drops to each lobe. I lifted my arms when directed, and a sheer gown was placed over my head. It was simple, the color an iridescent white like the pearls of my earrings. It hung over one shoulder, leaving the other bare, and pooled at my ankles in a long, unencumbered line of fabric.

Once the gown was on, they pulled the sides of my hair back, pinning them with a pearl clasp. Slippers of the softest white leather accompanied the outfit.

The servants left. I went to the dresser and opened the trinket box, curious to see what Ixia had seen. There, nestled atop a velvet lining, was an array of extravagant jewels. I closed the box. This life was so tempting. Things I'd never dreamed of owning where right here in front of me. Beautiful things. Gowns. Jewels. Leisure. Servants. All things my Anu family was accustomed to, but I was not.

A knock at the door made me jump.

I faced the door, drawing in a steady breath, before turning the knob. My father waited in the hallway. His presence took me by surprise, and I wasn't sure I'd ever grow accustomed to seeing him.

"Deira," he began in a reserved tone. "Supper is ready."

I studied his aged face and the fine clothes he wore. I remembered how hard it had been to walk away from Balen and wondered if my father had felt the same excruciating pain when he walked away from me. "What should I do, Father?" I asked suddenly. "Did you love my mother?"

He let out a weary sigh as we left my chamber and headed down the hallway. "Aye, I loved your mother very much. She stole my heart and my life here in Éire, but I cannot blame her for that."

"She would want me to save Innis Fail."

He nodded. "I believe she would."

"But you believe my place is here."

"I do." He paused. "Forgive me, Deira. I wanted to take you with me after your mother passed on. I intended to, but I would not have been allowed to pass through the Void with you, such was the bargain I made at the time."

We continued on. "Then why didn't you turn back and stay in Falias with me?"

"Because my presence there was precarious without your mother. Had I been discovered by those who were not loyal to her,

I would have been put to death. I could not have you witness such a thing and I was afraid for you."

We came to a door inlaid with ornate silver panels. My father knocked twice. "I have always loved you, daughter. Never forget that. Everything I have done, I have done for you." With that he placed his hands on my shoulders and kissed my cheek.

He left me as the door swung open. Soft music drifted from the room along with the rich aroma of food. The walls were sheets of gold and silver. A mural of battles, warriors in shining armor, and fire in their hands had been painted on the ceiling.

Two hounds sat on either side of a massive hearth, which blazed bright and hot. They watched me with their eerie red eyes and white ears alert. Placed in front of the fire was a large, gilded chair where the King of Annwn presided, his legs sprawled out in front of him, his elbow propped on the arm and his head bent, chin resting on his finger tips. He tapped one finger methodically against his temple as he stared into the fire deep in thought.

Dressed in a deep blue tunic and leggings, he made a striking figure. A gold band encircled his wrist and his long, blond hair flowed freely over his shoulder.

"Sit." He waved a hand toward a long, polished table in the center of the room.

I didn't move and neither did he. Finally, he rose from the chair.

His eyes swept leisurely over the gown, and my pulse quickened. Why did heat leap into my cheeks? I didn't care for him, not like I cared for Balen, and yet I could not deny there was something…

He said nothing about my appearance. His hand rested on the back of the chair. "Did you enjoy your visit with Balen?" he asked, studying me intently.

"No. Why do you make him suffer?"

"He made me suffer."

"Now you sound like the child." He'd called me a child in the courtyard, but I had forgotten about it until the words rushed out of my mouth.

Tense silence filled the room.

"Then it is agreed," Nox commented easily. "We both behave like children. Please sit."

He pulled out a chair near the end of the table. I sat stiffly, trying to calm my racing heart and curb my tongue. Nox settled at the head of the table and waited as servants placed our meals before us. After the wine was poured and left for us on the table, he excused them.

Their presence had created a kind of barrier between us, but now the silence was stark. I wished them back as I nervously downed half my wine. The fire popped and crackled. Sparks shot into the air. The hounds never even blinked.

Nox gestured for me to eat as he placed a bite into his mouth. "You haven't eaten since you entered the forest, Deira…"

My gut twisted at his words. I hadn't eaten since the quick meal of bread and cheese Balen and I had had on our way to Cathair Crofin. I was hungry. Painfully hungry, and as much as I didn't like being there, I needed to eat. The roasted fowl tasted wonderful. It felt wrong that I liked it, but I kept eating.

"Are you like them, Deira?" Nox asked at length. "Do you despise me, condemn me before you even know who I am? Would you be so angry with Balen for chaining *me* to the stone?"

I swallowed my bite and took a moment to form my words. "He told me what he did to you. I know there are rules in battle, especially when it comes to nobility. No one of your station should have been treated that way."

"Do you know how long I stayed chained to the stone?"

I shook my head, not wanting to know.

"Three hundred years," he answered to my astonishment. "Should Balen receive the same sentence, you think?"

"You have given me your geás," I reminded him carefully.

"Ah. That I have." He saluted me with his wine glass then took a long drink.

"Will you let Innis Fail die?"

Nox shrugged. "Depends."

"Could you restore the Lia Fail to our world?"

He eyed me thoughtfully. "Now why would I want to do that? Restoring the Light means restoring power to my enemies. They're becoming so weak now. Soon it will be easy to take control. You believe the Light still exists then?"

"I don't believe I'd be here if it didn't."

"Because you're the Light Bearer." He sat back with cold satisfaction. "A *lie*. You're here because I brought you here. Balen has staked his life on a foretelling that never existed. Ironic is it not? The entire House of Sydhr believed the words of Balen's mother. Granted, she was a gifted oracle, but not so gifted to see the words in her head as mine and not those of her god."

His words sank in and I knew they were true.

He'd entered her mind just as he'd entered mine. Shaken, I set my fork down.

Balen had sacrificed everything on the chance that Innis Fail could be saved, placing all his hopes on me, someone who was not, as it turned out, special in any regard. And while I never wanted to be my world's savior, the disappointment I felt was deep and stinging.

"Don't look so disappointed," Nox said. "I went through an amazing amount of trouble to make Balen pay for what he did to me, and to find you. After being chained for three centuries one develops an amazing amount of patience." *Or they go mad*, I thought as he went on. "You were born at just the right moment and everything fell into place so much better than I could've imagined. That little foretelling brought you both here to me."

The food turned sour in my gut. I pushed my plate away. "That *little* foretelling," I shoved away from the table and stood abruptly, "gave hope to an entire world."

He set his cup on the table and rose. "Innis Fail can rot. Don't expect me to feel sorry for them, Deira. They've lived in wealth and warmth and daylight for as long as I can remember." He slammed his palms down on the table. "It is *my* turn."

Angry beyond caring, I placed my hands on the table. "Then take your turn in the Light and get someone else to rule the

House of Annwn. You can do that without destroying an entire world."

His eyes narrowed, and I felt the distinct gathering of energy in the room. He leaned in as well, his pale eyes as cold and harsh as the snows that blanketed the island of Murias. "And who would want Annwn? Who would agree to take a turn ruling the dead? Balen? Your grandfather? Mael? No one. They'll fight to the death *not* to rule what I've had to rule for millennia."

"You must set Balen free."

His look turned menacing. "The last one to order me about had his eyes plucked out by the ravens."

"A far better fate than living with you," I shot back.

The hairs on the back of my neck stood. Nox's pale eyes clouded over in hard, gray silver. Dead and blank. I stepped away from the table as he straightened, immediately regretting my words.

To my horror, his body burst into a swirl of energy that shot across the table and shoved me against the wall before becoming solid again. My pulse thudded hard and fast. His body pinned me to the wall.

His hard glare penetrated my soul and sent a cold wave of anguish through me. I cried out, the loneliness of it too much to bear, the raw hopelessness and darkness, like the Void itself. Nothing but blackness. Emptiness.

"*That* is what I feel every day," he forced through gritted teeth. "*That* is what lives inside me."

I couldn't breathe, stuck in the darkness and nothingness. I wanted out.

"That is just the barest *hint* of what I endure. Do you condemn me for wanting respite from it?"

My chest heaved, and my lungs strained for air. He pressed so hard against me, that I didn't fall when my knees buckled. Tears sprang to my eyes.

His fingers dug into my arms, his voice demanding an answer. "Do you?"

"No," I choked out, crying. "No. I don't."

He eased his hold, let out a heavy sigh and then rested his forehead against mine. "I was going mad in the Deadlands. I'm losing myself in the darkness." He drew back to look at me, his voice raw. "I need to be free. I need light too."

Those words broke me, confused me. How I could I hurt for him? But I'd felt the darkness he lived with and I knew I'd do anything not to have that inside of me. No one should have to exist with that terrible cold, nothingness. I understood why he wanted out. I understood his hurt.

With a few devastating words, he'd weakened the shield I'd built around myself, thin cracks that began to spread and break. I no longer felt I had the will to fight, to stand against all this confusion and pain. I just wanted it to end, to give in.

Time stretched.

His body pressed tightly against mine, I heard the soft sound of his breathing and smelled his skin, as though he'd just come in from the snow and ice.

The air changed, becoming still and tense, waiting. He sensed it too. The eerie silver was gone from his eyes. His hand cupped my cheek, the thumb rubbing first my skin and then my bottom lip. His gaze snagged there and held.

His hips, his thighs, his stomach were flattened against me. There was no retreat. Guilt rose with desire. I blinked hard, confused by my thoughts and wild reactions. Nox of Annwn had tempted me with his voice, his invasion in my mind. He'd awakened a part of me I didn't want to admit was there; a sensual creature, a dark creature, one who'd found, in him, someone similar.

Balen was a champion, good and honorable and valiant. Nox was shunned to darkness and death. Where did I fit in? Where did I, with my dark powers, belong? Did I even deserve someone like Balen?

Part of me wanted Nox to erase the memory of the blackness, to make me feel alive and warm. My lips tingled. I licked them. His eyes went molten silver. He lowered his head.

The moment our lips touched, lust rolled over me with such force that tears stung my eyes. I grabbed onto it, desperate, as though it would somehow save me. He kissed me hard and deep and long. My heart banged. Adrenaline sang through my veins, wild and reckless.

And then I felt them. Hot tears sliding down my cheeks and mingling with our kiss.

What was I doing? I couldn't do this.

Nox broke off, his hands trembling slightly as he placed them flat on the wall on either side of my head. Our loud ragged breathing was the only sound in the room. "Not while you cry for him," he whispered in a raw voice, more to himself than to me.

He stepped back, scrubbing a hand down his face. "Go." I didn't move and his voice turned cold and lethal. "Go *now*, Deira. Before I take you against the wall."

I jerked, struck by his vulgarity. I knew it was meant to shock me, to scare me, to make me leave. And it worked. I pushed away from the wall and ran, not stopping until I was back in my chamber where I slid against the closed door to the floor, pulled my knees into my chest, and cried.

Chapter 23

Shame and guilt hounded me for the remainder of the night. I curled up on the rug by the door, sleeping intermittently. During the waking hours, I came to several conclusions about my behavior only to strike them out and start all over again.

I was lost. I had no previous experience to help me deal with the feelings I had for Balen and Nox. I wished my mother was with me, wished I'd had some education, some guidance on the affairs of the heart and body.

It seemed so impossible, and yet... My heart ached for both of them. I hated myself for it. And I didn't know what to do. I didn't know if my reactions were solely my own or if Nox had used his power to heighten my awareness and senses. I was caught in the middle of their war while an entire world and civilization was dying.

I thought of Balen chained to the stone, cold and alone in the fog of a past he'd created.

I thought of Nox and the suffering he'd had to endure in the bleak, hollow darkness he'd been relegated to rule.

Rising from the rug, I removed my gown to dress in a tunic and leggings. A dull ache pulsed in my head. I closed my eyes and pressed my palms against them to ease the dryness. I was spent. But it didn't matter; I had to press on. Had to do what I came here to do.

That was one thing I *wasn't* confused about.

Donning shoes and cloak, I left my room and made my way toward the stairs I'd seen earlier. They curved around and took me down to the first floor where I found the inner courtyard.

Dawn had not yet broke. The birds slept. Dew covered the stones. It was so still, like walking through a painted landscape. There was no sunlight breaking through the clouds, yet a radiant glow surrounded the tree as though it existed in perpetual summer.

Seeing it there made me think of life, of happiness, of summer, and of all the living things that depended upon and thrived in the light. The tree was life. I felt honored to step into the ring of grass and into the soft yellow light of the Lia Fail.

I closed my eyes and embraced it, envisioning being filled with all things good and right, all things wondrous and hopeful. Light must be returned to our dying world. Balen was right. It was all that mattered. Drawing in a deep breath, I moved closer and placed my palm on the rough bark.

And then I was sucked into the Light.

Images flashed before my eyes. The Old War. The Lia Fail, a black cloth thrown over the stone where it resided. I saw it being taken from its tower on the highest peak in Innis Fail, Bren Cara. I saw it shatter, hacked by a man who tried to divide it and use it, but to no avail. I saw it being set into a pillar stone. I saw Nox standing before the stone and calling the pieces together again and then burying them in the ground where the shoot of a tiny tree sprang.

I stumbled back, coming out of the visions.

A sense of fulfillment came over me as my mind snapped back into focus. One of the round fruits hung nearby, golden and full. Compelled, I picked it. It was heavy and smooth. It smelled sweet and ripe. I tucked it in my pocket.

I picked a second one and ran with it across the garden to the entrance that led inside of the hill and then out into the battlefield from the past.

It was odd I hadn't been discovered, but I didn't question it. I just ran.

The mist blanketed the field. I wasn't daunted. Energy surged through me, bolstering my courage and hope. I felt like I could run forever. But I didn't need to. The shadow of the pillar stone lurked in the mist, a mist that parted as I drew near.

Nox turned around to face me, a spear in his hand, as I staggered to a stop, my heart giving a hard, desperate thud.

Dread dropped like a heavy stone into my stomach. My hopes were lost.

He didn't seem surprised, as though he'd known all along that I'd betray him just as everyone else had. I didn't want to reaffirm that belief, to be that person, but I had to.

"You're just in time," he said, grimly, the pale gray of his eyes swirling like a frothy sea.

"I can't let our world die, Nox. Surely you must understand."

"I understand, Deira. You've made your choice. To keep me in darkness to save Innis Fail. You'd sacrifice my chance at freedom. Just as your *hero* sacrificed you to do the same. Perhaps you are more like him than I thought." Nox moved away, revealing Balen still chained to the stone, slumped, and as pale as winter snow.

"You gave me your geás," I reminded him, more steadily than I felt. "You cannot break it."

"I have not broken it."

"But he's…" I forced myself to stay calm. Balen was trying to lift his head, to look at me, but he had no strength to do so. And he was so pale…

"He's not dying today, Deira. His precious raven, however…" Nox pivoted and flung the spear straight and true at a pillar stone nearby.

It was then I saw Drem tied to the stone.

Balen's last bit of strength sent him surging up, fear in his eyes, a shout on his lips.

The spear pierced Drem's chest. A horrible shriek rent the air and sent every bird in the trees flying.

I ran past Nox, but he grabbed my arm.

Drem's screeches subsided, going pathetic and small, as the life ebbed out of it.

Balen slumped down, shocked, his life force fading away.

"*No.*" I jerked from Nox so hard I fell on my rear in the wet grass and stayed there, stunned and unable to process what had just happened.

"If one dies, the other dies... That is the legend, isn't it?" He sighed. "I am Lord of the Underworld. I have learned a thing or two. Two half-souls just went into the Place of Souls. The other two halves reside in Balen, who is not mortally wounded."

I didn't understand.

"He'll sleep forever, unable to die, unable to live, so you see, Deira, he is not exactly . . . *harmed* . . . is he?"

He grabbed the fruit from my hand, but I held on tight, surging up to grapple with him. "No, you can't take it." I needed it, needed it to save Drem. I could feed it to him. It would heal him and heal Balen. I had to try.

"Damn it, Deira, let it go."

I leaned all my weight back, refusing to give in. "No." Tears clouded my vision.

His grip became stronger on my hand, unbearable. My knuckles squeezed together, making me cry out in pain.

"Let it go."

I shook my head. I couldn't. I wouldn't.

Then, the bones in my hand snapped. Pain shot up my arm. I sucked in a stunned gasp and let go. I couldn't breathe—the pain stealing my breath. I fell to my knees and cradled my hand. It was my writing hand, the crooked fingers still stained in ink.

"Deira," Nox said, anger and regret lacing his tone.

He cursed, hesitated a moment as though he'd help me, and then he marched away, disappearing into the mist.

Balen was lost to me. Nox was gone. The fruit was gone. And it felt like there was a gaping hole in my chest.

I held my broken hand against my chest, taking in the pain and the hot throb. Silent tears slid down my face as I went to Balen. There was a faint rise and fall to his chest. I cleared the hair from his noble face, kissed his lips, and then covered him with my cloak.

"I'm sorry. I'm so sorry." I lay over him, rested my head on his chest and grieved.

After some time, I rose and went to the raven, removed its body from the pillar with my good hand and then placed it next to the pillar where Balen lay.

Then I left. Again.

The hounds blocked my path near the entrance to the underground caverns, but I'd expected it. I'd already accepted my path and the things I must do.

A calm came over me.

There was no insecurity or wondering if I could. I just did.

Standing there, grief-stricken and hollow, I left Deira D'Anu behind, opened myself to my tainted blood and let my dark power overtake me.

It lashed out, an angry, black, greedy force, surrounding the hounds and stealing every bit of life they had within them. It relished this. It thrived on the taking. It fed me, made me stronger, made the pain in my hand go away. The hounds' strength and blood lust, their life force, zinged down my limbs, raced through my veins and filled me with power.

I stepped over their corpses and entered the hill.

Those whom I met along the way, I disposed of with a swipe of my hand, using the dark power to lash out. I had no need to kill, just to render unconscious. While the power of the hounds was in me it was a simple thing to do, but it was already ebbing away.

I didn't stop until I came to the golden tree.

There, I drew in a deep breath, expelled it, and opened myself once again to my power. Warm tears trailed down my face, but inside I wasn't crying. I was lost in a black, empty, hurting void, filling up with a golden power that was not my own, sucking the tree dry, taking its glow, its luster, its life…

In the back of my mind, I knew it was too much, too much life for one body to hold. But I was drunk on it and didn't care. I swayed on my feet. My mouth opened. I screamed, but heard nothing. The world titled and I fell back, eyes wide open, staring at the sky.

* * *

I sat up, pulse pounding. I was in the courtyard. It was still early morning, still quiet. My hand throbbed hot and numb, but the bones had mended back together thanks to the power that now resided within me.

The tree loomed in front of me, an old, withered, gnarled thing. The golden glow was gone from its leaves. The fruit, now rotten, littered the dry, grassy circle at its trunk.

The remains of the Lia Fail had left the tree and now clung to me, surrounding me in golden light. I blinked a few times, trying to clear the drowsy warmth away.

I felt . . . lighter. A faint hum echoed in my ears.

"Deira?"

Father stood behind me, his eyes shining with regret and pity. And love. He shook his head, as he'd often done when I was a child and had done something foolish, and then lifted me to my feet to wrap me in his arms. I held on tight and wept, love and sorrow in the tears that dampened his shirt.

"Come," he said at length, his voice thick with emotion as he withdrew from our embrace and held out his hand. I hesitated, still a bit disoriented. "Come. I will show you the way back to Innis Fail."

I frowned. "You? But—"

"You were right, Deira. The time of making decisions for you was over a long time ago. You are a grown woman, capable of making your own choices. You are the best of both of us, your mother and me. Brave. Strong. Kind-hearted. Beautiful. *Glowing.*"

I glanced down. Indeed I was.

"It *is* where you want to go, is it not? Back to Innis Fail?" he asked, studying me.

So many thoughts and emotions weighed on me. I remembered the seeds in my pocket and a faint stirring of hope woke inside me. Balen would want me to finish. "Aye, I want to go back."

Approval settled over his features. "I thought so." My father slipped his arm around my shoulder and together we walked away from the garden.

"And Nox?"

I sensed the worry in my father. I heard it in his soft sigh as he opened a servant's door off the courtyard, revealing a long corridor. "You care for him, don't you?"

I didn't reply.

"He is . . . a lost soul. Weary of this life. He is hard, volatile, mad at times. But he has good in him too. I do not always agree with his methods, but he is desperate to find his place in the living world, instead of the dead."

"What will he do when he finds out you've helped me?"

"I am old, child. Old and tired. I have lived to see you grown and I am proud. It matters not what Nox does or does not do. But you must be careful. You have hurt him. For a long time, he has watched you, loved you even. He believed he'd found an ally, someone like him with dark power, someone who would truly accept all of him. For now, he takes out his rage in the Underworld, but when he learns you have taken the Light..." A soft chuckle escaped him. "He will be as shocked as I am that you were able to do such a thing."

Shocked was putting it mildly.

"Why doesn't he walk away, abdicate his throne? He could live in Éire among the living, in daylight."

"The Underworld *must* have a ruler, Deira. In order to be free, Nox must pass his power to another willing to take it. They must first taste the darkness and then decide. He cannot ask, plead, coerce, extort, or threaten another to take it. When the Lia Fail was stolen, Nox realized it could work in his favor. So he sought it, found it here in Éire."

"But why would he put himself so close to the Light? It weakens him."

"Aye. It weakens his dark power. But he is Sydhr, too. He needs the light just like every Danaan. Once he found it, he began his assault against the other houses. He wants them to pay for shunning him, to push them to the edge of destruction. The houses, the council, they know what he really wants. They know without him asking. For Nox to return the Light someone must take his place. He is patient. He will sit back and wait. And once the land is truly in peril, someone will come willingly to take his place. It is only fair. Perhaps those who refuse to take their turn in the darkness are just as guilty as Nox."

"But he brought me here," I said. And I'd changed everything.

"Well, I don't believe he ever considered you'd be able to do what he foretold. There was no reason for any of us to think you could."

"Come with me," I said suddenly as we entered a store room. "We can return to Innis Fail together. Be a family."

"I cannot leave Cathair Crofin." He paused, making sure I understood. "I would go to the ends of the world with you if I could, Deira. But the bargain I made… I cannot leave the forest. You understand?"

I did. He'd die if he left. I gave a pained nod before crossing to another door.

"I have hidden your warrior in an old mound within the forest," he informed me as we came out of the palace on the west side. At my surprise, he winked. "I am not without friends here. These were my woods long before the King of Annwn laid claim."

Father led me down a small path into the woods. The glow around me had faded somewhat, but I feared any trace would allow Nox or his hounds to find me. My father could not run or move as fast as I could, but he knew secrets about the forest and ways to stay hidden that he'd learned from his time with Nox.

"What of the hounds?"

"They're coming fast," he said. "I feel them behind us and in front of us. But they are no match for you, Deira D'Anu. They exist on dark power and death. You possess the Light. They cannot defeat that."

And he was right.

Nothing with dark intent was able to withstand the Light within me.

In time, we made it to the edge of Cathair Crofin.

It was there that I said goodbye to my father. A proper goodbye this time. Words of love. Tears shed. And a warning given. Nox would seek revenge.

Perhaps he'd already begun.

But I planned to seek *him* out. For I needed to gain entrance into the Place of Souls, to retrieve Balen's half-soul and wake him from eternal sleep. And I already knew how to make that happen. I'd made a vow to myself that the champion would not die because of me, and I intended to keep that promise.

I left my father and didn't stop until I crested the hill where the tall grasses bent in the wind, where Balen and I had first looked upon the dark forest.

As I stood on the hill in Éire, power surged through me, the Light of the Lia Fail existing in me as full and as bright as the shining sun.

I'd done what Balen had set out to do. What I, in the end, chose to do. I found the Light. And I'd save my world.

And perhaps, one day, I'd learn to use my power to summon that pesky raindrop I'd always wanted.

Or, I thought smiling, *a deluge*...

Author's Note

Thank you for reading Deira's story! Obviously, I have taken great liberties, using and twisting elements of Celtic and Irish legends to suit my purposes and build my world. Éire (Ireland) and Innis Fail (Inis Fáil), for instance, are considered one and the same, but I have made them two separate worlds and placed my characters in a time *before* the myths of the Tuatha Dé Danann's appearance in Ireland.

I have always been fascinated by fate and choice, and by reluctant heroes who struggle with the responsibility placed upon them. Deira is such a heroine. She is young, still trying to figure out her place in the world and what she wants out of life. I hope you've enjoyed her journey in Embers.

All the best and happy reading!

~ Kelly

About the Author

Kelly is a multi-published author who lives in North Carolina. She writes the YA series, *Gods & Monsters* (Simon & Schuster), and the *Charlie Madigan* urban fantasy series (Pocket Books), which are written as Kelly Gay. She is a two-time RITA® Finalist, an ARRA nominee, a Goodreads Choice Award finalist, and has landed on the Southern Independent Booksellers Alliance's Okra Picks list. Kelly is also a recipient of North Carolina Arts Council's fellowship grant in Literature.

You can learn more about Kelly at www.kellykeaton.net. To keep up with all the latest book news, events, and giveaways join Kelly's Facebook Page and Twitter at @KellyKeaton.